RETURN OF THE KNIGHT

Gentlemen of Knights
Book Eight

Elizabeth Johns

Dragonblade Publishing, Inc. is an imprint of Kathryn Le Veque Novels, Inc.
P.O. Box 23
Moreno Valley, CA 92556
ceo@dragonbladepublishing.com

Produced in the United States of America

First Edition August 2023
Trade Paperback Edition

ARE YOU SIGNED UP FOR DRAGONBLADE'S BLOG?

You'll get the latest news and information on exclusive giveaways, exclusive excerpts, coming releases, sales, free books, cover reveals and more.

Check out our complete list of authors, too!

No spam, no junk. That's a promise!

Sign Up Here

www.dragonbladepublishing.com

Dearest Reader;

Thank you for your support of a small press. At Dragonblade Publishing, we strive to bring you the highest quality Historical Romance from some of the best authors in the business. Without your support, there is no 'us', so we sincerely hope you adore these stories and find some new favorite authors along the way.

Happy Reading!

CEO, Dragonblade Publishing

Additional Dragonblade books by Author Elizabeth Johns

Gentlemen of Knights Series
Duke of Knight (Book 1)
Black Knight (Book 2)
Knight and Day (Book 3)
Dark of Knight (Book 4)
Shining Knight (Book 5)
Dangerous Knight (Book 6)
Holiday Knights (Boxed Set)
Lord of the Knight (Book 7)
Return of the Knight (Book 8)

CHAPTER ONE

HOW DID ONE return to something one had sworn to leave forever? Nothing ever could, nor ever would, be the same.

Gabriel Lloyd stood in the shadows, the place where he was most comfortable. The beeches, pines, oaks and chestnuts swayed in the soft breeze as accompaniment to the sing-song chirping of two goldfinches chasing each other through the dense canopy of the wood. A squirrel stopped to look Gabe over, then moved on, oblivious to the torment Gabe felt at being back. The outline of the great house stood tall in the shade of the forest of trees which protected it. It was still the same red brick, dressed stone and ashlar, with sharply gabled roofs intermingling with chimneys that almost equaled the height of the trees.

It was ten years since he had last been to Arden Park; a place he'd once loved, that had been his childhood home. Brief memories flashed through his mind, triggered by the mossy, earthy smells he had thought long gone. Fishing in the lake with his father, climbing trees, riding to hounds…it felt like an eternity, yet only a decade had passed.

Now the estate was his. He was the earl—the owner, the temporary steward of all it entailed. He did not want it. It represented everything that was evil in his life, and the man he had once idolized was at the heart of it all. His father had been a coward and a thief: a thief of honor and decency.

Unfortunately, it had all been uncovered very publicly, tied in with a case of murder and suspected treason, and even Gabe had been accused as a traitor in front of a crowd in Hyde Park. He had been trying to quietly investigate the matter in order to exonerate his father, but it had backfired enormously, ending in his father's ruin. Scandal had attached itself to the entire family like a parasite, and Gabe had escaped back to the Continent with the army to avoid his father.

But what was he to do now? It was difficult to be an absentee landlord. If he continued to hide and pretend he was not the earl, then others suffered, and that made him no better than his father. It was the only thing that had brought him back to England, though Napoleon had been defeated at Waterloo over a year ago.

He was no longer a fine gentleman. He had little idea of how to run an estate. The thought of settling down, and taking a wife and having a brood of children, made him ill. He already felt imprisoned by it all. Yet he knew that was the expectation. And if only there was no heir, it would be a simple matter of letting the title die along with him.

But the heir…the heir was a menace. His cousin Albert had also served on the Peninsula, but dishonorably in Gabe's opinion. It was unfair to inflict him on anyone. He would deplete the earldom's coffers and leave its tenants and servants to suffer. Gabe suspected his cousin would drink himself to death before long, and there was always a chance he would marry and beget a son first. It was just that sense of honor which Gabe felt towards his tenants that made him know he needed a wife.

The main problem was he did not know how to behave in the company of women except his sister, but she hardly counted. To most he was uncivilized, and he didn't know how to make small talk. He knew most people considered him dark and dangerous, and feared him because of it.

There had been ample time for him to come to terms with his fate, yet still he hesitated to go beyond the woods into the house. He had come to the same spot every day since he'd returned to

RETURN OF THE KNIGHT

Nottinghamshire, and soon he would have to cross the threshold. But not today. Slowly, he turned and walked the mile back to the village, reflecting that even there he was unknown. It was easy enough to hide in plain sight. If he had learned one thing in his years of spying for the army and Crown, it was that people saw what he wanted them to see. He'd been known as a chameleon amongst his peers, and being as changeable as the wind was how he had stayed alive.

When the time was right, he would know. He still did not have his bearings yet. He needed to know everything about the villagers and the tenants before they realized who he was. People were more apt to talk in anonymity to a stranger.

"Afternoon, guv'nor," the innkeeper said in greeting, placing a pint of porter before Gabe as he sat at his usual table in the darkened corner of the small room. "Would you like some meat pie? The missus has boiled potatoes and vegetables to go along with it."

Gabe nodded his assent and waited, watching, observing as he had every day for the past week. The taproom was cozy—a low-ceilinged room held up by heavy crossbeams with a wood floor covered in woven rushes. The room was dim despite the light flowing in the windows, and there were wooden tables and chairs throughout.

Usually, the smith and his assistant would arrive first and then, a quarter hour later, the haberdasher, and then the butcher. They always sat in the same chairs at the table next to him and discussed the village happenings that day. They were speaking about the assembly that night, and who would dance with whom—and people thought only ladies were gossips.

Gabe had learned the butcher and his missus were at odds. The smith was a bachelor and stayed at the inn every night, drinking until it closed and pining over one of the barmaids who paid him no mind. The haberdasher seemed a kind man, but his wife was apparently the town busybody along with a wealthy widow named Mrs. Winton. There was always at least one. The gentry in the area included a widowed rector, with his brood of six children, as well as a baron, Lord Foster, who had been friends with his own father. He vaguely remembered them.

Until the scandal involving Gabe's father, Lord Mottram, they had been the predominant family in the area, but had gone into hiding and had not emerged again until after his death. Gabe's sister, Maria, had married into a prominent family of the ton, and since that date had suffered no consequences due to their family's ruin. Maria had convinced their mother to reside with her after their father's death, and she seemed slowly to be recovering her spirits. Their father's shame had been a severe blow to her, Lady Mottram having been one of the leading matrons of the ton.

As Gabe sat and listened to the same stories he'd heard before, he knew he could no longer delay the inevitable. While he finished his dinner, he resolved to return to Arden Park for good.

Having packed his belongings and settled with the innkeeper, he was waiting for his horse to be saddled when he heard someone humming. He was drawn to the sound, and found himself pulled in the direction of the sweet melody like a moth to a flame. Around the corner of the stables, he found the source of song. A young lady was meandering down the lane, swinging a basket. She was wearing a practical gown of faded blue cotton, and a floppy brimmed straw bonnet that was well beyond its first blush of youth.

He watched her as she walked by, clearly at peace with her surroundings, and enjoying nature. Having recently come through London, he knew she would not be what was called good ton, but rather a country damsel. In the capitol, the ladies were polished, reserved, polite…and cold.

She looked like laughter and sunshine, the complete opposite of him. He could not tear his eyes away. He watched as she walked all the way to the end of the street, then lost sight of her as she rounded a corner.

Once she was out of sight, he picked up his bags from where he had dropped them and had walked back to the inn yard when he heard a scream from the other direction. Used to action, he dropped his belongings again and ran at once towards the noise.

AFTER LUNCHEON, ROSE left her younger siblings playing outside so she could deliver some fresh bread and fruit to those in the village who were invalids. It was a beautiful afternoon, and she could not help but hum as she walked along the high street, from the parsonage to the other end of the village. Chiffchaffs, wrens, and great tits seemingly chirped their tunes back to her as she lifted her face to be kissed by the sun. That evening the monthly assembly was to be held at the inn, and Rose always loved a good dance. There were hardly any gentlemen of an age with her in the neighborhood but she never minded anyone who would dance, regardless of their years.

It was where Bertie had swept her off her feet that summer he had been visiting at Arden Park. Had it really been five years?

It was time to accept the truth and move on with her life, however difficult it might be in a small village. There was rarely anyone new there, especially since the old earl had stopped entertaining, and now it looked as though his son would follow suit.

Suddenly, Rose felt the hairs on her neck rise. She had heard people say that could happen before a lightning strike, but there was not a cloud in the sky. She looked about, but saw nothing out of the ordinary. Mrs. Oldham was sweeping the path from the gate to her front door, the Miller's little terrier was yapping frantically, hoping Rose would come and pet him, and the rhythmic pounding of a hammer could be heard from somewhere distant in the village, along with the laughter of some children playing.

Yet the sensation would not go away. She stopped and turned around to look over her shoulder, but there was nothing there but the densely forested home wood leading to Arden Park.

Rose still felt a twinge of sadness when she thought about the happy family that used to live there. She had once had a dear friend in Lady Maria, but the old earl had somehow been shamed publicly and now he had been dead for a year. No one knew where Major Lloyd—now Lord Mottram—was, or if he was ever coming back. She remembered him, but she had been a girl of what, fourteen, when last she'd seen him? Even then he'd been cold and distant. At least there had been no warmth or friendliness to him, unlike like his sister and Lady Mottram.

Most of what she knew about Major Lloyd had come from Bertie, who was his cousin. He had not held a very high opinion of Major Lloyd from the letters he had sent home from the Peninsula. He had been in the major's regiment, and had thought him cruel and unfairly harsh to his cousin. Lady Maria, on the other hand, had nothing but praises to sing about her brother. Two such very different accounts made it hard to believe they spoke of the same man.

With so many men dead in the war, the life seemed to have gone out of the village. There had been no fairs or fetes, there being no earl or countess to host or support them. The village was full of mundane day-to-day business. Most of the young men were gone away with the army. Some were still off in the Americas fighting… and not all would come back.

Rose would not think about Bertie. She still could not accept that he was gone. Should she not feel it within her soul that he was dead? Before her thoughts could grow maudlin, she saw her brother coming towards her. Well, not her real brother in truth, but her cousin. Her uncle had taken her in, preferring to call her his daughter. She was his sister's child, but Rose knew nothing of her real father. It was not something Rose dare ask about, and truthfully, she was not certain she wished to know. After her, he had five others of his own. Thankfully, as the third son of an earl, he had a competence sufficient to afford the large family and live as a gentleman. They were not precisely wealthy, but they had enough.

She felt another twinge of guilt. At four and twenty, she should be married, thus relieving them of the burden she represented. Although she did her best to make herself useful, she knew Thomas was to go to school next term in addition to James who was already there. When her aunt had died of a putrid throat, Rose had taken on as many of the duties as she could, such as helping with the children and ministering to the needy in the village. The young ones had a nurse, but with five of them besides Rose, there was always someone who needed more than Nurse Crowder could give at once. Nevertheless, little Letty was now six and Bertie was not coming back. Rose knew her chances of finding a husband—and having children of her own—were slipping away.

"What is wrong, Tommy?" she called.

He was running at breakneck speed, his cheeks flushed and his brown curls windblown. When he reached her, he was breathing so hard he could barely speak. He pointed back towards the village.

"George fell out of the tree while trying to help Julia down and I think he broke his arm. And now Julia will not come down and is crying hysterically. I can fetch her but I thought you should come and help."

Rose had already joined him in running back to the house.

"Go and see if Mr. Watson is at home," Rose called as she ran. "Julia can wait in the tree." They did not have a doctor in the village, but Mr. Watson was the apothecary and his wife was the midwife. You had to go all the way into Nottingham for a surgeon or doctor. Rose prayed as she ran that the arm would not really be broken, or that it was a break that could be set easily.

When Rose arrived, however, she stopped short. There was a stranger kneeling before George, who was sitting on the ground. He wore a brown leather riding jacket and buckskin breeches with tall Hessian boots.

The gentleman appeared to be examining the arm and tying

bandages around the boy. George was bearing the ministrations valiantly as well as trying to behave like a man older than his ten years. Rose crept forward, trying to place the stranger, to no avail. He spoke quietly to George, then the man pulled hard on one of the bandages and Rose heard a loud crack, which made her feel distinctly unwell.

George moaned, but then he tested the movement of the injured limb. "You were right, sir. It does feel better now." She ran to the boy's side to see how well he did.

The gentleman did not look up at her approach. He spoke softly to her brother. "I would still have a doctor look at your arm to be certain nothing is broken, but hopefully, putting it back in place is all it needed. Rest it for a few days." The man was already standing, but he made a move to help George up.

"Where did you learn how to do that, sir?" Rose asked. It was not a skill a common man would have.

"The first time? Talavera," he answered without looking at her. He seemed to ignore them and walked to the tree.

He set his hat and jacket down on the ground before deftly climbing the tree to where Julia sat quietly. Rose had already forgotten about Julia by the time she had arrived and seen what was happening. Rose looked upward to watch, expecting hysterics from Julia. However, as soon as the stranger reached the girl, she put her arms around him and let him carry her back down.

When they reached the ground, Rose held out her arms to Julia, but she did not want to let the man go.

He whispered something to her, then she kissed his cheek before he set her on the ground. The child ran to Rose for a hug, but when she looked up to express her gratitude, the stranger had gone.

"Where is he? I did not even get his name and to properly thank him," she remarked, baffled.

"His name is Gabriel. He's an angel," Julia said matter-of-factly, looking up at her with wide brown eyes.

"He must be, to make you behave," Rose retorted, but still, she felt distinctly annoyed at his rudeness when she should be feeling grateful. He had mentioned Talavera. Perhaps the war could excuse his behavior.

CHAPTER TWO

G ABE WAS NOT ready to be seen, but his hand had been forced. He had recognized the girl immediately. His mind was uncanny that way– it seemed to catalogue every face and name. Her bonnet had fallen off somewhere between there and here, revealing sun-kissed, golden hair that was escaping the confines of its knot. She did not, however, remember him. He had heard her ask who he was, but he'd hidden, not ready to be recognized, although he had told the little girl his name.

Rose had been a bosom friend of Maria's, but she had been a girl then and was now a woman. She must be married by now, but those children seemed too old to be hers. They must be the rector's brood that he'd heard about. He knew that Rose was a lady, else she would not have been Maria's friend, but he did not recall she was a clergyman's daughter.

How had he missed her, this past week? He thought he had seen everyone in the village by now. It was just as well he had decided to go back to the Park, for he doubted his efforts with the boy would go unremarked in such a small place. A stranger putting a shoulder back in position certainly would be gossiped about.

Why had he not simply introduced himself? It would have made matters easier. Quite likely the village would have known within five minutes of his return, and it would have saved himself a lot of bother. Perhaps he should go back and do so, but he knew he would not. His feet were fixed in place as he watched the lady who had enchanted him earlier escort the boy and the girl back towards the parsonage.

It made him wonder, would there be any women to choose from in the neighborhood? He hated the thought of going back to London to seek a bride, but now that he had made the decision, he wanted it over with. He would prefer someone less sophisticated in the ton, because he would prefer to avoid it all together. He would have to consult Maria. Perhaps she would know of someone who would not mind his past and would be grateful for a marriage.

Once the trio were back inside their house, Gabe went to retrieve his horse and bags. He and his old chestnut stallion, Pedro, made their way back to the Park and this time went through the gates on the main drive. No one came out to greet him when he went by the front of the house, so he took Pedro on around to the stables himself.

HE DID NOT recognize any of the faces he saw there, but he was glad to see everything appeared to be in good repair as he had ordered. The stables were not full, but there was a team for a carriage and several work horses. He found an empty stall for his stallion, then went to find the head groom.

Thankfully, it was a familiar face. The man looked up from where he was counting sacks of feed.

"Bartle?" he said as a question, though he knew well it was the man who had first sat him atop a pony.

"Master Gabriel, is that indeed you? I mean, my lord." A smile lit his weathered face as he ducked his head. "It is good to have you home at last. Will you be staying long?"

"For good. I have resigned my commission and intend to take up my duties here at home."

"I am very glad to hear it. It has not been the same here for some time."

"You have not been neglected, have you?" Gabe furrowed his brow.

"No. You misunderstand me, my lord. We have been well attended to. There has been but little life here at the house, or in the village, that is all. It will be good to have someone here."

Gabe understood, but he did not know if he could bring Arden Park back to its former glory of house parties and entertainment, but perhaps he could find a mate who would be willing to try.

"I brought my army stallion home with me. I placed him and his temperament in the last stall," Gabe motioned towards the end of the stables.

Bartle filled a pail with oats and began walking towards Pedro. Gabe followed.

"That's a fine horse you have there, sir," Bartle remarked, as he looked at Pedro in his stall and hooked the pail of feed in its place. The horse went straight towards the treat.

"Aye. He has been through every campaign with me. I am considering breeding him."

Bartle's face lit up, which told Gabe everything he needed to know.

"That would be a fine thing to do."

"I will need to purchase some mares, of course, if you should hear of any suitable animals?" He left it as a question.

"I will be on the lookout, my lord." The stable master nodded respectfully. "It is good to have you home," he repeated as Gabe took his leave.

He walked up the long pathway to the house through the thick shrubbery, a route he had taken many times before, but he still felt like a stranger. As he gained the back door to the kitchens, he could smell fresh bread and roasting ham.

As he opened the door, he knew he should not be entering that way on his first appearance as earl, but he had never basked in the glory of rank, and he did not mean to start now.

He saw the familiar plump figure of Cook – Cookie – as she

was lovingly known to Maria and himself. Often, when their parents had been in Town, the two of them had been allowed to roam freely and Cookie would always have a treat waiting for them on their return. Not that he and Maria had had much time together as such, he being so much older, but still, it was a fond memory.

She turned and exclaimed, with a hand over her heart. "Why, Master Gabriel! Don't you be sneaking up on me and making my heart stop. At my age, too!"

Gabe felt a smile break out on his face– a rare thing for him.

"Now, come here and let me have a good look at you. Shame on you for not giving us any warning!" she scolded. "You don't talk any more than you used to, do you? Now, have a seat and tell me how you like these jam tarts. I'm taking them to the assembly tonight."

She placed a tray of warm currant tarts before him, which she knew very well were his favorite. "You will be attending, won't you?"

He held one up and looked at her, with what was very likely the horror he felt at the thought of attending the assembly.

She put her hand on her hip. "Do not tell me you mean to be a hermit?"

"It would be my preference," he admitted. "However, it had occurred to me that I cannot do so all the time." He sank his teeth into the old, familiar taste of home and closed his eyes to fully relish it. Had it been ten years since he had enjoyed such a treat? It had. He opened his eyes to see Cook watching him with satisfaction.

"Must I go to a party so soon?" he asked, wondering why he was seeking the advice of a servant, but he trusted her implicitly, and she knew him better than most.

"You should. If word gets out that you are here…" She left the rest unspoken.

He sighed. "Very well. Will you tell me who is likely to be there? I would hate to be completely ignorant."

"Indeed, as they will remember you well."

Gabe was skeptical about that, but they would remember who he used to be. He did not know if he could be that man any longer.

ROSE HAD BARELY had a good look at the stranger's face, but once she was home, and over the initial shock of what had happened, she felt more and more convinced she knew him from somewhere. However, since it was unlikely that she would ever see him again, she was soon swept away in the excitement of dressing for the village assembly.

Hopefully, she thought, a soldier would be passing through who would be obliging enough to dance with the young ladies. Would their mysterious Gabe still be in the neighborhood and join them?

"Do not be a goose." She laughed. "He barely spoke a word to you when there was good cause!"

Still, in such a small village, it was hard not to hope for a handsome stranger to arrive and sweep one off one's feet.

"At this point, it is my last hope!" she added for good measure to her own reflection. At one time, she had cherished hopes of having a Season in London, but then her aunt had died, and there had been no question of her going after that. Besides, she and Bertie had promised themselves to each other, so it had not mattered.

Yet, somehow, she had reached the advanced age of four-and-twenty.

"A hopeless spinster, already on the shelf!" she exclaimed, as she fastened a string of pearls around her neck. The necklace was one of the few things she had inherited from her mother, along with a pair of matching earrings.

She had chosen her cream-coloured satin—one of the three

evening gowns she owned—and dressed it with a light blue ribbon that matched her eyes. She tied another in her hair as a bandeau, to keep her curls off her face whilst dancing. Much though she tried to frame her face with them, like the fashion plates which portrayed young ladies of the ton, Rose was too lively a dancer, and the curls always became plastered to her face.

Perhaps it was just as well she had never had a Season. She would not fit in such a place as London.

Soon she and Thomas were walking to the assembly rooms. Papa rarely attended, since he preferred to spend Friday evenings working on his sermons.

Rose walked with excitement, and perhaps it was a sad testament to small village life, but as she heard the music drifting down from the large gathering room over the inn, she took Tommy's arm and pulled him forward.

"Rose, there will be plenty of time for dancing!" he chided, though he was laughing.

When they reached the room, it was already crowded, with a lively country dance in full swing. The small band of a violin, harpsichord, and flute played the merry tune.

Rose greeted everyone as they passed through the assembled. Before she could utter a protest, Quinn Foster took her by the elbow and swung her into the dance. He was a handsome popinjay of some two and twenty years—just younger than she— but as the closest neighboring nobility, had oft spent time together. He was like another brother to her and the others.

"Quinn!" she scolded, "That is hardly proper behavior!"

"When did you ever care for that?" he teased, his devilish chocolate eyes dancing. "I would not do such a thing in London, of course."

She glanced heavenward. He was right about her, of course, and only reiterated what she had told herself a few moments before.

"Did you hear the news?" he asked, eyes twinkling.

They were swinging so fast to the rhythm it was difficult to converse, but Quinn always did have all the gossip.

"What news?"

"They say Mottram is back."

"The new earl? Major Lloyd?"

"One and the same. I doubt he will grace us with his mighty presence tonight. I saw him in London. He is still as cold and haughty as ever—more so, if you ask me."

"How do you know he is here?"

"Servants, of course," he said, with a naughty smile that she did not care to contemplate. She took a few turns with other members of their set and found herself scanning the room in hopes of seeing Lord Mottram or their stern rescuer. Neither was likely to be in such a place, but still, she could hope.

She danced two more dances, and decided that Quinn was right – the lofty earl was not coming. It was a warm spring night and having fetched a glass of lemonade, she walked towards the doors to cool herself in the evening air. If only she had remembered her fan, but she was ever forgetting little things.

She watched as Sarah Foster flirted with Tommy, the poor girl. Perhaps, in a few years, she would grow into a beauty, but for now she was in the awkward early stages of womanhood, a little plump and a little spotted, and Tommy was about to embark on his next journey at school.

Rose scanned the room again when something made her look back towards the entrance. It was he: the stranger who had helped George and Julia.

He looked every inch the gentleman, in black breeches with a black coat, a dove-colored waistcoat and white neckcloth.

Without his hat, recognition dawned. Her stranger was the new earl!

She studied him from afar, noticing, even with his arrogant, aloof stare, that he was lean and severe, even dangerous-looking. His hair was blonde and close cropped, his eyes a cold, piercing blue even from this distance. She felt a shiver run down her spine as she recalled his competence with setting George's shoulder.

What else had war taught him?

Suddenly, those piercing blue eyes met hers. She had been staring blatantly, but she did not look away. She continued to watch as he walked past those that had just noticed him. Surely not? He was making his way towards her.

She took a sip of her lemonade, watching his approach, their gazes boldly connected all the while. He did not quite ignore those in his path, nodding to some, many still trying to ascertain who the man was.

Soon he stood before her, making a bow. Surely he did not remember the likes of her, a gangly girl then but a fourteen-year-old just budding into womanhood? Or perhaps she was simply the only familiar face.

"Miss Sutton, I believe, or has your name changed? Forgive my impudence after all these years away, but I remember you as a close friend of my sister, Maria. Do you remember me?" he asked.

Rose curtsied. "Yes, of course, my lord. Welcome home."

They both knew very well she had not recognized him earlier that day, but to be fair, George had been hurt, and the new earl had not precisely tried to make himself known. It was almost as if he were two different people—this finely dressed lord and the gentleman stranger of earlier.

"Is your next set spoken for?"

"No. It is not spoken for. We are not so formal here in Edwinstowe."

He did not respond with a smooth answer as Quinn would have done, but simply gave a nod of acknowledgement. He was a man of few words, clearly. Was she to be flattered that he was condescending to dance with her because there was no one else? Part of her bristled, but the other part was filled with curiosity, a desire to find out more about him. She was never one to take offense for long unless it was due to an injustice.

Once the current set ended, he offered her his arm and led her to the next set that was forming. It was another simple country dance. Did he remember that in Edwinstowe the commoners mingled with the gentry? Otherwise it would have been a very lonely place for those few who bothered to call themselves lords and ladies in these parts. His sister, Lady Maria, had not been at all pretentious. Something in the back of her mind warned Rose that perhaps he felt out of place, or even wary, because of his father's fall from grace. She determined to enjoy the dance as she would have any other and try to judge him on his own merits.

"How is your sister, my lord?"

"She was doing quite well last week when I saw her. She and her husband are expecting their first child."

"Please give her my regards when next you speak with her."

"You shall be able to do so yourself. They intend to pay a visit, with my mother, in a fortnight."

"How lovely!" she exclaimed as they came together in the dance.

"I have little doubt we will hold some entertainments. I do hope you will come."

Rose wanted to laugh at the formality of the man. He looked as though he had sucked on a sour lemon as he said the words.

"I would be delighted, my lord."

He made just a slight incline of his head as she took her turn with her next partner in the set. There was only one more turn to speak with him, and she had not even remembered to thank him!

"Forgive me for not thanking you sooner for helping George this afternoon."

His eyes started up to hers as though surprised she had mentioned it.

"I am very grateful you were there to help him so quickly," she continued. "He might have suffered for hours otherwise."

He appeared uncomfortable with the praise, so she said no more. The dance ended, and he made her a bow, then quickly made his way back through the crowd towards the doors. Was he leaving so soon? What a strange creature he was! Of course, it was her luck that the only eligible gentleman to come through the village in five years was cold and distant—the complete opposite of herself. No, she could not imagine being shackled to such a creature and pitied the poor woman that ever was.

CHAPTER THREE

WHY HAD HE thought going to a village assembly would be a good idea?

"Stupid, bumbling fool," he said under his breath.

He had never been good at seeking the company of and conversing with others, so why did he think that would suddenly change? And in a crowded room of strangers, no less? It was agony for him. Small rooms full of loud music and dancing, he thought, were worse than facing the front lines of the French any day. He avoided these situations at all cost. Just because he had decided to take on his duties as earl did not mean that he could suddenly become a different person and relish such occasions.

And Rose—it was hard to think of her as anything else, for she was as beautiful as the flower that defined an English garden in Gabe's mind, and was equally an enigma. Her friendly face across the room had called to him like a lifeline, like a fresh stream in a desert. He had approached her with all the finesse of one of Wellington's Regiment of Foot. Had he not marched straight into battle without reconnoitering properly?

As a rule, he would wage his campaigns with careful strategy, but he'd launched an attack and already bungled it. What a fool she must think him! Then, instead of dancing with others or joining the men in the card room, he'd beaten a hasty retreat with his tail between his legs like a coward.

Thankfully, Rose had been well-bred enough not to evince surprise, or remark upon their scarce acquaintance when he'd approached her. She had been even more beautiful up close, with her cheeks pink from exertion and her curls loose around her face. She had none of the pretense of the ladies in London. There he could remain quiet, bar a few practiced phrases and responses, and not worry. With her, he wanted to be clever, but instead was able barely to form coherent sentences. One would never know he'd spent a successful career in the army. That was much preferable to doing the pretty in Society.

When he had finished his dance with her and then looked up at the crowd of overly curious gazes, the walls had begun to close in on him and it had felt as though a pack of wolves was slavering to attack. Hushed voices had swirled around him; he felt rather than saw the whispers behind hands and the looks of judgement. He had just enough wherewithal to leave before he embarrassed himself.

Gasping for fresh air, he made his escape from the assembly room and found his way to Pedro. He rode back to the Park reliving every moment as he was wont to do after every engagement. When engaged in his military commissions, he was able to muster the composure to do his duties well with efficiency. Finding a wife was a duty, was it not? He knew his target, but why was it so difficult? He had made a career of studying people and learning their characters, their probable responses. It was easy in the shadows—so why could he not do so in the light?

The cool night air was soothing as he trotted back to the Park. A bright, waning gibbous moon lit the way as the trees seemed to wave comfortingly as he rode by, their scent also a balm to his hurt. Returning to civilian life was not for the faint of heart, he reflected dully.

Gabe was not so naïve as to think there would not be some sort of morbid curiosity about him. His carefully cultivated solitude was about to be invaded. There would be thinly veiled prying; he knew he would be the topic of discussion in drawing rooms and the tap-room for days to come.

But he could never reveal his real self to them, and likewise he could never become one of them or belong here. Just to dwell among them, his soldiering past would have to remain hidden. If one whiff of what he had spent the past decade doing came to their ears, he would be ostracized completely, much like his father had been, though for different reasons.

It was enough that his family name had been tarnished by the scandal with General Newsom, and Gabe had been the one to cause it to be made public. He had been searching for a traitor, only to be suspected and very publicly called one in Hyde Park by Newsom in front of hundreds at the victory celebrations. Newsom had been the real traitor, but in the process it was revealed that his father had allowed Newsom to get away with it, even covered it up.

Still, it was nothing to what Gabe had done in the name of King and Country. Spying was an all-encompassing name for necessary, but dirty, work. At least the Corsican monster was gone. Nevertheless, Gabe was still loath to face Society in London to see how he would be received. When he had been in Town to sell out, he had avoided large ton gatherings.

With the wounds from Waterloo still deeply imprinted on his mind and body, and the pain of too few survivors, he was barely able to maintain the façade of a gentleman. Those back in England had little idea of what dark deeds were necessary to bring them peace at home. Much of his campaign had been spent performing the tasks no one else wanted to do. He had become the one the generals called upon when they needed something unsavory done: reconnoitering behind enemy lines, rescuing prisoners, disrupting enemy ranks by interrupting supply lines— or even assassinations deemed necessary to cause chaos within enemy ranks.

He only hoped that his enemies would forget him now that the war was over. Torture in an enemy prison seemed easier than hiding behind fine clothes and suave manners. It was all an act—

and barely contained behind a thin veneer, at that.

He needed Maria to help him navigate this new way of life. Thirteen more days lay dauntingly ahead until his sister arrived. What was he to do in the meantime, stay at the Park and hide? He knew that would be an impossibility now that he had shown his hand.

ROSE WATCHED THE earl leave and shook her head. What was he about? That kind of behavior was not going to help him enter into life here... if that was even his intention, but he was lord of the manor and could lord however he saw fit, she supposed. She knew she had only a minute, perhaps seconds, until she became swarmed with questions. One could not blame those asking. Everyone was eager for any titbit of gossip or news to liven small country life.

Quinn was the first to her side.

"I say, Rose, what was that about?"

"I wish I knew." She was still watching the door, hoping Mottram was only visiting the necessary and would return. But she knew he would not.

"Come now, did he not speak? Did he just demand a dance and stare at you the whole time, expecting you to fawn over him?"

"That was not that the way of it," she scolded. "I was under the impression he was reserved. It cannot be easy to return here after everything that has happened."

Quinn scoffed. "If you expect me to feel pity for the man, you are wasting your breath. It is unlikely anyone hereabouts will feel such consideration."

"And why is that, Quinn?"

"He's an earl. He whole life has been one of privilege." He waved his hand in the air as though it was obvious.

"While yours has not?" she retorted. "He has served in His Majesty's army for at least a decade. I think perhaps you misjudge him, and I will decide for myself."

He scowled and folded his arms over his chest.

"Do not tell me, you have designs on him? You have refused all offers from me, claiming you were pining for your Bertie."

"What offers would those be? And yes, I have stayed true to Bertie. I cannot believe you would suggest I am such a fickle creature!" Quinn had always pretended that he would marry her one day. He was so used to saying it, that it was second nature even if neither of them had any intention of marrying the other.

"When will you accept he is not coming back?" he asked more softly, though clearly still annoyed.

"Perhaps I have," she answered, with more bravado than she felt.

"Then do I have a chance of your affections?"

She narrowed her gaze at him. "You are not serious in your attentions. You only pay me any mind because there are no other ladies to flirt with." No one ever said it aloud to her, but she knew he was looking higher than the likes of her.

He opened his mouth to protest, but they were now surrounded by others curious for news.

Tommy was next to speak. He slapped her on the back, then made her a deep, mocking bow. "Shall I start calling you my lady?" he teased, as only a younger brother would.

"Do be serious. I only danced with him!"

"I am only saying what everyone else is thinking. He did not speak to anyone else. He made a beeline straight for you, danced with you, and then left. What else are we to surmise?"

"That is not true. He spoke to Lord Foster when first he walked into the room."

"What was he like?" Sarah Foster asked dreamily. "He is very handsome."

Rose could not help but smile when she saw Tommy look sideways at Sarah. Perhaps he was not as indifferent to Sarah as he thought, when her attentions were on someone other than himself.

"He was very polite. As I told Quinn, I believe he is shy. Perhaps I was one of the few faces he remembered, due to my friendship with Lady Maria. Really, we should not speculate," Rose answered.

"A little late for that, is it not?" Quinn snorted. "Any gentleman knows that singling out a lady the way he did is not the thing."

Rose could feel her cheeks burn. Even she knew that, but somehow, she did not think that had been his intention. "Nonsense."

"But did he say anything?" Sarah persisted.

"He did mention that his sister and her new husband will be visiting soon and will be holding some entertainments."

"How lovely! I have never been inside Arden Park before." She rapped her brother on the arm with her fan. "To think you said he was a boor."

"I have no reason to change my opinion," Quinn countered.

"Papa will call on him tomorrow, I am sure of it. Then we shall see."

Rose thought it was naïve of Sarah to defend the earl without having met him, although doubtless she was also aware that no one eligible ever came to quaint little Edwinstowe. Not that that would stop her from indulging a fancy of being lady of the manor over the county in which she had lived her whole life! At least she would have a proper Season, and she was still very young.

Indeed, Rose knew there was another reason why any speculation about the earl having designs on her was ridiculous. She had been brought up as a lady, but she was only the orphaned niece of the rector, who was himself a third son. Earls did not marry ladies with no birth or fortune.

She danced until the assembly ended, trying not to think about the mysterious earl. Nonetheless, she found herself assuring everyone who asked, as an excuse for his having left so soon, that Lord Mottram had been tired from his travels. She could but hope it was true, and did not care to delve into why she was making excuses for him.

As she lay in her bed that night, struggling to sleep, it was hard not to ask herself why she had been singled out in such a fashion. Hopefully the village knew her well enough to realize she was virtuous, but she knew a girl in her position could not hope for more.

CHAPTER FOUR

T HE NEXT DAY Gabe was in his study, already having
welcomed Lord Foster and his son, Quinn. They lived in the
neighboring county, but it was less than ten miles to their estate,
and they were the closest neighbors of the nobility. Foster had
been a chum of Gabe's father in the past. In fact, he was one of
the few people Gabe had recognized at the assembly. He was a
jovial fellow—every inch the country squire—in his practical
brown leather riding coat and riding boots, and with his round
belly to match his bald, round head. He was fond of his hounds
and the hunt, as Gabe recalled from participating as a youth.

Lord Foster lowered his girth into the nearest of two burgundy leather armchairs flanking the fire.

"'Tis good to see you back, Mottram. Your people need you
here, as I tried to tell your father, but he barely received me at the
end."

Gabe nodded his understanding. "I am sure he appreciated
your friendship, nonetheless, sir." He found himself feeling the
need to comfort this man.

"You mean to do your duty?" Foster asked, as though decid-
ing whether to lecture Gabe or not.

"I have just sold my Commission and do not intend to be an
absent landlord. It took me some time to get my papers in order
and return. Nevertheless, I trust no one here has suffered from

neglect."

"Even your father ensured his tenants were not without."

"Don't badger the poor fellow, Father." Quinn Foster spoke from where he leaned lazily against the mahogany mantel. "He has said he is here to stay." Gabe assessed the young buck quickly. He was handsome and a bit of a dandy, no doubt recently down from school. His hair was swept into the fashionable Brutus style, his tasseled Hessian boots were polished to a high shine, and his shirt points high and starched, as was his elaborately styled waterfall neckcloth.

"There can be no harm in questioning his intent, can there?" He turned back to Gabe. "I mean well, lad. I've known you since you were a tot. I meant only to offer fatherly advice or help with the local dissenters, should you have need of it."

Gabe nodded appreciatively to the baron, and knew he meant well, but since he then heard a knock on the front door and footsteps coming toward the study, no doubt with more well-meaning visitors, he stifled a groan and kept his expression impassive. He had expected some visitors, but it was still early, and he feared it would be a long day.

"Reverend Sutton, and Master Thomas," Hobson, his elderly butler, announced.

Gabe rose and went over to shake the rector's hand. Catching Hobson's eye, he requested coffee, and signaled no more visitors for the nonce. He would soon be overwhelmed, he reflected, if he didn't set limits. The dark, paneled walls of the study were already feeling as if they were bearing down on him.

"Welcome, sir," Gabe said. "Please join us."

"Thank you. I see we are not the first to pay our respects. Foster, Quinn," the rector said, acknowledging the other guests and shaking his neighbor's hand.

He was a handsome man, most likely in his late forties, with dark hair and silver at his temples and whiskers. His twinkling gray eyes spoke of his good nature. The son, Thomas, was a younger version of the man, but at least ten years Gabe's junior.

Gabe wondered if he was to be reprimanded for his behavior at the assembly—as if it were any of their business—but as the highest-ranking man there, he did not know if they would dare. Then again, he reflected, Foster had just proclaimed his willingness to be a surrogate father.

Gabe still grimaced when he thought of the assembly. Would the reverend mention his having singled out the girl, Rose? He knew he deserved censure for such ungentlemanly conduct.

"We have come to welcome you to the neighborhood, and also to thank you for helping young George yesterday."

"It was nothing, I assure you. How is he today?" Gabe asked.

"None the worse for the experience, thanks to you. Those twins are always getting into trouble." He shook his head fondly.

"You should take a wife to help you with those children. The nurse is too old to look after them," Foster said, as though he had said it a hundred times.

"Rose helps with them," the rector answered with a dismissive wave of his hand.

"That lass needs a husband. You should let us take her to London for the Season."

Gabe could tell this argument had occurred before.

"She has my blessing to go, and she knows it. It is her choice to stay."

Gabe did not react. Outwardly, he was too practiced to do so, yet inside he wanted to scream. No! She was to be *his* wife! The trouble was he had a great deal of work to do to make that happen.

"You know, do you not, she will not leave you without a nudge?" Lord Foster stroked his whiskers.

Reverend Sutton furrowed his brow as if it was the first time he had considered it.

The man seemed a little distracted, though harmless, Gabe thought. He wondered if Rose had sent him on this errand. It did not seem likely he would have thought of it himself.

"It would not hurt for you to take a wife either, Mottram,"

Baron Foster continued in his vein of well-meaning advice. "There is too much to be done on the estate now that your mama has gone. Unless she is coming back? No? You need a wife to continue the name at all events."

Gabe said nothing. Even though he agreed, he had no intention of telling Lord Foster of his intentions until Miss Sutton—Rose—agreed.

"Is there anything we can do for you, my boy?" Foster asked, doggedly persevering. "My lady wishes to invite you to dine with us this week or the next, if you have no other plans."

"I thank you for the offer. Perhaps the week after this. My sister is bringing her husband to visit," Gabe said cautiously. Surely he would have his bearings by then?

"They are all very welcome. Lady Foster will be pleased." He forced himself out of the chair. "I must be off. I have bitches about to whelp, you know."

"How many are breeding, sir?" Thomas asked. Gabe at once gathered Foster was referring to his beloved hounds.

"Just two this time." He looked at Gabe. "You could do with a hound or two around here. Yes, it would be the very thing! I will send for you and you can have your pick of the litter as my welcome gift."

Gabe stuttered a thank you. He would not know what to do with a dog, but he also realized he would be offering the highest insult if he refused.

"We will see ourselves out." Lord Foster clapped Gabe on the back as he and Quinn walked from the room, leaving him with the rector and his son.

Thomas eyed Gabe knowingly and with a hint of sympathy in his eyes. There was silence for a minute, as though they all needed a brief reprieve from the ebullience that was the baron.

Reverend Sutton cleared his throat. "Besides offering our thanks, Rose wanted me to extend an invitation to dinner tonight, but if you are otherwise engaged...it would be only a family affair."

"Do take note that he did not say 'small'," Thomas teased.

The rector shuffled from one foot to the other. "Well, indeed, and you have met almost everyone now except for little Letty and James, my eldest son, who is away at school."

"I would be pleased to come to dinner."

"Excellent! Excellent. Well, then, we shall not keep you any longer. If there is anything at all with which you may need help, please do not hesitate to ask. I hope you now realize we are pleased to see you safe returned." The rector stood and shook Gabe's hand before he made his way to the door.

Gabe contemplated asking, then and there, for permission to court Rose, but he would prefer to do it without the knowing brother hearing every faltering word.

He was thankful to have an excuse to see Miss Sutton again tonight, but he was not used to being in company with children. At least there would be only one family to contend with. He knew he would have to do something to convince her—he was not a complete fool. For some reason he did not think his title and wealth would hold much sway with his country lass. Did she even want to marry? The reverend had not sounded convinced.

Gabe closed the door just as Hobson arrived with the coffee. Gabe leaned his head back against the door with a heavy sigh. At least he liked coffee.

ROSE RETURNED TO the parsonage later that afternoon after teaching at the village school. Two afternoons a week, she helped with Bible lessons and reading.

She lifted her head to consider the ominous sky as she entered through the creaking wrought-iron gate and hurried up the stone path, reaching the kitchen door as a crack of lightning flashed while thunder boomed. Almost at once, the skies opened and the threatened rain poured down.

Leaning against the back door with a sigh of relief, she smiled at Cook while she simultaneously smelled roast beef cooking and the telltale aroma of Cook's renowned apple pie.

"Is someone coming to dinner?" she asked, shedding her bonnet and pelisse.

Cook looked somewhat harried as she buttered the top of the fresh bread she had just pulled from the oven. "The new earl, Rose!" she answered shortly.

Rose groaned, but stepped across the chipped red tiles to reassure the family's beloved retainer.

"Everything will be wonderful as always. Do not fret so."

"But an earl, and with no warning! How am I supposed to lay a fancy table for the likes of an earl in only a few hours?" She threw her hands in the air and hurried off to another task.

Rose was not concerned about the fare, but she did suffer some qualms about the guest. She hastened to the rector's study, where he was most often to be found.

"Must we have him to dinner, Papa?" Rose asked as she entered the cozy, dark room, even though she knew what his answer would be.

Her dear Papa looked up from his Bible, peered over his spectacles and waved her to a well-worn damask wingback chair that had once been a deep green but had faded into more of a mossy hue.

"Besides Christian charity, Rose, he saved us a great deal of bother with George. Who knows how long it would have been before his arm was set, and that could have led to many other complications, as you well know."

"Yes, Papa."

But he was not done with his gentle reproof. "We also want to encourage him in his new position as Earl. It will not be easy for him, especially with what happened with his father. He has been a soldier a long time, and has no wife to share his burden."

"Burden?" Rose thought uncharitably of the glamorous Lord and Lady Mottram's way of life, and the way Lord and Lady

Foster lived. Burden was hardly the word that sprang to mind—not when many of the villagers lived day by day.

"Indeed. It is a huge responsibility, and I, for one, intend to shepherd him through this time. He seems a good man, though, if not one of many words."

"He singled me out for a dance last night, Papa. Or had you not heard?"

He looked up at Thomas, who had appeared in the doorway. Her brother gave a nod of confirmation. He must have heard their conversation and come to join in.

"He marched in through the crowd, danced with me and then left without a by your leave. He barely spoke a civil word to anyone else!"

Her Papa scratched his head in obvious consternation. "I am certain there is a good explanation."

"Perhaps he has been too long from Society," Thomas offered. "He did seem reticent."

"I would rather say pompous and arrogant," Rose retorted.

"That is unworthy of you," her papa scolded gently.

Chastised, she willed her temper to subside. "Perhaps, but you know I cannot afford any bruises to my reputation."

"Now, now, I am certain no one thought that of you because of his attentions."

Rose looked at the ceiling in exasperation. What must it be like, always to think the best of everyone? When her eyes returned to her papa's, he was watching her intently.

"Leave us, Thomas, and close the door," he directed gently.

Rose had no idea what this was about. As the latch clicked on the study door, she wondered if she was to be reprimanded.

"I promise I will be civil to him, Papa, if that is what concerns."

He shook his head and pushed back his chair, moving from behind the desk. He walked towards the windows, which overlooked the church cemetery, with his hands clasped behind his back. She waited for him to speak.

"I think, perhaps, I have been remiss with you, my dear."

"Never! How could you think so?" She defended him vehemently.

He sighed heavily. "You are a very good girl, Rose. I have always been honest with you about your mother."

"Yes," she said hesitantly, wondering what he was trying to say.

"However, I never intended to give you the impression that you were a... natural child. When your mother was dying and asked us to care for you, we had not been able to have children of our own and were happy to bring you up as our beloved daughter. It was never meant to bring shame upon you, as it must have done. Have people been cruel to you?"

"Not precisely cruel, Papa, but I have heard whispers."

He turned back to look at her. There was agony in his eyes. What was he trying to tell her? "Is this why you have refused to go to London?"

Was it? "Perhaps a little. But when Mama died, I felt my place was here, to help you."

"Oh, Rose. There is much I need to tell you. Wait here a moment."

Her papa left the room, his distant footsteps climbing upward towards the attics. She could only frown and wonder as she waited. He returned, several minutes later, with a small, dusty box, which he placed on the oak desk. He brushed the dust from the top and lifted the lid.

"Your mother was very beautiful, like you. She was my baby sister—you look exactly like her. She took the ton by storm in her first Season and had many offers, including one from a very old but prominent duke."

Rose waited. Her pulse thrummed through her veins with anticipation—of what, she knew not.

Her father pulled out an old, worn leather Bible. "I meant to give you her things sooner, but when Violet died, it slipped my mind." He opened the pages and pulled out an aged piece of paper, yellowed and worn at the edges. "Your parents' marriage certificate."

Rose took the paper with trembling hands. "Why did no one ever tell me?"

"It is a very long story, but one you deserve to know. Your mother was very beautiful, as I told you."

Rose listened, wanting to unfold the small piece of paper, but afraid to.

"She could have had any gentleman she wanted, within reason. She had a respectable dowry and was the daughter of a viscount, which was enough for most."

Rose knew something unpleasant was coming, otherwise she would have known.

"Of course, she fell in love with the son of a duke. The family did not approve, as they already had someone selected for him. My sister did something very rash and eloped with your father. They thought his family would accept the marriage once the deed was done."

While eloping was considered scandalous, it was not unforgiveable. Surely, Rose wondered, there was something else?

"His family was outraged and immediately called for an annulment. The duke's brother was an archbishop. They threatened to cut him off if he did not comply."

Rose winced. "What happened?"

"The damage to your mother was done. His family was very public in their renunciation of the marriage."

Rose could see why her parents' marriage was not spoken about.

"Lord Edward joined the army to spite his family. He said he would never marry another. Violet came to live here with us while he went away, for by that point she was already increasing with you."

"What happened to my father?" she whispered, though her throat was constricting with tears.

"Your mother received word that he died on his way to India… but he died before the annulment went through."

It was a small comfort to know she was not a bastard, but the price had been very dear. She felt the pain of their loss very acutely. Rose felt tears welling in her eyes, for she knew what had happened to her mama. She did not need that piece of history repeated.

The gentleman she knew as her papa walked over to her and put a gentle hand on her shoulder. "Forgive me for keeping this from you. Never has there seemed to be a right time to tell you, and I have always loved you as my own. Your mother asked us to bring you up as our own so you would not feel burdened by the knowledge."

"You have, Papa." She threw her arms around his neck and hugged him tight until he pulled back and spoke again.

"But you see, Rose, you have another family. You are rather well-born, and it is your right to take your place in Society. I have never thought to keep that from you."

"I do not care anything for Society." She pulled her handkerchief from her sleeve and blew her nose.

"I can write to your father's family," he went on. "After twenty-four years, I would think they would be willing to let bygones be bygones for your sake. I know from experience most people regret the rash actions of their youth."

"I do not know if I could be civil to them for the way they treated my parents."

"I know it is a lot to take in. Think about it, and if you change your mind, I will write the letter." He picked up the box and handed it to her. "I believe there is a miniature of your father in there somewhere."

Rose was torn. "I cannot think that I will change my mind, Papa."

"Do you not want to marry one day? Rose, I do not think your suitor is returning. It is time to get on with your life."

"I realize he is gone," she whispered.

"It is very honorable and dutiful, how you have helped me to care for the younger ones, but it is not fair of me to keep you here any longer, my dear."

"If I were to go, who would help you?"

He ran his hands through his hair, disheveling it, and making him look very dear. "I have been thinking of marrying again, myself."

Those words from his mouth were almost as shocking as learning about her parents' marriage. The bells on the church rang out, signaling the hour of six in the evening.

"It is time to dress for dinner," he remarked, as though she needed the reminder. "Our guest will be here soon. If you have any questions, I will do my best to answer them nevertheless."

Rose stared at what was left of her mother's possessions, feeling as if the world as she knew it had all been false. She wanted to lock herself in her room and absorb everything her papa had said, along with her mother's belongings, but instead she had to dress for dinner with the cold and unapproachable earl.

CHAPTER FIVE

G ABE FELT MORE nervous now, going to dinner alone with this quaint family, than he had when awaiting the French across the battlefield the first time. At least there he had known what to expect. Of course he had attended family dinners once upon a time, but that was long ago. The officers' mess was always guaranteed to be full of lively conversation, but he had never been required to participate if he did not wish. He suspected he would not simply be able to sit there and eat his food tonight.

Pedro was already saddled and waiting for him, and they rode at a gentle canter through the woods into the village.

He hoped that Rose was not too angry with him.

Considering this, he supposed that if she was in a miff he would have to apologize. He should do that anyway, he reflected. Rose had not seemed embarrassed at the time, but then he had left the assembly room. If he were sufficiently fortunate, no one would have remarked upon it, but deep within he knew better.

He had to find a way to accustom himself to such gatherings again—not that he had ever liked them.

When he reached the parsonage at the edge of the village, he dismounted and tied Pedro to a post. The wrought-iron gate creaked when he opened it and he let himself into a charming garden in full bloom.

A graveyard sat between the house and the church, with

flowers neatly placed before each stone and monument, but this was a riot of flowers, untamed as vines grew this way and that over trellises and benches, up the side of the house and even along the fence.

Although he knew he was being ridiculous, the stone path felt as if it was leading to an enemy trap. This had to be done, and if he could not accomplish a small family dinner with the village man of God, he would resign himself to being a recluse and manage alone as best he might. With each step he took a deep breath and, closing his eyes for a moment to gather his courage, knocked on the door when he reached it.

The door was opened by the son, Thomas. Curious. Perhaps they had no servant. Gabe relaxed a little.

"Good evening, my lord. Come this way."

He was led into a small study, directly off the entrance hall, where the reverend was seated behind a large oak desk, writing. He stood up when Gabe and Thomas entered the room.

"Welcome, my lord. Forgive me, I was putting the finishing touches to my sermon for tomorrow. I hope you will join us." There was a hint of query in his tone.

How could Gabe say no? He frequently went into churches— alone and when they were empty. Taking his place in the family pew on a Sunday, however... Nevertheless, it was something he would need to do in his new role. "Of course, Rector." He nodded in what he hoped was a polite fashion.

"Excellent. Rose will be down shortly, I expect. We were delayed in dressing for dinner."

"May I offer you a drink?" Thomas asked from beside a cabinet in the corner.

"Thank you." Gabe inclined his head. He had just taken a seat with a glass of sherry in his hand, when heavy footsteps accompanied by giggles were heard coming, like a herd of sheep, down the stairs.

A stern voice called after them, presumably a nurse who was incapable of properly controlling her charges. "Children!"

Giggles followed before three children rushed into the room and stopped abruptly.

"George, Julia, Letty," the reverend said sternly, "Are these good manners?"

"No, sir," they answered in unison.

"Please make your bows to Lord Mottram. George and Julia you have met before, if you recall, my lord. And the youngest is Letty."

The three freckled children with auburn hair and green eyes made their bows and curtsies, respectively. They were in their Sunday best, a far cry from the dirty urchins he'd seen near the tree the day before. Had that been only yesterday?

More footsteps sounded on the stairs—light this time—and brought Gabe out of his thoughts. Rose stood in the doorway, looking lovely in a pale green gown. It really was a miracle she was not yet wed. Upon closer inspection, her eyes looked rather red. Had she been crying? Gabe quickly rose to his feet and made her a bow. "Miss Sutton."

Her cheeks flushed at his gaze, but she lowered her eyes and made him a pretty curtsy. "My lord."

"Now that everyone is here, why do we not go on in to dinner? As you can see, we stand on little formality here. I told the children they could join us, as a treat, as long as they behave themselves." The rector gave the younger three a pointed look.

"Yes, sir," George mumbled.

Gabe felt a small hand touch his arm and looked down to see Julia staring up at him from large green eyes. "I will show you where to sit," she whispered.

Unused to children, he was surprised when she took his hand and led him across the hall to the dining room and took the seat beside him. The room was rectangular with a table for twelve, still light from the evening sun. These children were no strangers to adults or family meals. It was hard for Gabe to fathom the warmth he felt in this family. Perhaps if he had been more of an age with Maria, they would have shared a similar bond.

The children chattered amiably with each other, clearly with no fear of reprisal for speaking without being spoken to. Dinner was served by a male servant—a large roast of beef with buttered potatoes, glazed carrots, and French beans topped with bacon. Plates of fresh bread and fresh plums filled the table.

Reverend Sutton cleared his throat and everyone bowed their heads. Gabe followed suit as the food was blessed. It was such a picture of domestic bliss as Gabe had never experienced.

"Amen," the children echoed their father's completion of the prayer and each began to serve the food that was nearest to them.

Gabe accepted slices of roast beef from the rector and vegetables from Rose. He, in turn, passed the bread around the table.

"Is it true you were in the war?" a young voice asked.

He looked up, to see that George had asked the question.

"He may not wish to speak of it," Rose whispered in her brother's ear. That did not deter the young man.

"Why can I not ask that? I want to be a soldier, too."

"It is a fair question. I do not mind," Gabe answered, though he hated speaking of his occupation. He had also thought it would be glamorous when he was a lad. If he had only known.

"I served on the Peninsula and then through to Waterloo."

"What regiment were you in?"

"The 1st Lifeguards, but I often performed other duties away from the regiment."

"I say, was that not your beau's regiment, Rose?" Tommy asked.

Gabe looked at the girl across from him, startled to hear she had a suitor. She did not look pleased.

"It was, but he is gone now. Let us speak no more about it," she said quietly.

George, muttered an apology and turned his attention to his potatoes.

"Hopefully we will enjoy a long period of peace henceforth," Mr. Sutton said. "The Lord knows, England's men are much depleted."

"Indeed," Gabe agreed.

"We lost nearly thirty men from our parish alone," the rector explained.

Gabe had not realized that. It was a severe blow to so small a village of only five hundred.

"Rose helps the widows and children as much as she can, but having you back will be a boon, I am sure."

"I will do anything I can to help, of course," Gabe answered, humbled by this knowledge. Why had his steward not spoken of these matters?

"Thomas has been doing what he can, in ways of mending fences and such, but he leaves soon to join James at Oxford."

"Do you mean to study for the church as well?" Gabe asked the boy.

The lad shook his head. "James is for the church. My uncle has promised me a set of colors in his regiment."

"I was mad to join the army at your age too."

Gave fielded several more questions from the rector, Thomas and George about the army and the war, but he noticed Rose was very quiet and withdrawn. Was she pining for her beau? Or was she angry with Gabe himself for his behavior the night before? If only he could have a moment to speak with her, although he did not know how he would ask such a thing.

He survived the meal, and the children were sent upstairs to the nurse amidst a few protests. Rose withdrew to see them on their way.

"Shall we repair to the drawing room for a drink? Unless you have had your fill of my boisterous brood?" Mr. Sutton chuckled. "You would not be the first."

"Drink is always welcome. I've been without too many times to refuse."

Gabe hoped Rose would return soon, and prayed he had not missed his chance to speak with her. Thankfully, she arrived and took the seat next to him by the time the tea tray arrived.

"How do you take your tea, my lord?" she asked, though she

was still not her usual sunny-tempered self. She had certainly been more friendly at the dance.

"Milk, no sugar, thank you."

She served him first, and then her father and brother. They were having a discussion amongst themselves, and he knew this might be his only opportunity.

"Miss Sutton, I wish to apologize for leaving straight after our dance. I did not mean any insult, I assure you."

She set down her tea cup with a nervous click.

"No apology is necessary, my lord. I am sure you had your reasons for such a precipitate departure."

"No reason would be excuse enough to cause insult to a lady. I am afraid I am not accustomed to being in a crowd or going about in Society," he offered, recognizing it as the lamest of excuses.

She looked at him, then, with a hint of surprise. "I would have thought," she said carefully, "that you were often subjected to worse than a village assembly during your time at war."

"I would not say the situations were comparable," he replied.

"No, of course not. Now I beg your pardon." Her cheeks flushed red a moment before she looked down quickly, evidently embarrassed.

Gabe cursed to himself—his wretched tongue in the presence of women! He seemed to make matters worse instead of better. He finished his tea, then excused himself, feeling as though he had only dug a deeper hole for himself.

ROSE HAD GONE straight to bed after Lord Mottram had left. In addition to the confusion engendered by his visit, her thoughts were so disoriented after what her papa had told her about her parents, she could not help but wonder about her real father's family.

Would they still refuse to acknowledge her parents' marriage after all this time? If so, then what of her own situation? Rose was not optimistic about them forgiving old grievances. Perhaps they might regret the events which had led to her father's death, but people of their rank often did not care to admit they were wrong, and felt justified in their actions. Besides, why would she want to live with those who had torn her family asunder? Her real family was in Edwinstowe.

Of all days, her thoughts ran on, why had it been today that her papa had invited the earl to dinner? Normally, she could have been more composed, but his cold aloofness made it difficult for her to think well of him—especially when so much of his behavior had confirmed what Bertie had always said.

Then, when her brothers had started talking about the army, it only made her think of Bertie, and all that she had lost. Bertie, the fun-loving soldier whose life was snuffed out far too soon.

This morning was church—another place she was not quite ready to face. She walked the well-worn path in front of the cemetery to the church, still brooding about everything happening. Part of what had kept her awake the night before was thinking about the earl's apology and what to make of him.

Faced with a row of parishioners at the church door, she had to force a smile to her face. It would not do to show them that anything had affected her. At least she knew now the truth of her parents' marriage, which comforted her insecurities a great deal. Why had she never thought to ask her papa before? She knew he had not intentionally kept it from her, but also understood it was likely he had not realized she was ignorant of the facts.

Rose shook hands and asked after everyone's health and children, the infirmities of the elderly, and the farmers' new calves. Mrs. Winton was chatting with Papa, thankfully, because Rose could scarcely abide the widow. She could not say why, but something about the woman grated, as if she tried too hard. She was overly friendly with Papa and the children, yet was always quick to point out Rose's every fault. Oh, dear Lord, was Mrs.

Winton the one whom Papa was considering taking as his new wife?

Rose tried to think of all of the conversations she had been privy to, and with a sinking feeling, she realized it must be true. She watched the way her papa looked down at the woman and felt sick. How had she not seen it before?

"Are you well, Miss Sutton? You look pale." She turned to see Lord Mottram standing beside her.

"Good morning, my lord," she replied, curtsying. "Yes, I am quite well. How do you do?"

Without answering, he offered her his arm, and she noticed everyone else had gone inside.

"Let me escort you to your seat, if you are certain you do not need to return to the parsonage."

How could she refuse such solicitousness? Everyone would see her on his arm. If the tongues were not already wagging, they soon would be. What could she do? Trying to ignore the stares from the congregation, she placed her hand on his arm and allowed him to lead her down the aisle to the front pew, to her seat beside her siblings. With a stiff bow, he took his place in the long, vacant pew across from theirs, which had not seen anyone since the old earl's retirement from all society.

The organ began to play, and Rose forced herself to sing, wondering how her life had changed so much in a few short hours. One thing was for certain—she would not be able to stay at the parsonage if her father married Mrs. Winton.

When Mama had died, Mrs. Winton had been a young widow, but she had at once tried to take over as many of her duties as possible, it seemed. Rose liked almost everyone, but there was something about the woman which unsettled her. If only she could place it, perhaps Rose could overcome her dislike. She was sure the woman disliked her equally.

Rose had conceded the sewing circle to the woman, because she herself had little patience to sit quilting when there was so much else to do. Besides, the other ladies were far older than she, and liked to gossip.

The woman's brittle laugh echoed through her thoughts, as other uncharitable memories of Mrs. Winton joined the list of reasons Rose could not like her. For some reason, she did not treat Rose as well as the other children. Perhaps she did not realize Rose was not a baseborn child, but it should not have mattered. Certainly not for a woman who proclaimed Christian charity and aspired to be the reverend's wife. Rose could see it all clearly now.

She felt an elbow in her ribs from Thomas, and quickly stood up to join the rest of the congregation. She scarcely heard a word her papa said, which pricked her conscience with guilt. Papa was an excellent preacher, and they always enjoyed discussing his sermons later in the afternoon. Today she would not be able to participate. Perhaps she should plead a headache and take a tray in her room. Truly, she felt one coming on. She did not want to deal with these changes to her ordered existence.

When the service ended, she noticed the earl seemed as reluctant as she did to leave the church. How ironic if she were to find herself in sympathy with him after mentally criticizing him for his reticence.

Their gazes met, and turning slightly away, she offered a polite, if half-hearted, smile.

He stepped forward, still looking concerned. "Are you feeling improved?"

"I believe I may have a slight headache, sir, that is all."

"I have no such excuse. I am afraid to be mobbed." Was that humor he was attempting?

"I can act as your shield." She stepped forward and walked down the aisle, not waiting for him to offer his arm. That would be too much for her wits at this moment—and for the congregation most likely still standing outside, deep in conversation.

Unfortunately, Mrs. Winton was speaking with Papa just down the steps, and Rose saw she could not avoid her. Their conversation should not have surprised her, however.

"I wish you had been there to see, my dear Reverend. It was quite scandalous how he singled her out at the dance, and then to lead her into church this morning! We both know he can only want one thing of a girl so below his station."

"I am sure he means no harm, my dear." Her papa patted the woman's arm while leaning over to listen.

"I say this not to meddle, but because she has no female influence at home. I am sure most gentlemen do not notice these things."

Rose felt her cheeks flame and prayed the earl's hearing was not as acute as hers.

"Is something wrong, Rose?" Her papa looked at her in concern.

"'Tis merely a little headache, Papa." And a desire to strangle the woman with ambitions to wed her dear father. She tried not to glare.

"Who have we here?" the vulgar woman said, knowing full well who he was, of course, and rudely waiting for an introduction instead of asking after Rose.

"Lord Mottram, may I introduce to you Mrs. Winton, a lady of long standing in the parish," the reverend said with a smile.

The earl inclined his head and Mrs. Winton curtsied. "Madam."

"We are so pleased you have returned, my lord. Is it true our Lady Maria is to visit soon?"

Rose looked up and the cold look on the earl's face indicated he had heard her disparaging remarks. Rose would not at all mind his cool aloofness towards Mrs. Winton. In fact, she would relish it.

"Indeed." He turned towards Rose. "Miss Sutton, I hope your headache is not too severe and goes away quickly." He bowed towards her and abruptly left.

Rose wanted to smile and applaud, but instead excused herself to lie down and rest, feeling more in charity with the earl for his championing of her—even if it was only a little.

CHAPTER SIX

I T WAS PITIFUL how much Gabe was looking forward to his family's arrival. To say that the last fortnight had been painful was an understatement. He felt like a fish out of water—or one struggling to swim upstream at the very least.

He had tried to stay away from the parsonage so as not to draw any more attention to Rose, after overhearing that harpy outside the church last Sunday. He feared Rose would want nothing more to do with him. It would hardly do, now, to announce his attention to court her, even though he had been tempted to tell the Winton woman he would be proud to have Rose for a wife. He decided to wait for his sister's advice.

The wait felt interminable. It was mid-afternoon before they arrived. The relief he felt when he saw the carriages draw up the tree-lined drive was like taking a breath after holding it for too long. He went out to greet them.

Lord Philip Everleigh, his new brother-in-law and long-time colleague, stepped out first. They shook hands warmly.

"Everleigh! You are very welcome to Arden Park."

For many years, Philip had been their neighbor, and child-hood friend of Maria's, at their other estate but he had often visited Arden Park as well.

"Gabe!" Maria, visibly increasing, was already climbing down from the carriage with Philip's help and threw her arms around him.

In a rare display, Gabe returned her affection. "You can have no idea how happy I am that you are here."

She pulled back and looked at him suspiciously with her tawny eyes. "Has something happened?"

"Everything is well," he reassured her. Then, recollecting his duty, pulled back to assist his mother from the carriage. She seemed hesitant to alight, yet he sensed grim resolution within her to accept her fate.

"Mother," he said in greeting as he handed her down and kissed her on the cheek.

She smiled. "You look well, my son. I hope you are settling in."

"I am, though how well is arguable. I shall certainly appreciate advice from all of you," he said as he led them into the house.

"Would you care for refreshment?" he asked.

"Certainly. I am parched," Maria said. "First, I must excuse myself for a moment, but will be back directly."

Gabe looked at his sister's rounded belly and smiled. In her present condition she looked very handsome and blooming.

All of them took a few minutes to refresh themselves, but his mother was first to return.

He had not seen much of her since his bitter parting with his father, and her appearance shocked him. She had aged a great deal, and instead of her formally cheerful manner, she seemed sad and withdrawn.

"Are you happy, living with Maria?"

"I am happy enough," she answered.

"You are always welcome here, or at any of the estates. There is a Dower House at…"

"I do not enjoy being alone, as you know," she interposed, "and once the child is born, I am certain it will lift my spirits Maria wishes to go to London from here."

"The offer is there if you should wish to avail yourself of it," he reiterated. At that moment, Hobson brought in a tray laid with tea and an array of foodstuffs, from sandwiches to fruit and their favorite currant tarts.

"What offer?" Maria asked as she sailed back into the room.

"If Mother ever wishes to live at any of the estates, or with me, of course."

"She does not wish to go to London, but I think it will be good for her. I had not meant to mention it so soon, but I also think you should join us, Gabe." Maria sank onto a gold damask sofa and helped herself to a tart.

Gabe raised his brows at her as if she had asked him to jump off the Dover cliffs.

"Have you not considered taking a wife to help you? You know it is your duty to produce an heir."

"Of course I know. I have thought of it." In truth, he did not wish to speak about it to anyone, but especially not in front of his mother or Philip. Perhaps if he could draw Maria off on her own, he might find it easier to explain his plans.

"Well, you are hardly likely to find someone while buried here in the country, are you?"

Gabe remained silent as Philip strode through the door, saving him from answering—for the moment, at least.

"Have you warned him, yet?" Philip asked.

Gabe was immediately wary. He turned his gaze on his sister and waited for the axe to fall.

"I have not had the chance," Maria said, looking guilty as she twirled a lock of her chestnut hair.

Gabe knew that look. He waited for her confession.

"We are to have a few visitors. I hope you will not mind, but you know all of them well. I have already informed Hobson and Cookie. I have brought my housekeeper and extra servants to help."

"Who?" Gabe growled, furious.

"Lord and Lady Marsden, Philip's parents, of course. Aunt Jane and Uncle Severn, Cousin Bertie and Louisa with one of her friends, and Jack and Kate."

Gabe was speechless.

"I knew you would not agree if I asked, so I decided it would be better to beg forgiveness rather than permission."

Gabe looked to his brother-in-law for help, but he only shrugged. Gabe was too stunned to reply. Years of training to restrain himself instantly came to the fore, luckily, or his sister would have been in dire straits.

"Say something, Brother."

He walked over to the windows and looked out at the lake, seething. He had hoped to have more time to get his bearings, but it seemed as though he would have no such luxury. His sister, however, should have known better than to do such a thing to him.

"What is there to say? It is already done. How long must I endure their company?"

"Only a week, then we go on to London," she said sheepishly.

Gabe closed his eyes. Nothing was going according to plan. He had hoped to invite Miss Sutton to the Park under the pretense of seeing Maria, then to slowly make her acquaintance before asking permission to court her. Not only was a week not enough time, but now it was to be such a large party.

Gabe remained where he was, silent, while the rest of them took their tea, and chatted about what needed to be done before the visitors arrived.

His mother left to rest in her chambers, then Philip begged leave to do some work in the study. That left Gabe alone with Maria.

"Please say something, Gabriel."

"You have already arranged this party of yours."

"I do beg your pardon, but you would not have agreed."

"You are correct in that, at least. What do you hope to gain by forcing me to accept these people in my house?"

Maria had the grace to wince. "Gabriel, they are family and friends. They want to welcome you home after a long absence. What is wrong with that?"

"Nothing, if it had been on my terms. You know how I have spent the last ten years of my life—well, you know some of it. You cannot expect me to change the color of my feathers overnight."

"You are worried about your reception?" She frowned.

"Not only that, but I find it inordinately difficult to… in short, it is not easy for me to be in a crowd, or to converse trivially with strangers."

"Then this will be excellent practice."

"Maria," he growled in a warning tone.

"Please, Gabriel. Try. For me, if not for yourself."

"I had other plans. Do my wishes not count?"

"Of course they do!" She rose and walked over to stand beside him at the window, then put her arms around him. "I do not wish for you to be angry with me. We can leave for London sooner."

He shook his head. "I do not wish for you to leave. I wanted to have time alone with you."

"Oh, Gabriel, I can send everyone away. I can make some excuse."

How he wished it was as simple as that, but he knew the guests would already be on their way. Some may well having been traveling for days already.

"I will endure their presence for your sake—but please, do not force me to do the pretty with any young misses."

"I had no intention of that… only to begin introducing you to one or two eligible ladies." She sighed heavily when he did not respond. "Have you begun to reacquaint yourself with the people in the village?"

"A little. It has not gone especially well." That was a gross understatement, he reflected dourly.

"What do you mean?" She walked back to retake her seat on the sofa, then patted her hand for him to come and join her.

Gabe hesitated, then sat down beside her. It was not easy to confess one's inadequacies. He sighed deeply.

"I will start at the beginning," he uttered at last, and then paused again. Despite his need to seek advice, this was almost unbelievably hard. "It took me several days before I felt I could enter the house, so I stayed at the inn in disguise— reconnoitering, as it were."

Maria raised her brows at this, but said nothing.

"I had finally resolved to return – I had called for my horse and was awaiting his arrival when I heard a scream. Naturally, I went to help."

"Naturally," Maria said, with a hint of sarcasm.

"It was only a dislocated shoulder that was simple enough to put back in place, but the victim was one of Reverend Sutton's sons. Do you remember the eldest, a girl called Rose?"

"Of course! She is still here? I thought she was expected to wed."

"I cannot be sure, but I think someone may have mentioned that he was a soldier and did not return."

"How sad. I must call on her. Do go on."

"Once that had occurred, Cook told me I could not hide until you arrived, since I had been seen."

Maria watched him. She looked wary. "What happened?"

"The village assembly was that night, of all things. I went, and tried to be proper. I recognized Rose and asked her to dance."

Maria frowned. "Did she refuse you?"

"No, no. She was all that was kind. But when the dance end-ed, everyone was staring… moving in on me."

She put her hand on his for comfort.

"I could not remain. I had to leave before I made a fool of myself."

"So you left straight away?"

"Yes. After just the one dance." He did not dare look into her eyes. "I was invited to dinner at the parsonage the following evening and I did manage to apologize. I even attended church the next day."

"Did you?"

"I told you I was trying to make myself amenable."

"But?" She prodded for further detail.

"Miss Sutton did not appear well and I escorted her to her seat. Afterwards we overheard a busybody telling Reverend Sutton he needed to mind his daughter better because my intentions could not be honorable towards one of her station."

"Well! How vulgar! I will wager that was Mrs. Winton, was it not?"

"I believe that was her name."

"She has been trying to convince the reverend for years that she should be his next wife. Poor Rose. What else?"

He shook his head. "Nothing else. Since then I have stayed at home so as not to cause her any more trouble."

"I am sure everything will blow over quickly, but I will call on her to make sure."

"Thank you, Sister. Do put in a good word for me, if you will. I do not think she likes me. You know I am not one for smooth words and fancy phrases."

"No, indeed." Her eyes twinkled. "Why should I put in a good word for you?"

"Because I intend to make her my wife."

⟫⟫⟩⟨⟨⟨⟨

ROSE WAS TRIMMING the dead blooms from the roses in her garden when she heard a carriage approach. She looked up at that, because there were not many people with carriages in the small village.

It was not one she recognized, and she watched as it grew closer. Soon she saw a friendly face at the window. "Rose!" Lady Maria waved.

Rose waved back as she set down her tools. Standing up, she pulled off her dirty gloves and apron, straightening her gown and bonnet as she walked towards the carriage.

"How are you, my lady? It is so good to see you again!"

"My lady? There will be none of that. You are still my oldest friend," Maria scolded.

Rose smiled, and then gasped as her friend climbed down from the carriage. "Congratulations on your marriage and your happy news!" she declared. "It suits you very well. You look beautiful."

"Thank you. I am lucky, indeed."

"Would you like to come in for tea?"

"I was actually hoping you might walk with me a little," Maria said. "I have been in the carriage most of the day."

"Of course. Let me tell someone where I am going."

Rose hurried back to the house and told Cook where she was going and then she joined Maria. It was surprising that she had come to visit so soon after her arrival. Once they were clear of the parsonage gates, Maria spoke again.

"Gabe told me what has happened since his return. He feels dreadful."

Rose was shocked by the plain speaking, but she supposed it was for the best. "What did he tell you?"

Maria waved her hand. "'Twas like plucking feathers from a robin, but finally I drew from him the tale of the assembly and about Mrs. Winton."

Rose grimaced. "He did overhear, then, did he? I was not certain, but he was delightfully cold to her when she tried to toady him."

"He has stayed away because he does not wish to cause more trouble for you, but he also feels the two of you may have had a bad beginning."

Rose could not deny it, but why did it matter to one such as he?

"I must say, my brother has never been a man of many words, nor one of empty compliments. He has had a difficult time of it—especially since he exposed our father's dishonor."

Rose was not certain why Maria was telling her this. It was

true, she did not care for the earl, but she did not precisely hold him in dislike. She did not quite know how to respond.

"How have you been? I was surprised to return and find you unwed. The last news I had from you, you were promised to someone."

Rose looked away. Had Bertie not mentioned her to his family? She felt too shy to say anything. "I had a beau who went away to war, but he did not return. It has been five years, long enough for me to move on."

"Forgive me. I cannot imagine what it must have been like for you... here... waiting. I was in Brussels just before Waterloo. Many of our friends were lost."

"We are fortunate in that your brother and husband survived."

"Yes," Maria agreed solemnly.

They had already meandered around the village green and back, and stood again near the parsonage gate.

"But that is not what I came here to say." Maria stopped and turned to Rose.

"Indeed?" Rose could not imagine what else there was to say. Theirs had always been an easy friendship, one able to pick up the thread when they met again as though no time had passed.

"I would like you to stay at the Park for the next week, if you are able. Unbeknownst to my brother, I have invited a few friends. I would be most grateful if you would come to even the numbers. I am sure my brother would appreciate another friendly face."

"I do not know how to answer you, Maria. You must know I have no refinement, no *Town bronze*, as Tommy would phrase it. I should not wish to embarrass you in front of your friends."

Maria dismissed Rose's concerns with one word. "Fudge!" she declared roundly. "You will do well enough. We are not in Town so you need have no fear on that score. Please, do come. It would be for just a week. 'Tis the only way I may be assured of your company long enough for a proper cose!"

"You are making so short a stay?"

"It is but a brief visit because we are going to London for part of the Season. I am hoping to convince my brother to come in the hopes he may find a wife."

"I daresay that is only natural," Rose replied.

Suddenly, Maria clapped her hands. "Why do you not come with us? You would, of course, come as my guest. I should so enjoy having you with me!" Maria offered handsomely and with what seemed to be genuine pleasure. "It would be the greatest of good fun, and, as I recall, there very few eligible gentlemen to choose from in Edwinstowe."

"I fear your memory does not fail you," Rose conceded, more tempted by the idea of going to London with a friend than by that of begging her unknown grandparents to take her in. Yet how would she fund such a venture? She could not allow Maria to do so. "I confess, I am tempted."

"Excellent! I will convince you by the week's end!"

Warily, Rose looked at the house, then pulled Maria through the gate and to the far end of the garden, where a cast-iron bench afforded some privacy. Maria followed without question. Once they were seated, however, she demanded, "What is it?"

"My father told me he is considering remarrying." Rose almost wailed the words. Taking a long breath to compose herself, she continued, "It is hard to imagine, but I fear Mrs. Winton has at last worn down his resistance."

Maria gasped.

"I know. The thought alone is repulsive, but at least she treats the children well."

"Poor Rose. Then there is no alternative. You must come to London with me. I will not hear otherwise."

"Do but consider, Maria! I have little enough standing in Edwinstowe. How I should go on in Town, I cannot say. I should be thought horribly provincial, you know. I have not a single gown suitable for even…" She broke off, searching her mind for an appropriate comparison. "Even a garden party." She waved her hand at her friend's latest fashion. "I am a veritable dowd, Maria!"

"Pish!" Maria dismissed her concerns with some vehemence. "I shall love to dress you and you need have no qualms for the cost. However…" she continued quickly, raising one hand against Rose's imminent protest, "as you can see, I will soon be unable to wear my gowns. Indeed, my dear, you will be doing me a good turn by wearing them. They will no longer be the style by the time I can fit into them again and it would be a waste to let them remain unused all Season!"

"You are very kind in making light of your charity, but I cannot like it. Unfortunately, I am afraid I will soon be in a position whereby I may be unable to refuse. I know I shall find it intolerable to be under the same roof with that woman, and I could not bear for Papa to know I disapproved of his choice."

"It is hardly charity," Maria argued, "but I do agree it would be best if you were to leave because you wish to do so."

Rose laid her hand on Maria's arm as suddenly all the consequences occurred to her. "Whatever shall I do if no gentleman offers for me?"

"Rose, dearest, you need have no fears of that, I assure you."

"How can you be so certain? I have very little to recommend me."

"Your sunny disposition and pretty face are quite enough. Why, only look at me! I am quite plain, and yet I made a brilliant match. My husband, of course, makes up for my lack of beauty. Indeed, he is too handsome by half. I still cannot believe he chose me." She shook her head, but looked dreamily happy.

"Nonsense, Maria! You are one of the prettiest ladies I know," Rose protested, and meant it.

"You are very kind to say so, but I cherish no illusions and never have. Thankfully, Philip is able to see all of me, not just my face." She stood up. "I must be going. Philip will wonder what has become of me. Shall I send the carriage for you in the morning?"

Rose could not believe this was happening, yet was it not just what she had been praying for? "I cannot believe my good fortune! Thank you, Maria. I will do my best to be ready."

Maria clapped her hands with giddy excitement. "I could not be more pleased. You must help me convince Gabriel to come to London."

Rose doubted anything she said or did would move such a pillar of stone, but she smiled back at her friend as that lady signaled to her coachman that she was ready to depart.

"I hope you can work a miracle in a week, Maria." Rose kissed her friend's cheek and watched her climb into the carriage before waving as it rolled away. For several minutes she remained where she was, watching the conveyance shrink into the distance, disbelief at her change in fortune having stunned her into immobility.

Rose went directly to her bedroom, collected the small chest of her mother's belongings from her wardrobe and set it on the bed. Sitting down, she removed and then opened the marriage certificate.

Lord Edward Robert Byrne to Violet Rosalind Sutton
21 June 1791

Her surname was Byrne. She said it aloud, but it felt foreign on her tongue. Would it be wrong to continue using the name Sutton? She knew from being the daughter of a rector, that only legal names could be used on a marriage certificate for it to be valid. She would have to ask Papa about that. In her heart she felt like a Sutton, but she also did not want to dishonor her real father's name either.

How would she feel if she met her grandparents? Were they even still alive? She doubted they would know who she was, especially if she kept Sutton as her name.

She looked through the rest of the trunk. There was a bundle of letters, tied up in a red ribbon, which had been exchanged between her parents. It would be a while before she was ready to read those. A small velvet pouch contained a few pieces of jewelry that Rose could wear. She doubted they were worth much more than sentimental value, but it would help her to feel that her mama was with her.

Next, she found her father's miniature. He was very handsome, his large blue eyes and honey-gold hair a mirror image of her own. What had he been like? Besides fiercely loyal and in love with her mother? Rose feared she would never know a love like that.

She closed the trunk and decided now was as good a time as any to tell her papa. She knew he would not prevent her going, but it would be difficult to leave, for it was unlikely she would return again as more than a visitor.

"Papa?" she asked, from the threshold of his study. He looked up at her and smiled.

"Come in, Rose. Is something on your mind?" He set his spectacles down.

"I have been thinking a great deal about what you said. Lady Maria was here earlier and has invited me to their house party this week, and to go to London thereafter. She has offered to be my patron."

"I see." He wrinkled his forehead, then scratched his brow. "I hope you did not think I wanted you to leave."

"Not at all, Papa. It did, however, occur to me that if you are resolved on marrying again, it might be difficult for me to stay here."

"No, no, my dear," he quavered. He looked crestfallen at the idea. "I am certain that my future wife would be pleased to have you here."

Rose shook her head. There was little point in arguing. He did not see Mrs. Winton's faults, and Rose did not wish to drive them apart. Her papa's happiness was of supreme importance.

"Papa, I am four-and-twenty. I may not have another opportunity. In the eyes of many I am already an ape leader."

"What nonsense. You have my blessing, of course. You will

be deeply missed, my dear."

"And I will miss all of you." Rose felt tears threatening.

"It is hardly goodbye, poppet," he said gently, using her childhood nickname.

"I know." But they both also knew nothing would ever be the same.

CHAPTER SEVEN

L ATER THAT EVENING, after dinner, Gabe joined Philip in a drink in the study. His mother and Maria were upstairs— plotting something or other, he was sure. He poured himself a glass of cognac, then sat in a chair to brood over the invasion of his home and privacy that was to occur the next day.

"Is it really so bad?" Philip asked, from where he was sitting, in a chair across from him, nursing his own brandy.

"You know me well enough to answer that for yourself." Gabe sank down into his chair, stretching out his legs and crossing his ankles.

"If it is any comfort to you, I sent a note to my parents, informing them we would call on them in London next week instead."

"That was not necessary," Gabe remarked. "I like your parents better than I do most persons of my acquaintance."

"I understand, but as you know full well, Maria is inclined to be exuberant and fails to understand why others may not love the company of people as much as she does."

Gabe barked a short laugh. "That is an understatement. Can you wave a wand and make the others disappear as well?"

Philip shook his head in mock sorrow. "I fear even I am not so skilled."

"Has Wellington been keeping you busy?" Gabe changed the

subject.

"Not really. Things are quiet at the moment. Now Maria is increasing, I have been considering following your lead and selling out."

Gabe was surprised to hear it. He would not have sold out had he not had the earldom to oversee. "What will you do?" he asked, intrigued in spite of himself.

Philip waved his glass in the air in a gesture of vagueness. "I suppose I shall take over the estate my mother is leaving to me. It has been vacant for some time now, anyway."

"What has the world come to? Jack first, then me and now you."

"In point of fact, Knight was first, but he is still a diplomat. I daresay, if I grow too bored, that is always a possibility."

"Poor Wellington. What will he do without all of us?"

"Hopefully he will not need us anymore."

Gabe raised his glass to that.

"There you are!" Maria said, coming into the room without ceremony and looking full of energy despite her condition. Both of them began to rise to their feet, but she waved them back down, then went to perch on the edge of Philip's chair. "What are you two discussing? Mother has gone to bed, and now I have no one to talk to."

"My poor darling," Philip teased.

"At least tomorrow I will not have that problem," she beamed.

Gabe was hard-pressed not to scowl.

"Mother and Father are going to join us in London instead," Philip remarked.

"Did you tell them not to come?" She looked affronted. "I invited them for Mother as much as for you."

"I understand, but a few more days will do no harm." Philip's voice was gentle yet commanding.

"Never mind, I shall forgive you." She made an airy motion with her hand. "I have invited a neighbor to join the guestlist to even up the numbers. She is one of my oldest friends, so I will enjoy having her here. She will get on wonderfully with Kate."

Gabe tried to remain impassive. He had not expected his sister to facilitate matters quite so much. He raised his brows at her, to which she smiled impishly and winked. "I have even convinced her to come to London with us. Is that not marvelous?"

"Why would you do that? I could more easily court her here," Gabe protested. He saw Philip's eyes flicker back and forth as he watched this interchange between the siblings, but wisely, his friend held his tongue.

"Are you certain of that, after what you overheard Mrs. Winton say?" Maria countered. "Rose thinks her father means to marry the harridan."

"'Tis no wonder she wants to leave, then," Gabe muttered.

"Therefore, I see it as my duty to help my friend," Maria added innocently.

"You intend to be her patron?" Philip asked.

"Of course!"

"I will not have you overexerting yourself in your condition," Philip warned.

"Nonsense. I have never felt better. And I will be careful—of course I will."

"Perhaps Mother would care to help. It might give her a new purpose… she still seems…" Gabe searched for the right word.

"Withdrawn?" Maria suggested. "Out of sorts?"

"I am hoping a grandchild will lift her spirits," Philip said. "Hopefully, too, once she sees her friends still receive her, it will ease the burden."

"I pray you are correct, Husband."

"What is she like, this friend of yours, wife of mine?" Philip raised his brows in cheerful query. "If she has caught so discerning an eye as Mottram's, I am intrigued, because 'twas my belief you had in mind several young ladies to parade before him."

Gabe glowered at the idea.

"Well, he appears to have done much of the work for me already," Maria said wryly, while Gabe tried not to protest at their discussing his marriage prospects in such a calculating manner. He did need help, after all.

"I soon realized it behooved me to marry, and I should prefer a girl who is unaffected. I do not believe I shall be comfortable with a society marriage."

"I can understand that," Philip conceded.

"Rose is very unaffected," Maria agreed. "She is also very beautiful."

"Is she, indeed?" Philip asked, feigning interest. Maria slapped him on the arm. Gabe knew Philip was only teasing. He was completely devoted to Maria, Gabe was pleased to acknowledge of his former colleague, who had once been considered a consummate rake.

"Her beauty is secondary to her good nature. It was what I noticed first about her. London is full of superficial beauties." Gabe felt the need to defend his choice, as if he had not considered it fully.

"We shall do our utmost to help you. I would be delighted to call Rose my sister—as long as you are certain. There may be some talk."

"Why would that be?" Gabe asked. "Surely, it is not be such an unequal match. She is the daughter of a gentleman."

"I know not the circumstances, but when we were younger, there were whispers about her birth. I know she is not Reverend Sutton's true daughter, but his niece. However, I know no more than that. You would have to ask her or the reverend."

Did the manner of her birth trouble him enough to raise such a question? Gabe was unsure. It would be to insult the family, yet he certainly did not want his children whispered about. Rose had been reared as a lady. "I cannot think there is aught to cavil at in her demeanor. How could I ask such a question? Every feeling must be offended."

"Perhaps I could discover more of the circumstances," his

sister responded. "I will reflect upon the best way to proceed."

Despite the fact Gabe was now questioning whether he had been too hasty in his choice, he could not yet envision any other lady as his bride.

"You have time to make your choice, Brother," Maria assured him. "You will be at liberty this week to determine if you and Rose will suit. Would I be correct in assuming you have said nothing of your interest, either to her or her father?"

He shook his head. "I have not." *Although I almost did so without a single word of courtship*, he added to himself. He now realized he should take a softer approach.

"Well, then, you may take such time as you need to get to know each other before making your decision. We will be making a prolonged stay in London when we leave here, should you wish to join us and broaden your search."

Most assuredly, Gabe did not wish to do that.

Maria stood up, holding her back. "I think I am for bed, my dear," she said. "We may not have too many opportunities to retire early for a while."

"I daresay you are in the right of it, as usual, my love," Philip agreed. "Indeed, I believe I should be wise to join you."

Rising, Gabe kissed his sister good night, but he did not follow them up to bed. His mind was too unsettled to sleep.

As had been the case with his military operations, he tried to consider the situation from all angles, and anticipate what could happen. Courting a lady was completely beyond his sphere of experience.

While the enemy was not always predictable, at least he could normally see most of their options and calculate their likely reaction. The female mind was a complete enigma to him.

With regards to Rose, he had thought he had many advantages on his side: position, wealth, acceptable looks. There were not many gentlemen in the village to choose from and he thought, at her age, she might be at least willing to look favorably upon his suit. However, if Maria were to take her to London and be her chaperone, Gabe knew his odds would be considerably lessened. Given Miss Sutton's beauty and sunny nature, and with his sister's connections behind her, she would soon be the toast of the ton.

Gabe was not unaware of his faults. He knew people thought him haughty and cold—perhaps even arrogant and aloof. Perhaps he was, although he did not behave that way intentionally. He did not have the gift of easy charm. Most things were distinctly black and white to him – right and wrong; except, that was, for wooing a lady. That, he reflected, could be termed as being in many shades of gray—no more like mud with mystery mixed in.

He had not thought anything could be harder than dealing with his father's scandal, yet he sensed this would be a challenge like no other. Somehow, he knew Rose was the right helpmeet for him, untainted as she was by Society. But how was he to convince her? Indeed, was he the right man for Rose?

The more he considered, the more Gabe wished he had asked his sister for more specific help, although he suspected she was already aware of what needed to be done. He knew quite well she had invited Rose to Arden Park on his behalf.

He thought of Rose's warm smile and husky laugh, and knew she was too good for him, but it did not keep him from wanting her. Perhaps some deep need buried inside craved to know such joy in his life once again—that innocence which had been stolen from him long ago. He would have to be very careful not to drag her down into his darkness, he determined broodingly, feeling his brow pinch in response. Nevertheless, the thought of trying to court anyone else was repugnant.

THE NEXT MORNING, Rose was nervous but resolved as she rode in the carriage sent for her by Maria. Her siblings had not realized her leaving was very likely for good. That circumstance was partially her fault, since she presented her departure to them as being somewhat of a holiday. Letty and Julia had shed many tears, however. It could not be helped. Looking back, she should have done this long ago. She was not so naïve as to believe her chances of making a brilliant match would be good. Papa had given her a hundred pounds to spend, though she doubted it would have stretched very far had it not been for Maria's generosity in lending her gowns. Papa had also saved a small dowry of five hundred pounds for her. It was little enough when compared with the fortunes of those among the ton, but she was touched nonetheless.

It was hard not to wonder what options she would have—if any. There was always a chance no one would want her to wife, but she could not enter into this venture without being sensible.

Besides possessing no fortune, she had no town sophistication. The last thing she wanted was to embarrass Maria when she had had the goodness to offer her patronage! Of course, Rose had been taught basic manners, but people in the country would laugh if she tried to put on airs above her station! Why would she wish to do such a thing?

Before long, the carriage rolled through the gates of Arden Park. The beauty of it struck her with wonder. It had been years since she had been there on a visit, and she was torn between fascination and fright. If she were being honest, the latter was mostly due to the earl. He had scarcely been present during her previous visits, and something about him unsettled her. As his forbidding face loomed in her mind's eye, she remembered Maria's words and resolved to give him a chance, though why he should be concerned with her opinion of him, she could not fathom. Surely, he would not trouble himself with one such as she! Even Quinn, for all of his pretty words, had no real interest in the rector's ward. She meant no more to him than a comely damsel with whom to practice his flirting and flaunt his dandy ways.

The trees opened up to reveal an imposing red-brick house

with steep gables, a common feature amongst old abbeys that had been transformed into manor houses. The carriage drew to a slow stop before the house. A footman opened the door for her and handed her down from the vehicle. As she walked hesitantly to the house the butler opened the door to greet her. Truly, Rose thought in wonder, she was being treated as an honored guest. It was humbling. For someone who had never been beyond twenty miles from home and had never attended a house party, she had little notion of what to expect.

"May I bid you welcome, Miss Sutton?" Hobson said with a bow.

"Thank you, Mr. Hobson. It is good to see you again," she returned.

"I will have your trunks brought up to your chamber. The family is in the drawing room." He held out his hand, indicating for her to go before him. She knew the way, yet she was still feeling shy and overwhelmed.

When they reached the door, Hobson stepped inside and announced her. "Miss Sutton."

Rose blushed at the formality and the attention drawn to her as several unfamiliar faces turned to look. The gentlemen stood up, and Maria came forward from the gathering, arms stretched out wide.

"Rose! I am so glad you are here. Let me introduce you to those you do not know." She took her hands then went around the room. "You know Mama, of course."

Rose curtsied to Lady Mottram. "My lady, you are looking well."

"You are kind to say so, Rose. I am pleased you could join us."

Maria was already leading her on. "This is my dear friend, Kate, and her husband, Captain Owens. You must not take too seriously anything Jack says."

Jack, a handsome man with blonde hair and a devilish twinkle in his eyes, bowed over her hand. "I am afraid every word is true." He winked roguishly. Rose laughed.

"I am very pleased to meet you," Kate said kindly. She was a very striking lady with a mass of red hair and blue eyes, and Rose tried not to feel intimidated.

"And this scoundrel," Maria said, pulling her away without ceremony, "is my dear Philip." Maria had not been exaggerating when she had said he was almost mythologically handsome. "Do you see what I mean?" Maria whispered in Rose's ear.

"I am pleased you have joined us, Miss Sutton. Any friend of my wife's is a friend of mine." He smiled at her and Rose could only wonder at Maria's good fortune. Of course, she was the most beautiful person in terms of character, but she was not a ravishing beauty, as one would expect to find on this man's arm. Rose liked him all the more for choosing her dear friend.

"And of course, you know Gabriel."

The earl bowed. "You are most welcome, Miss Sutton."

Rose curtsied and looked up into his pale blue eyes. His intense stare was unnerving. What did he mean by it?

"Thank you, my lord."

"I shall ring for tea," Maria said, leaving Rose standing alone with the earl. Desperately, Rose searched for something interesting to say—she, who was never at a loss for words.

"My sister tells me you are going to London with her," he said, at last interrupting the interminable silence between them.

"Yes. She has been kind enough to offer her escort. I had hoped to spend a Season in Town when I was younger, but my mama died and the opportunity was lost."

"I am sorry for it."

The poor man truly was not a gentleman of many words, was he? "It has been a long time. Papa and the children will do very well without me."

"Have you visited London before?"

"No, sir. I have not been beyond the county of Nottingham-shire." She laughed, feeling self-conscious, which was a strange sensation for her. "I imagine you have been all over the world."

"Mostly Europe," he corrected. "It would have been more pleasant to have seen it in times of peace."

"Forgive me. Of course, you were not there for pleasure."

"There is nothing to forgive."

Their gazes met and Rose tried not to squirm. The intensity in his eyes seemed to see more than most, although she had nothing to hide. Why was conversation with him so difficult? She was certain that somewhere, deep inside, he had fascinating stories to tell, but he seemed reticent to share them.

"Where do you prefer to be, my lord, in Town or in the country?"

"That is difficult to say. I enjoy parts of both."

She tried to smile encouragement for him to elaborate.

He seemed to be trying to accede. "I enjoy the quiet beauty of the country, but I also enjoy the architecture and inner workings of the city."

"I have seen pictures of some beautiful churches of Europe in one of Papa's books."

"Maybe one day it will be safe to travel and again see them at first hand," he said quietly.

The refreshments had arrived by this time and Maria handed each of them a cup of tea. "I am glad the two of you have found something to talk about," she said, dimpling.

Rose was not about to contradict her friend, but it was exhausting trying to draw words from a brick wall.

"I do hope you can convince him to come to London with us," Maria said.

"You are not going?" Rose asked before she could properly consider how impertinent she sounded. She had thought all peers went often to Town, for Parliament at the very least.

"He does not appreciate the crush of persons to be met with during the Season."

"I do not appreciate a crush of persons at any time," he muttered.

Rose knew that to be true, the poor man. Had he not apologized for that very thing? She felt another surge of sympathy. To have been thrust into his position with such an aversion, he must indeed be daunted.

"Perhaps you may commiserate with each other as you search for your companions in life," Maria teased. "You know, exchange notes and that sort of thing."

Rose felt her cheeks burn with embarrassment at her plight being spoken of so casually, but she supposed it was no secret that the Season was, in effect, the Marriage Mart. It seemed so callous to speak of a lifelong commitment in terms of a business arrangement, but she supposed that is what it was to most members of the ton. With a sinking feeling, she wondered if finding a spouse she enjoyed, respected, and liked was even possible—yet what other option did she have?

She looked up at the earl to see he was as uncomfortable with the notion as she—and by the look of anguish in his crystal blue eyes, she believed he was.

"After all, Gabe, how do you expect to find a wife if you do not look for one?" his sister continued.

"I daresay you are correct," he conceded, "but I hardly think this is the—"

"A suitable bride is hardly about to fall from the sky in Edwinstowe, Gabriel."

"Enough." The earl coughed discreetly. Rose took it as a warning to his sister. She was being unusually bold, as siblings were wont to do.

"Maria," her husband, Philip, called to her, at the same time beckoning with a finger. Rose wondered if he could tell she and the earl needed rescuing.

"It seems your sister is intent on managing both our hereafters."

"Ah, is that what they call interference nowadays?" he asked wryly.

Rose laughed at his slight show of humor.

"If we wish to avoid our lives being ordered for us, Miss Sutton, it would seem we may have to help each other after all. May the good lord preserve us from well-intentioned sisters."

Rose knew little about sisterly good intentions, but she was surprised at how brazen Lady Maria had been in her evident determination to find them suitable matches.

"Unfortunately, my sister is a kitten compared to Society ladies. When they hear tell of an eligible *parti* they are relentless."

"How so, my lord?" Rose was fascinated despite herself.

"They think it is their duty to see every eligible bachelor leg-shackled," he grumbled.

"It is not so unlike life in a village, then," Rose remarked.

"Perhaps, but on a much grander scale. Watch and see. If a young miss is caught without a chaperone, her reputation is instantly ruined. The cats like nothing more than to hear of a peer caught alone with a young lady, and then force the pair to wed. I have seen many a man fall into such traps."

"That sounds dreadful, my lord. No wonder you have no desire to go to Town."

"Nevertheless, my sister is correct. I do have need of a wife. It is my duty."

"And I have need of a husband." She said the words before she had properly considered. Gasping as she felt heat rising in her cheeks, she looked away. There was a long silence but he did not move from her side. She found herself loath to admit the necessity to this man for some reason. It all felt so mercenary.

At last he spoke. "Mayhap we might be of assistance to each other," he suggested quietly. She glanced swiftly at him. There was no discernible warmth in his features but he had raised one brow as though he thought she might recoil from the show of friendship.

Rose found herself agreeing with a gentleman she was still inclined to dislike, yet she could not but feel it would be prudent to have him on her side.

CHAPTER EIGHT

G ABE HAD NOT minded the first day of their guests. He rather liked Jack and his wife, Kate, and their new daughter, Josephine. She was too small to do anything more than sleep, but her presence did make Gabe think about having his own children. It was not something he'd done more than consider in a theoretical sense until now. Seeing a real child, however, and the offspring of one of his fellow soldiers, somehow made the notion different, especially now that he knew he would need an heir.

As the thought crossed his mind, he remembered his current heir was due to arrive that day. He had not known Bertie was back in England, and had been shocked to hear that Maria had invited him. She had little idea of her cousin's behavior on the Continent, of course. Not only was she asking him to be civil, but also to entertain him at his home.

Gabe gripped his mug of coffee almost hard enough to break it. He was to act as though nothing was wrong, as if a pretense of civility would somehow erase Bertie's sins. Not that Gabe was without fault. He had certainly committed acts for the army and Crown that he was not proud of, but at least it had been done for the greater good and under orders. If only he could say the same about his cousin.

"Good morning, my lord. Am I disturbing you?" Rose asked softly.

Gabe looked up from his coffee. He had not even sensed that she was there. She looked fresh and lovely in a simple yellow cotton frock. He stood up quickly. "Not at all. I was not expecting anyone else to awaken for hours."

"I am always up with the singing of the birds," she confessed sheepishly. "There is always work to be done."

"Yes, of course. Your father is lucky to have you to oversee his household."

A look of sadness marred her charming features, and he wondered what he had said to distress her.

"Would you care for some coffee?" he asked, not knowing what else to do.

"No, thank you. I prefer tea."

Gabe rang the bell, and a footman appeared shortly afterwards. Gabe did not take food this early in the morning, so he did not require anyone to wait upon him. "Order anything you like."

"Just tea and toast, please," she said to the servant, who bowed and withdrew.

An awkward silence followed.

"Please do not feel obliged to wait on me," she said. "I would not wish to keep you from any plans you may have."

He was hard-pressed not to laugh, but she would probably take it amiss. How could he explain to her that he felt as though he had nothing meaningful left with which to occupy himself? That there was a team of competent stewards, solicitors, and bankers that needed very little direction from him to manage the estates and earldom? That he was tempted to shed his neckcloth and plow the fields so he might feel he was doing something useful? She would hardly wish to hear that he would prefer fighting battles to playing the idle gentleman... but that brought another thought to mind. "I know you are soon to leave for London, but your father dropped me a hint there were those in the parish lacking certain necessities. If it would not be too much trouble, would you tell me who requires help? It seems you are well acquainted with the needy in the village."

He had expected her to look pleased, but instead, she appeared skeptical.

The footman placed a rack of toast and a pot of tea before her. Gabe waited while she added a splash of milk and one spoonful of sugar to her tea, and stirred with a few faint clinks of silver against the fine porcelain. She set the spoon down on the saucer and looked up at him. "I think it might be better if I show you, my lord."

"When would be convenient?"

"Now?" she returned, taking a sip of her tea. "Unless you are otherwise occupied this morning, of course. The villagers, as I am sure you will be aware, will already have been at work for hours."

Gabe was well aware of the early habits of country folk, having spent time in Edwinstowe before returning to the Park. Soldiers rose at dawn as well. Nonetheless, he wanted to know what details he had missed—which persons he had neglected to assist in their time of need.

"Do you ride?" he asked. "Or would you prefer to travel in the carriage?"

"Actually, sir, a cart would be more to the purpose."

He watched, mesmerized, as she smoothed some fresh butter across her toast. "Whatever you wish."

"Thank you, my lord."

"Of course." Gabe never said anything he did not mean, which was why he said very little.

"Then you will not mind if I ask your Cook to prepare some baskets?"

Ah. "How remiss of me. Of course, my mother was used to give provisions to the sick and elderly. I presume no one from the Park has seen fit to fulfil this duty in her absence?"

He could see from the look on Rose's face that they had not. Gabe would have thought his old retainers would have known he would wish all such niceties to be continued as they had been before.

"I have done what I could," she said softly.

"Please finish your breakfast. I will go now and speak with Cook. Please join me when you are ready. Do you know the way to the kitchen?"

She nodded. "I do."

Gabe did not know why he felt as if he had been scolded, and he tried not to feel anger for his servants having not carried out his unspoken wishes. As he entered the kitchens, Cook turned and evidently saw him scowling.

"Dear me, whatever is the matter, Master Gabriel?"

"Baskets. We must prepare baskets for the needy in the village. What were we used to send?"

"Preserves, vegetables, bread..." She waved her hand. "Whatever we had spare."

"Why did it stop?"

Cook wiped her hands on her apron and leaned against the work table. "All the old ways stopped when your parents returned from London."

"I presume the needs of the villagers did not cease?"

"You know they did not, sir." She looked as guilty as he felt. "For a time I was able to continue gifts to the poor, but your father let so many of the servants go, there was no one to deliver them."

Ah. At least now he understood.

"Do you have enough maids to provide for my guests? You have my full authority to hire whatever under-servants you have need of."

"We can put up some baskets for today, my lord, but if I might hire some of the older children in the village, it would be a great help to many of the families. Several of the eldest have already left to find work in other places."

"Then do what needs to be done." He turned away, wondering what he should do next.

"Master Gabriel?" Her tone took him straight back to the nursery and those occasions when he had neglected to wash his hands before mixing the dough for his favorite biscuits.

He turned once more to face her, his eyebrows raised in gentle irony.

"If I might be so bold, sir, her ladyship always felt it her duty to lend a hand in preparing the baskets as well as delivering them. As we are short-handed, perhaps you might see your way to fetching the baskets? You will find them on the top shelf at the back of the larder." She pointed, but he knew the way. He felt a reluctant smile twist his lips at how neatly she had turned the tables, and at the same time given him occupation. The smile she gave him on his return was well worth the labor and the impertinence.

Willingly, therefore, Gabe began to follow Cook's instructions, and before long, over a dozen baskets were spread out on the vast table.

"How may I be of assistance?" Rose appeared next to him.

Gabe looked up at Cook for his own orders.

"Miss Sutton." Cook bobbed a curtsy, but did not seem surprised to see Rose in her kitchens.

"Mrs. Marks," Rose responded politely.

"There are jars of preserves in the larder, if you'll be so kind as to fetch those, my lord," Cook suggested. "If you would help me wrap these loaves," she said to Rose, "that would clear the table a little." She indicated a jumble of fresh bread. No doubt, Gabe mused, on his return from the larder with an armful of jars, the loaves had been made that morning for himself and his guests.

"If you know of any girls capable of kitchen duties who could be of help to me this week, I should be obliged," he overheard Cook say to Rose.

"I know of at least two who might be glad of the work, Mrs. Marks," Rose replied. "If you wish, I could speak to them this morning."

After adding preserves to each basket, Gabe left Rose and Cook to finish filling the remaining space with bread and fresh vegetables while he went to send a groom for a cart in which to transport the offerings.

The last thing he had anticipated, when he awoke that morning, was to be sitting close to Rose while he drove them into the village.

"I must thank you," he said.

"Thank me?" she repeated, looking surprised.

"I did not mean to neglect my people."

"You were abroad and could not have known," she answered quietly. "You are here now."

They drove on for a few moments with only the sound of the horses' hooves clopping along. Then it occurred to Gabe what she was risking by being seen with him alone again.

"Are you certain you should be seen alone with me?"

She hesitated before answering. The yellow ribbons of her floppy bonnet fluttered in the wind. "Perhaps we should have brought along a groom or waited for Maria to join us, but it is the right thing to do regardless of what people say or think. Most of the people we will be visiting are not gossips. They will be only too happy for these baskets. They could mean the difference between living in their own cottages or the workhouse."

The reminder of his neglect made Gabe wince. It was a well-deserved barb whether she intended it as such or not. She still did not seem to like him despite the friendliness he had thought they had achieved the day before.

"Very well. Where to first?" he asked as they neared the village.

"Turn left along the old gatehouse road."

Gabe slowed the cart to turn on to the old road. It was rutted and narrow, overgrown with hedges, yet another instance of neglect he would need to attend to. He wondered what else had been overlooked in his absence.

"Up ahead lives Mrs. Hoskins. She lost her husband in the war and has three small children: two boys, and a baby girl born after her father's death."

At the end of the lane was a ramshackle cottage with a sagging roof and an overgrown garden. A few chickens wandered aimlessly, pecking at the ground, and some goats were munching on the overgrown weeds. Gabe felt as though a knife were twisting in his heart. This was one of his properties and should never have been allowed to fall into disrepair.

Two dirty little urchins came out to greet them.

"Miss Sutton!" The boys greeted her with a wave as Gabriel drew the horses to a halt and pulled the brake into position on the cart's rear wheel.

"Good morning, Danny and Johnny. Is your mother at home?"

"No, ma'am. She's gone to sell the milk and eggs."

"What have you brought?" Danny asked, standing on tiptoe to try and look into the wagon.

"Just a few things for your mother."

Two toothless, disappointed faces looked up at her.

"I am certain she will show you when she returns, but you must wait until she comes home. Do you understand?" Rose said firmly. She spoke and behaved like a school matron, Gabe mused.

"Yes, Miss Sutton," the boys chorused.

"I have missed you at school lately," she added, resolving Gabe's pondering.

"Sometimes Mama needs help here," Johnny said, looking at his feet.

She ruffled his hair. "I understand."

"Who is that gen'lman?" Danny asked.

Gabe stayed back after pulling a basket from the cart for them, watching and learning.

"This is the new Lord Mottram, boys. He has just returned from the war. Make your bows." The boys complied awkwardly and Gabe inclined his head in return.

"Our papa was a soldier, but he didn't come home," Johnny said.

What was Gabe to say? He already felt enough guilt for returning from the war alive when so many others had not, and now he felt responsible for their poverty. He vowed to make it right.

Gabe was mostly silent as he and Rose spent the next few hours visiting the sick, infirm and elderly in the village and surrounding countryside. All were effusive in their thanks and generous with the little they had, offering meager hospitality when in truth they had nothing. Humbled by the experience, Gabe began to formulate a plan of action. At least now he had a purpose.

>>>><<<<

ROSE HAD FORGOTTEN about the house party. They had spent several hours delivering baskets, but the whole while, the earl had been very quiet. Three hours they had been out, and he had scarcely said as many words at each house! She was disappointed, but why she had expected more of him, she could not say.

By the time they returned to Arden Park, she was not prepared for the new visitors. She was exhausted from doing all the talking, and wanted to be alone. For the next several weeks at least, she feared she would have no time to herself whatsoever.

Maria came out to greet them as the cart stopped. "There you are! Did you forget more visitors were arriving today?" she asked her brother.

"How could I forget?"

"It is my doing, Maria," Rose interposed despite her annoyance. "I took his lordship to the village to show him some repairs which needed to be done. He was kind enough to help me deliver baskets to some of the needy. Time escaped us. You know when I start talking, I do not know when to stop."

"I wish you had told me you were going. I would have accompanied you," Maria said, softening her tone.

"These are visits I make often. It was so early we did not wish to disturb you," Rose explained.

"Our aunt, uncle, and cousins are in the drawing room," Maria told Lord Mottram.

"Would you think me terribly rude if first I wash my face and change my gown?" Rose asked. The earl's family would hardly be interested in her, and she felt quite disheveled.

"Of course not. Take your time," Maria insisted. "I fear my brother, however, should make haste," she added with a teasing smile.

"I would not wish to appear in all of my dirt, either," Lord Mottram remarked.

Rose didn't know why she felt the need to defend him. Even though he had not spoken a great deal, at least he had been willing to help with the charity baskets—a duty which customarily fell to the lady of the manor—and seemed remorseful for the estate's oversight during his absence.

As Lord Mottram left to go to his chambers, Rose turned to retreat to hers when Maria stopped her. "I have placed some gowns in your room. They are not the latest fashion but they are of good quality, should you wish to make use of them. I will send my maid in to help you. She is adept with a needle and will make any small alterations in the twinkling of an eye!"

Rose nodded and smiled gratefully. There was little use in denying that she needed the charity, even though such largesse was still difficult to accept. As she climbed the polished marble stairs, the irony of her visits to the poor neighbors that morning could not be lost on her. Was it even right for her to dress in borrowed clothing, and pretend to be something she was not? The fact that she had no alternative was disheartening and she felt deceitful.

When she entered her chamber, it was a large, luxurious apartment of pale pink and cream with a picturesque view out over the lake. Several beautiful gowns were spread out across the bed for her selection. Relishing the softness of the fabrics, she ran her fingers across one of lavender silk and another in a pale green muslin. As she did so, a knock sounded on her door. "Come in," she answered.

Maria's maid, Bisset, entered the bedchamber. "Good afternoon, miss. Have you made a selection?"

"Not yet. What would you suggest?" Rose knew that Maria had been in some of the finest drawing rooms and ballrooms in the world. This was hardly of the same echelon, yet Rose felt just as intimidated.

"Your coloring will look well in any of these. I think perhaps the light green muslin would be suitable for today."

The maid helped Rose into the appropriate undergarments to fit the gown, then helped her with the intricate laces on the back. Rose had never had a maid, and therefore her gowns were fashioned on a simple pattern so she might dress herself. Thankfully no alteration was needed.

She picked up her brush and ran it through her wavy hair. Releasing a deep breath, she was then ready to face the newcomers—well, as ready as she would ever be.

"Tsk. You do not mean to dress your hair?" Bisset asked.

"My hair will never stay in any sort of fashionable arrangement. The best I can do is to wear a bandeau."

The maid curled her lip and waved Rose into the seat before the dressing table. "Give me but a moment."

Rose dared not argue with the intimidating French maid. She brushed and pulled and braided and pinned until Rose was afraid to look in the mirror.

"Voila! Now you are ready to be seen." Bisset beamed with satisfaction.

Rose looked up and almost did not recognize her own reflection. "This is necessary for me to take part in a country drawing room?" she asked. "I look fit for Almack's!" Getting to her feet, she walked towards the door.

"You look parfait. Now you may go and enchant the earl."

Rose paused at that statement and turned back. "I have no ambitions towards the earl," she said quietly. "A quiet country gentleman will do." She smiled sadly, hoping even that was not too much to ask for.

"Do not make light of your charms, my lady."

Rose did not correct the maid's slip of the tongue. She made her way to the drawing room, sharing the chatter from the guests which wafted up through the house. She wondered what the talk in the servants' quarters might be, to make Maria's maid say such a thing! She vowed to be more careful with her reputation in the future. How could she have been so foolish as to go out, unaccompanied, with Lord Mottram? While it was true she was beyond the age of needing a chaperone, and she had been going about on her own in Edwinstowe for some years, Mrs. Winton had already made it clear she thought Rose to be reaching far above her station. She snorted with derision. As if the earl would even consider someone like her for a bride! For herself, she could only think of Bertie and how opposite he was in nature to his cousin. Her throat filled with emotion, but she resolved to be strong. If she was not mistaken, it was his family which should have arrived.

She did not relish seeing Bertie's parents, for it would be difficult to pretend she had not known and loved him. If Maria had been unaware of Bertie's promise to Rose, then she doubted his parents or sister would be.

Pausing before reaching the open doors to the drawing room, she inhaled a deep breath for courage, then stepped inside. The normally large drawing room felt small and crowded with the new arrivals, clustered in groups of gold and cream chairs and sofas around the room.

Maria came forward and took her arm as she had done the day before.

"Please forgive my tardiness, Maria."

"You look beautiful. Is Bisset not a wonder?" Maria led her to an older couple; the gentleman looked very similar to the old Lord Mottram. "Uncle Severn and Aunt Jane, I believe you met my dear friend, Rose, some years ago."

"Indeed. Reverend Sutton's gal?" he asked, rising to his feet to bow.

"Yes, indeed. It is lovely to see you again, sir." She dropped a curtsy. It was on the tip of her tongue to speak condolences to them, but Maria pulled her to the nearby sofa where two young ladies sat.

"Here are my cousin Louisa and her friend, Lady Alice Montgomery. They will also be having their first Seasons in London," she remarked in introduction.

Rose curtsied. Lady Alice was very beautiful, with golden curls and bright blue eyes, and Rose had little doubt she had been invited as a prospective bride for the earl. Rose felt rather sorry for the young girl, who must be around sixteen years of age. In her situation, she would be bartered off to an older man for wealth and position. At least Rose did not have concerns on that score.

Louisa had grown into a pretty young lady, having chocolate-coloured hair and matching eyes. She had been much younger when last Rose had seen her. She was no beauty, unlike Lady Alice, but she was warm and friendly, much in the way her older brother had been.

Jack and Kate were sitting nearby, alongside Lady Mottram who was doting on baby Josephine. The child was cooing and blowing bubbles and Rose could not resist patting her soft downy hair and stroking a finger down her round cheek.

"She is perfect. You must be so proud."

"Indeed," Kate said softly, and looked knowingly at her, as if she understood why Rose was about to subject herself to the rigors of the Season. Maria had told her that Kate had grown up as the ward of Jack's crotchety old grandmother, and had been treated like a servant.

Rose faintly registered Lord Philip speaking to another guest in the corner, but Maria pulled her away from adoring the baby in order to finish introducing her. Rose smiled as she disentangled her finger from the tiny fist that held onto it.

"This is my cousin, Lieutenant Albert Lloyd," Maria said, as

Rose turned and looked, and almost stumbled into Maria when she recognized the other guest. "Are you quite well?" Maria asked. "You look as though you have seen a ghost."

"Bertie? You… you are alive?" Rose whispered, not answering her friend's enquiry.

Her eyes sought his, and he paled when he saw her. "Miss Sutton," he sputtered, bowing. It was truly he! Those golden-brown curls and hazel eyes she had dreamed about were there before her in the flesh. How long had he been returned to England? Was he ever to have told her?

Rose clutched Maria's arm for dear life. She had to escape before she made a greater fool of herself.

"I must leave," she said quietly to Maria and turned away.

"Very well, but wait a few more minutes so the others do not notice anything amiss. You shall tell me what is wrong later. I assume my cousin has treated you ill in some way?"

Rose managed a slight nod and swallowed hard. Maria led her to a seat near the window, thankfully not asking anymore questions.

What a complete fool she was! For five years she had been pining over the man—for gentleman she would not term him—and waiting for him to return. Now here he was, very much alive and laughing with Lord Philip. It was of little comfort that at least he had had the decency to remember her name.

"Would you care to tell me what he did?" Maria asked quietly, looking concerned.

Rose blinked back tears. "I cannot stay here. Please make my excuses." She stood up, smoothed her gown and walked as calmly as she could from the room. Once beyond the threshold, she escaped through the rear of the house and out of the back door into the garden. Picking up her skirts, she began to run toward the lake, desperately trying not to fall into a fit of despair.

CHAPTER NINE

G ABE HAD JUST finished speaking with Philip and Jack about the idea he had had to help the villagers. He was pleased with the possibilities, and hoped Rose would approve. He dared not bring veterans into the village without first considering the possibility that they would not be well received, but he hoped they and the villagers would be able to support each other. After speaking with Rose, he would then seek an audience with the rector. Some things could not wait for the veterans.

When Rose had walked into the drawing room, Jack had moved back towards his wife and daughter, and Philip had gone to speak with Bertie. He was glad someone could be civil, because he had little to say to his wayward heir.

He was struck anew by Rose's beauty when she entered and watched quietly as she charmingly greeted everyone in the room—until the interchange with Bertie. Then he knew his cousin had done something very, very wrong.

It had been difficult to hear over the other conversations in the room from where he stood by the windows, but he overheard Maria ask Rose if she had seen a ghost.

With a sinking feeling, he realized Bertie must have been the beau she had referred to as being lost in the war.

He wanted to go to her, but he knew he had no right. Besides, she would want smooth words of comfort that he did not possess. Even so, she would not want them from him. He was keenly aware that she did not seem to care for him. The easy smiles she had for everyone else were unnatural and strained when turned towards him.

She left the room fighting tears, although he did not think anyone else had noticed.

What could he do to help? The only thing he could conceive of was to ask Bertie to leave, yet he needed confirmation that this was what had upset Rose. While he was happy to have any excuse for his cousin to leave, it would be better to have a good reason.

He waited until the company began to disperse before he stopped Bertie at the door. "A word, if you please."

He saw the distaste on his cousin's face before he formed it into a sort of smile. "What can I do for you, Cuz?"

"We need not pretend to like each other," Gabe replied.

"Very well." Bertie folded his arms over his chest.

"Would you care to explain your previous relationship with Miss Sutton?"

"I do not know what you are implying, but I met her a few years ago when my family was here for a visit. We became friendly." He shrugged.

"Friendly enough to raise expectations in the lady's mind?" Gabe saw no need to prevaricate, and caught the look of guilt before Bertie disguised it, but he wanted to see him wriggle his way out of this corner.

"It was a mild summer flirtation, that is all—youthful folly. You know how it is when one is young."

Gabe raised his brows.

"She could not have thought I wanted to marry her!" he whined.

"It was quite clear to me that she knew you well enough to be shocked, having evidently been led to believe you died in the war."

"I cannot be expected to inform every female who harbored a

tendre for me that I was *not* killed in the war!"

"You may, however, be expected to inform those who had promises from you before you left."

"Who says I made promises to her?" Bertie blustered.

"Did you?"

Bertie did not answer directly but his words offered the truth. "What do you expect me to do? Apologize?"

"Did you ruin her?" Perhaps Gabe did not have the right to ask, but it was clear no one else was prepared to defend her, or hold his cousin accountable.

"No," he scoffed. "The virtuous rector's daughter would not let me touch her."

Thank God. He did not want Rose to be burdened for life with such a wretched specimen.

"I am deeply touched that she waited for me, but unfortunately, my tastes have changed over the years."

That was a gross understatement. It took a great deal of will for Gabe not to plant Bertie a facer then and there. It certainly would have been satisfying.

"As Miss Sutton has been invited by my sister to spend the week with us and go to London afterwards, I think it best if you keep your distance from her."

"Why should I do that? I may wish to renew our friendship," he drawled.

"You forget, *Cousin*, that the allowance the earldom pays to the heir may easily be withdrawn."

"A pittance." He spat. "Are you threatening me?"

"You do not seem amenable to my request from any sense of common decency. An honest man would leave Arden Park at once."

"Is it not enough that you have the title and the money? No, now you must lord it over me in every aspect of my life, just as you enjoyed doing in the regiment!" he shouted.

"Had you behaved in a proper fashion in the regiment, you would not have needed to see me above once in a while." Gabe maintained his calm with great effort.

"You held me to a higher standard than every other soldier," Bertie sneered. "Not everyone is just such a paragon as you."

"Enough." Gabe tried not to scowl at his cousin in a like manner to the way Bertie was scowling at him. Why could they not have a civil conversation? Perhaps the answer was because, no matter what, he could not like his cousin's sense of entitlement to anything and everything that gave him pleasure at the expense of whatever he destroyed in its path. Was there any hope of redemption for someone like that? Gabe did not know why he allowed himself to continue to feel disappointment in his heir. He needed to stop giving the cur so much power, he reflected. The interview certainly firmed his resolve to marry and produce his own heir, as this one would never be fit for anything.

"I think you should make your excuses and leave. You had forgotten some very pressing engagement in Town—perhaps a meeting with the East India Company about a prospective position?" Gabe suggested.

"You are surely not serious?"

"I have never been more so in my life." Gabe used the tone he reserved for enemy prisoners.

Bertie laughed as though he thought Gabe had lost his mind.

"I should have reined you in long ago."

"You cannot just dismiss me like this because of Miss Sutton." Bertie's face was red with anger and humiliation.

People like Bertie never understood why the world did not center around them. It was only because of his respect for his aunt and uncle that Gabe had not done anything so drastic before.

"If it were but the first time. Do not insult me by making me recite the long list of offenses on the Peninsula."

"If you expect me to disappear for the Season, you will have to pay for it."

"I will have some funds transferred into your account, but there will be no more after that." Gabe just resisted growling. If he ever saw Bertie again it would be far too soon.

"I'll leave you to make my excuses to my parents." He stormed out, slamming the door behind him.

Gabe would deal with that problem later. First, he wanted to check how Rose did—if she was still on the estate. He went out into the entrance hall to find his butler.

"Hobson, did you see which way Miss Sutton went?"

"I believe she went towards the lake, my lord."

Gabe did not want to know how the old man knew everything, but he hoped the butler was right. Gabe ran across the terrace and down the steps beyond the parterre garden towards the lake, breathing a sigh of relief when he saw Bertie galloping away down the drive. Good riddance.

He scanned the shore of the lake but could not see her. He cursed under his breath. Was he too late?

The village was in the other direction, and he did not think she would leave without her belongings. Hobson would have known. Where was she?

He kept walking, trying to think of what else he could do. He wanted to run to her and tell her he had removed Bertie from her sight. He reached the edge of the lake and still could not see her. The bench was empty, as was the folly. Perhaps he should let Maria tell her the good news.

Looking out over the still water, he thrust his hands in his pockets, feeling a foreigner in his own home. He had never felt as though he truly belonged in the army, either, but at least there he had been able to blend into the shadows and do his duty.

Gabe doubted he would ever be able to blend into the fabric of Society in his new role. Perhaps he should abandon his quest with Miss Sutton. She deserved better than such a misfit. Doubtless he should go to London and coldly choose a bride from among this Season's hopefuls, as everyone expected of him.

"My lord?"

Gabe turned to see a red-rim eyed Miss Sutton standing before him.

"There you are. I came to see if you were quite well."

Her expression told him he had not been looking very hard. The unspoken reproof was just. He had become lost in his thoughts.

"Please forgive my abrupt departure from the drawing room."

"There is nothing to forgive. I understand why you left."

"You do? Did Maria…" Her voice faltered.

"Maria said nothing. I deduced for myself the cause of the situation. My cousin's behavior…" He shook his head." I will not make excuses for him, but he served under my command, and I understand fully what he is capable of. Allow me to apologize for the distress he has evidently caused you."

"You need not apologize for him, sir. It is entirely my own fault. It is clear to me now that I misread the situation very badly."

"Knowing Bertie as I do, I am quite sure he gave you every reason to believe him sincere in his affections."

He saw tears welling in her eyes, and wished he could comfort her.

"I… I should go and pack my portmanteau."

"No," he said abruptly. "That will not be necessary. My cousin is gone and will not bother you again."

"You sent him away?"

Curtly, he inclined his head. "There is no occasion for you to leave."

"I do not know what to say." She looked around as though confused, unsure of what to do.

"Say you will stay." He hoped he did not sound as desperate as he felt. He held out his arm, hoping she would accept it. Tentatively, she placed her fingers there. She still did not wish for his company, he could tell, but it was a start.

ROSE HAD FULLY intended to leave Arden Park, but she could tell the earl was trying to help, so she accepted his arm and they walked slowly back to the house in silence. So many thoughts were running through her head, she did not know how to separate them.

Not but ten minutes ago, she had been entertaining thoughts of becoming a governess, or a companion. She could not face the prospect of staying under the same roof as Bertie, knowing he had lied to her; that he had made false promises with the intention of dishonoring her. She could not consider that to be anything less than the truth. Now that she looked back upon their meetings, she realized how gullible—what a *fool*—she had been. For a moment she closed her eyes. The horror of what could have been her situation was unthinkable. Thank God she still had her virtue!

Nevertheless, the reality was a bitter pill to swallow. If an untitled gentleman like Bertie had not wanted her, then it was unlikely anyone in Society would. Yet she knew she could not go back home for long. She did not wish to burden her papa, and she did not wish to tell them what a simpleton she had been.

"Does anyone else know of this?" Rose asked quietly as they neared the house, Lord Mottram walking companionably by her side. "I pray the whole house is not agog over the tale."

"No, and your secret is safe with me. Maria may suspect, but my cousin left immediately, without even speaking to his parents. I will make his excuses for him. You need not feel it is your fault. This is wholly his doing and his shame."

Rose found it difficult to believe some of the fault was not hers. At the very least, she had been remarkably naïve. Yet there was little alternative to staying here, unless she crawled home with her tail between her legs.

"Thank you, my lord." She curtsied, he made her a bow, then walked into the house alone, wishing she might seek the sanctuary of her bedchamber. The first thing she needed to do, however, was find Maria and explain her behavior in the drawing room. Her spirits dropped further, for she doubted her friend would wish her to go to London when she had heard the whole.

Maria was with Kate in the nursery. It was a bright room with dormer windows, and other bedrooms off of the main room which was full of books and toys and cheerful scenes of animals on the walls. The new mother was rocking a sleeping Josephine while the ladies chatted comfortably.

Maria looked up at Rose's soft knock on the open door. "Am I disturbing you?" Rose asked politely.

"Not at all. Do come in," Kate said.

"I should not wish to wake the baby."

"There is little fear of that. She sleeps like her father. Nothing short of a cannon exploding wakes this one." She laughed. "But if you wish for privacy, I am happy to tuck her into the cradle and leave you together."

"No, indeed." Rose took her head. "I would appreciate your opinion as well."

Maria patted the window seat next to her; Rose walked over and joined her.

"I would have followed you," Maria said, "but it looked as though you needed a little time to yourself, and I did not want to draw attention to you."

Rose smiled appreciatively. "Thank you. I must beg your pardon. My behavior was inexcusable, and I wish to explain."

Kate looked a little confused, but she remained quiet.

"When your cousins visited here, about five years ago, I was a silly young girl, and thought I had fallen in love. A handsome young soldier made certain promises to me. Well, I took them as promises."

Maria's hand reached across, took one of Rose's and held it. "I remember that you were fond of each other, but I had no notion there was an attachment."

"I waited for him, of course. After Waterloo, I did not hear from him again. Indeed, I assumed he was lost there."

Beside her, Maria sucked in a breath. "Then you saw him for

the first time again today." It was a statement, not a question.

Rose nodded. "I was going to leave. In the circumstances I could not stay, of course, but your brother has asked him to leave. He is already gone, apparently. Please believe me I had no thought to cause a rift within your family."

"You have done no such thing. It seems my cousin has brought this upon himself. I will tell you one thing, however. There is no love lost between Gabriel and Bertie."

"I knew Bertie had written some unkind comments about being under the earl's command in the army." Now, of course, she could not but question if anything he had ever said to her was true.

"My cousin wrote to you?" Maria looked surprised.

"Yes. Up until the battle at Waterloo."

"And yet this afternoon he barely acknowledged you. What an utter scoundrel! I am glad Gabe has sent him on his way!"

Rose was a little shocked to hear that both Maria and her brother supported her. "Please forgive me," she said again. "I did not mean to come between you and your family. I am quite prepared to leave at once." She paused and looked down at Maria's hand, squeezing her fingers in silent entreaty. "May I beg you to write me a reference?"

"Certainly not, Rose Sutton! You will come to London as my guest, and I will hear none of such a notion, if you please. I will not entertain it. If you have not, by some mischance, secured an offer by the end of the Season—which I very much doubt—then we may reconsider finding you a suitable position, but *not a moment before!*"

Kate, seated in the chair across from them, was chuckling. "She was just as heavy-handed with me, I am afraid. It is pointless to argue."

At a soft knock, all the ladies turned towards the door. Mr. Owens and Lord Philip stood on the threshold.

"We do not mean to interrupt, ladies, but we thought you would care to know are going into the village to help Mottram with a little problem."

"I was wondering why you were dressed for common labor," Maria remarked. Rose had not even noticed.

"That is because we intend to labor," Jack quipped.

"On what, pray tell?" Maria asked.

"There is a widow whose roof needs mending, and it seems there are too few men to help," Lord Philip answered, as if this was a normal request.

"Do not hurt yourself," Kate ordered.

"Do you think we did not mend fences and dig trenches in the army?" Mr. Owens looked offended.

"Not often," Maria answered, lifting her cheek for her husband's kiss. "Do be careful."

"Always," Lord Philip said, with a mischievous grin.

"Hardly." Maria shook her head, watching fondly as the two gentlemen left again.

Rose listened with interest, because she suspected she knew exactly where they were going.

"I, for one, am glad they have something to keep them busy," Kate mused.

"Indeed," Maria agreed. "It is not an easy transition from life in the army to that of a gentleman."

Rose worried her lower lip while mulling this over. It seemed she had perhaps misjudged the earl yet again.

"Are you feeling more the thing, now, Rose?" Maria asked.

"I believe so. I am relieved your cousin is gone, but I am still not quite comfortable with the notion of accompanying you to London."

"Fret not, we will be by your side every step of the way. Between ourselves, I had had little training for Society either," Kate said. "With Maria as your patron, you will go on very well. She knows everyone."

"Perhaps… as long as I do not have to dance."

"What do you mean? Of course you will dance!" Maria exclaimed.

"I only know simple country dances and reels. I would make a spectacle of myself if I were to try a minuet," Rose argued.

"We can remedy that."

"That is what I was afraid you would say," Rose muttered.

"Are any of your brothers at home?" Maria asked. "Should they not be of an age?"

"Thomas is at home. James is away at school."

"Perhaps Quinn Foster would come to make up the numbers? We can hold a small dinner and dance here, so we might practice." Maria clapped her hands happily.

"I am not certain the gentlemen will wish to dance after laboring upon a roof," Rose argued. "Besides, is it not too late in the day to send out invitations?"

"Nonsense! They need as much activity as possible, I assure you. Cook will not object to an extra setting for dinner. Since Bertie was supposed to be here, that is all it will be. I will send a note to the Fosters, if you will send one to your brother?"

Rose did not waste breath in arguing. Maria was doing this for her benefit, after all. They went downstairs to Maria's apartment, where she availed herself of a pen and paper from her writing desk.

"I am happy to deliver the invitation to the Parsonage in person," Rose offered. "I miss the children. It will be good to check all is well with them."

"Of course. You are welcome to a carriage, or one of the horses if you prefer to ride? I will have one brought around for you."

"I will ride. Thank you," Rose answered. She did not possess a proper riding habit, but reflected it could do little harm since she was only going a short distance.

When she was mounted on a gentle bay mare and on her way, she turned up the old Gate House Road and cantered towards the Hoskins' farm. It was not precisely on the way, but she needed to see the truth for herself.

She pulled the horse back to a very slow walk, and could not believe her eyes, even though she was expecting the sight before them. The three gentlemen were on top of the roof, busily repairing it. Tears sprang to her eyes. She did not go close enough for them to see her. What would be the point? If the earl had wanted her to know, he would have told her—or not. At least he was a man of action, if not words, and villagers certainly needed the former more than the latter.

CHAPTER TEN

H E HAD TO go to London. Gabe leaned back in his chair in the drawing room, nursing a glass of brandy, eyes closed, trying to accept the inevitable. He, Philip, and Jack had spent the afternoon patching the worst of the holes in Mrs. Brown's roof, but it was not enough to weather a significant storm. Very soon he had realized he would need more workmen. His vision of bringing veterans here to live and work would only happen quickly if he saw to it himself. Letters back and forth to his man of business, and the War Office, would take too long. Along with Jack and Philip, they would have far more success finding suitable men themselves. Ergo, London.

That is not the only reason, his conscience whispered. *Rose.*

And now his sister had organized an impromptu dinner and dancing party for that evening. Miss Sutton needed practice, she had said, knowing he would not argue with anything she suggested regarding Rose. He felt his sense of self slipping, and wondered if all this trouble was worth the cost. What was it about Miss Sutton that made him do things he had never thought he would?

Yet he still did not know if, at the end of it all, she would have him. He did not know if he was capable of convincing her even to like him, but his pride would not allow him to ask for her hand unless she did.

The thought of asking someone else, however, was still repulsive.

When he heard the wheels of a carriage coming up the drive, he finally rose from the chair, ready for the evening. Quinn Foster and Thomas Sutton arrived together and were shown into the drawing room.

"Good evening, Mottram," Foster, the young dandy, greeted him. Gabe tried not to scowl at the pup's elaborate neckcloth and collar points that stood to his cheeks, to say nothing off the bright blues and greens of his costume. He was of a similar age to Miss Sutton, Gabe thought, but the differences in their maturity were quite wide. Next, he greeted Rose's brother, who looked more the country gentlemen in a subdued black coat, breeches and grey waistcoat.

"Welcome to Arden Park. Thank you for accommodating my sister's whims at such short notice."

"You are not the only one with a sister," Thomas said with a sympathetic smile. "Although, I will say, we do already miss her."

Gabe suspected there was a great deal of truth in that, Rose having been, in the past few years, more of a mother to those children than a mere sister.

"I think I hear her now," Thomas said, looking eagerly toward the door. Gabe could sympathize. He felt silly for how much he looked forward to the sight of Miss Sutton and her smiles. Would he ever be able to put one of them on her face?

Immediately she entered the room, she cast her ray of sunshine upon her brother. She was dressed more formally than Gabe had seen her before, in a beautiful evening gown of gold and cream which seemed to flow about her. She was strikingly beautiful, and would fit perfectly into a London ballroom, yet Gabe preferred her as he had seen her that first day. He suspected that was the real her.

As he watched her chat animatedly with her brother and Quinn Foster, he could only hope she would be unaffected by London. He knew other men would want her as much as he did.

He had not expected to have to compete with them and did not know if he could become someone he was not in order to win her.

Soon, the others had filled the room. He noticed how Thomas and Quinn's faces had brightened when the other two young ladies joined the company. At least he would not feel obligated to make meaningless conversation with them.

He was grateful the party was still relatively small. When they sat down to dinner at the head of the long table, he was fortunate to have Maria on one side of him and Rose on the other, no doubt Maria's doing. The latter's beauty was only accentuated by the golden walls of the room and the candlelight glowing from one of the sconces behind her. Cook had outdone herself with the meal, and Gabe was glad when he saw the array of dishes. The girls Miss Sutton had hired in the village must have helped, he mused. The first course consisted of pea soup, prawns, stewed oysters, pigeon pie, and turbot in a lemon glaze.

"Rose," Maria said across the table, even though it was not quite the thing at a large dinner party to do so. Gabe assumed this did not qualify as such. "Please convince my brother to come to London."

"That will not be necessary," he said, as he finished his soup and placed his spoon down.

"Does this mean you will come?" his sister asked.

"There are some matters I need to attend to in Town, yes."

"I hope that includes looking for a wife." She could not resist tormenting him, clearly.

"It is not my primary concern."

"I suppose I should be content that you are going at all," she said, before being drawn back into conversation with Jack Owens.

"Do you really mean to make us dance after all our hard work this afternoon, oh cruel one?" Gabe overheard Jack tease Maria. "I am now a gentleman of leisure, you know."

Maria looked heavenward and gave Jack a slap on the arm.

"Remind me not to trifle with you!" Jack rubbed his arm,

pretending to be sore.

Gabe could not help but envy Jack's ease with words and manner. He looked back at Rose, who was also watching the exchange and no doubt wishing she had Jack for a dinner companion instead of himself.

"Thank you for what you did today," she said, turning to look at him.

"It was very little, I am afraid."

"Not to Mrs. Hoskins, nor her children."

Gabe looked down at the next course placed before him, not seeing it. He was unused to praise and did not know how to react. Yet he would do anything to have more kind words from her. He must remember to ask Maria for help. Perhaps she would give him a few phrases, suitable for various situations, which ladies might like to hear. "I am glad you showed me what needed to be done. I regret it was not dealt with long before."

"Why do you dislike London so?" she asked, thankfully changing the subject.

"'Tis not London itself I dislike, but going about in Society," he corrected.

"That does not comfort me at all." She laughed nervously.

"Society will love you, Miss Sutton. You have nothing to fear."

"You should wait to pass judgment until you have seen me dance," she teased, and offered him a real smile.

Gabe had thought he was enchanted with her smile before, but when one was cast directly at him, it threatened to stop his heart. No one had ever smiled at him thus. "I have seen you dance," he reminded her.

"Oh, yes. How silly of me." She blushed and Gabe did not know what he had said wrong. Had he embarrassed her? Or reminded her of his own folly that night?

"You are not silly at all. You looked very beautiful." It was as much flattery as he knew how to speak, but he meant it.

"Oh." Lowering her eyes, she fidgeted with her napkin. "I

fear I become rather carried away."

"I envy you that," he said softly, and she looked up at him again with that grayish blue gaze which reminded him of the sky just before it rained.

"I will be like a thorn amongst the roses in the ton, I am afraid. I have none of the sophisticated polish or ennui to be successful, but it is kind of you to say so."

He wished to reassure her more, but the flattery would not form on his tongue. "I hope you will save a dance for me in London."

"Thank you, my lord. I imagine you may take your pick of the ladies present."

Without making a conscious decision to do so, he felt himself smile and shake his head. "I believe that is where you must wait and see."

⟫⟫⟫⟪⟪⟪

ROSE SUPPOSED SHE should be grateful to try some of these dances before being expected to perform them in a London ballroom. The dancers formed a small group, and there was a lot of laughter. Certainly she did not feel either inferior or gauche, as she would have expected.

They removed to the ballroom, which seemed a cavernous place for so few dancers. The windows around the perimeter had been opened to admit a breeze on the sweet night air of late spring, and was lit by two large chandeliers in the center of the room. Lady Mottram had agreed to play for them and Maria began to assign partners.

"Since we are not in London, I think we may dispense with the silly rule that husbands are not to be danced with," she said, casting a knowing smile at her handsome spouse.

The two young ladies tittered and smiled coyly at Thomas and Quinn. Rose could already foresee the outcome, and if that was the expected behavior of a debutante, then she was doomed. There was little she could do, she reflected, but accept it graciously.

She looked over at the earl, and he seemed to realize the same thing, as he cast her a wry look.

"I am afraid you are to be subjected to my exuberance," she remarked apologetically. "I will do my best to dance with propriety, but I do so love to dance. It is unfortunate for us both that I do not know how to perform them all." She waved her hand at the empty floor as though it would explain.

"Perhaps we shall balance each other, then, because while I know how to execute the steps, I do most decidedly lack exuberance."

Rose laughed, feeling more comfortable with the earl than she had before. He was trying to put her at ease, an unexpected kindness she had not thought to find in him.

"Shall we start with the minuet?" Maria asked of no one person.

"I do know of the minuet," Rose whispered to his lordship, "but I confess we do not dance it at the village assemblies. Perhaps we should take our places near the wall to prevent my disturbing the other couples," she suggested sheepishly after the tiniest of pauses.

"I am at your service." Mottram bowed slightly.

He was a very competent dancer, and seemed unaffected by her clumsiness when she would stumble or misstep. She found herself watching the others and slowly recalling the steps. When she began to turn in the wrong direction, he issued gentle commands and used light pressure to steer her back the right way. She found herself surprised at yet another kindness.

"Excellent!" Maria said when the dance came to an end, and Rose could only feel relief. The stiff formality prevented her from fully enjoying it as she would a lively jig.

"Thank you, my lord. You do indeed excel at the steps."

"And yet I detected no excessive exuberance," he countered.

"That is because I was concentrating on where I should put my feet."

"I do not believe you were doing so by the end. You seemed quite proficient."

"Shall we try a waltz?" Maria asked.

Lady Alice gasped.

"No one will tell the patronesses of Almack's, Alice. How are you supposed to learn the steps if you do not practice?" Maria questioned reasonably.

"Have you ever danced the waltz, Miss Sutton?" the earl enquired.

"No, my lord." But she had heard it spoken about in scandalous whispers! Although it had become commonplace in London a few years ago, the dance had never reached popularity in the small villages.

"It is quite simple. Try not to think, just follow my lead. There are only a few positions to learn."

As the earl stepped close to her, and took her hands, then his left arm rounded with hers as to form an arc. She felt her pulse start thrumming and her palms sweating. The countess began to play an unfamiliar song.

"It is easier if you keep your chin up, Miss Sutton."

She had not realized she was looking at her feet. She was too unsettled by the strange sensation of him being so close to her. The sensation only grew when she looked up at his face.

"Watch the others for a moment. There are three steps to a bar, in three-quarter time," he tapped his foot as the others twirled about. "Are you ready to try?"

She nodded and concentrated on his hands as they stepped forward.

"Step, slide, step." He spoke the steps until she found her rhythm, then led her through the other various positions.

"Excellent," he praised, as they completed a clockwise circuit without her treading on his toes. "You have it, Miss Sutton. It is as simple as that."

It was a lovely dance, she had to admit, though she did not believe she could have performed this dance with just any stranger.

"I have an excellent dance master," she said, daring to look up into his eyes.

Small crinkles around his eyes grew into a smile and it felt as though a thousand butterflies were floating about within her chest.

"There is one more move, if you possess sufficient daring," he teased, as their gazes held.

Before she could answer, gentle pressure on her hip and against one of her legs was the only hint she had before he spun her about.

"How was that?" he asked.

"Oh, quite wonderful. Again, please." She laughed. A strange look came over his face before he obliged.

Quickly she shed her fears and allowed herself to enjoy the dance and, dare she admit, enjoy the earl's company? The music ended before she was ready. She thought she could have waltzed for the rest of the night.

"Shall we exchange partners?" Maria asked. "I expect it would be good for the ladies to practice with other gentlemen."

Rose found she did not wish to change. It was with great reluctance that she let go of Lord Mottram's hand and curtsied. Perhaps she had been too hasty in her harsh judgment of him.

"A pleasure, Miss Sutton," he said, as he bowed over her hand before he released it. Only then did she realize she had forgotten herself again to exuberance.

CHAPTER ELEVEN

G ABE RODE ALONGSIDE Philip and Jack beside the carriages as the party made their way to London. His long-time colleagues took great joy in plaguing him about Rose.

"It looked as though Miss Sutton was warming towards you," Jack commented.

Gabe gave him a withering look. "If we were still in uniform, Captain, I would put you at the front of the line for that."

Jack laughed.

"I assume my little sister is the one who informed you of my intentions, since she is the only person I have told," Gabe grumbled.

"She is also my wife," Philip said, in a mild warning tone.

"Nonetheless, it was not her confidence to share."

"To be fair, to those of us who have known you for years, it is quite obvious," Philip responded.

"Thank God I don't know the other guests well," he said sardonically.

"May we be of assistance in your quest?" Jack asked.

"The very thought is appalling," Gabe shot back.

Jack laughed. "I am serious. There are many things we could do to aid your endeavors."

"I have heard that before," Gabe drawled.

"Much though I am loath to admit it, Jack is correct. There

are subtle ways in which we could help," Philip agreed.

"Before you ask, I am capable of being subtle," Jack retorted.

"Being helpful to me would be if you could find veterans willing to remove to Edwinstowe and work as laborers, field hands, and tradesmen." It was the main reason Gabe had been willing to leave Arden Park.

"I assure you, Major, that will not take nearly enough of our time." The twinkle in Jack's eye made Gabe feel sick.

"I take it from that you mean to make me your project?" Gabe was incredulous.

"Think of it instead as our doing a good deed for both you and Miss Sutton." It was a backwards compliment, perhaps, but Gabe knew it was kindly meant.

"I will be sure to inform you if I think of anything," he retorted.

"Promise me now, while Jack is here to bear witness, you will not take it amiss if I go beyond what is acceptable. Wife's orders, you understand." Philip held up a staying hand before Gabe could protest.

Gabe knew well his sister's powers of persuasion. He would do better himself to warn her from too much interference, little good though it might do.

"What is your plan?" Philip asked next.

"Plan?" Gabe asked, confused.

"Come now. Major Lloyd always has a plan," Jack teased.

"I confess I should have had one," Gabe admitted. "I realized too late that I should have reconnoitred as if it were Waterloo. I completely bungled the first encounter."

"Then how did you decide upon Miss Sutton? Not that I question your taste. She is delightful," Philip added.

"Instinct," he replied. "I saw her, and I knew."

"How very touching. Poetic, really," Jack mocked, holding his hand over his heart.

"I would take great pleasure in unseating you at this moment," Gabe growled.

Jack sent his horse prancing sideways to taunt him.

"I like her," Gabe muttered. "She is happy and unaffected—everything I am not. I daresay you think me too much of an opposite for her." He might as well hear the truth now, he reflected, stiffening in readiness.

"Not at all, I think she might be good for you," Philip said with a wry twist of his lips. "However, if I may, I suggest a few romantic overtures might not go amiss."

"I am not completely obtuse," Gabe protested. "I wished to make sure they were welcome first. I am not certain she cares overmuch for me."

"She did not seem to object to being your partner when we were dancing," Philip countered.

"She had little choice in the matter, after all, but is too well-bred to openly display aversion."

"Nevertheless, it would be a highly advantageous match for her. According to Maria, her father has said he intends to remarry and she feels a pressing need to leave," Philip remarked.

"At the moment, I am not certain she would consider marriage to me advantageous, and I should not wish for her to accept me because she has no other choice." To think he had intended to ask her father permission to court her from the very beginning! What an arrogant idiot he had been!

"I am surprised you have not already asked her father, being wont to be all business once you are determined upon a course," Jack teased.

Gabe felt his ears burn. It was exactly what he had intended until Rose became more to him than a pretty face. "The thought had crossed my mind," he admitted sheepishly.

They all laughed.

"I expect you are going to tell me no one has done that since the Dark Ages," he said, realizing his lack of finesse when it came to matters of matrimony.

"No, no, I am certain it was a regular occurrence only last century." Jack shook his head.

They rode on to London in amiable camaraderie. Gabe wished conversing with Miss Sutton could be as easy.

When they arrived, Gabe separated from the rest of the party, and went to his own town house. It was a cavernous mansion of gray stone, and to Gabe it felt more like a mausoleum than a home. He had always kept his own rooms in Town, and wished he still had them. He had never minded being alone, but something about this house made him feel unusually lonely.

A large household was no longer maintained, but the servants were prepared for him. A new butler opened the door. He had been hired by his secretary while Gabe was abroad.

"Good day, my lord. I am Bromley," said the man, who was middle-aged with dark brown hair and a kind face. "Your secretary sent word you would be arriving today."

Gabe inclined his head. "I trust you are settled in your situation, Bromley?"

"Yes, my lord. Your chambers are prepared. Is there anything you require? Some refreshment, perhaps?"

"Not at the moment, thank you. I am expecting my trunks to be delivered soon. They were on my sister's baggage coach."

"Very good, my lord."

The house smelled clean, and there was not a Holland cover in sight. Gabe retreated to the study, but it was difficult to think of it as anything but his father's. It looked as though all of that gentleman's old things were still there, as they had been the last night Gabe had seen him. A pair of spectacles sat atop his favorite copy of Donne on the side-table; the ormolu clock stood upon the mantel with a portrait of the old earl above; the large mahogany desk still filled one corner, its standish waiting for its contents to be picked up.

Gabe regretted how matters had ended between his sire and himself, but he could not go back and change anything. He opened the window to the back gardens to let in the evening breeze, then poured himself a brandy before sinking into a cognac-colored leather armchair which stood across from the one his father had always sat in.

He tipped his head back against the chair, wondering why he had come and how soon he could leave. There were too many bad memories in London, and being there alone only made him dwell on them more. It was too late to go to the War Office that evening, and thus Gabe had little else to do besides think of Rose and the formidable task of wooing her.

There was a knock on the front door, the harsh sound echoing through the empty house, and Gabe assumed his luggage had arrived.

Footsteps resounded on the marbled entrance hall floor and grew closer to the study before there was a knock on the door.

"Enter," he called.

"A note has been delivered for you, my lord. A messenger awaits your reply."

Gabe frowned. "So soon?" He accepted the note and broke the seal. It was in Philip's sprawling hand.

My dear Mottram,

Unfortunately, when we arrived at the town house, we found a rather nasty surprise.

It seems a chimney has fallen in and must be repaired before we can inhabit it again. The servants have all gone to stay at my parents' house and thus there is little room for us. Maria and your mother would prefer to stay at Mottram Place instead, if that is acceptable to you. We will await your word.

Everleigh

Gabe rose, walked over to the desk and pulled out paper on which to pen a reply.

You are all very welcome.

Mottram

Once dry, he folded the note and sealed it with wax before handing it back to Bromley.

"Please advise the housekeeper that the countess, my sister and her husband, and a Miss Sutton will be joining us shortly. Please have suitable chambers prepared."

"Yes, my lord." The servant bowed and left to direct his underlings to the various tasks.

Gabe sat back in his father's chair, pressing his fingers together before his face. *Be careful what you wish for.* He supposed he should be thrilled at the prospect of having Miss Sutton in such close proximity. If only he were not so afraid of making a mull of the whole, he would be delighted at the turn of events. It seemed almost more difficult to try to woo someone under one's own roof than by sending poems and flowers to them in the traditional fashion. It would be hard to make a grand gesture when she was staying there, although it might make her feel more comfortable in his company.

Ah, well, he mused, the choice was no longer in his hands. He would have invited them to stay had Philip not had his own town house. It was only natural that his mother and sister would wish to come to his father's house—his house. At least he would be able to put off the feeling of loneliness for a while longer.

ROSE WAS DELIGHTED to see more of England than simply Nottinghamshire. Maria and her mother chatted amiably most of the way, sometimes reading, sometimes embroidering, but Rose was content to take in the passing scene. For the most part, the countryside varied between forests and farmers' fields, rolling hills and flat stretches, among which they made regular stops to change horses and stretch their legs. They stopped overnight at The George coaching inn in Northampton, a large wooden building surrounded by stables. Grooms ran to meet carriages and change horses, servants hustled about their business, people wandered about stretching their legs, and inside, passengers crowded the dining room to catch a meal and drink a pint while awaiting the stage. It was a novel scene, but they were quickly ushered to private rooms away from the commotion and chaos.

ROSE HAD DIFFICULTY sleeping due to the noise of the inn that seemed to run day and night, so different from her quiet country home. She was grateful to resume their travel the next day.

When the country started to turn into the city—where houses became situated more closely together, along with more people and more conveyances—she felt anxiety mixed with anticipation. It was really happening.

As the gates of the city drew near, the skyline indicated a very dense populace by the number of church spires, palaces, towers, and buildings seemingly large enough to put the whole of her village inside. As they entered the City itself, the streets were crowded and dirty, with a mixture of people the likes of which Rose had never imagined. Traffic filled the streets in both directions and pedestrians lined the pavements. Vendors' carts filled every corner, with every shop imaginable in between.

Rose realized she had taken for granted the air she had breathed throughout her life, as the stench from the Thames mingled with smoke and sewers to swirl about the coach in an unpleasant odor. The way ahead cleared and they drove on through what Maria called tenements to Mayfair.

When the traveling coach pulled to a stop before an elegant stone town house, Maria could barely alight from the carriage fast enough, and Rose was not far behind.

Rose stood for a moment, looking around her at the square in which Philip and Maria resided. It was hard to credit so much grandeur in the one house, yet every single one was of equal elegance.

"What do you think?" Maria asked from beside her.

"It is very grand," Rose replied, not knowing what else to say. She felt so very small and insignificant amongst the fine architecture.

"You might be surprised, then, to hear it is very modest in comparison to most of what you will see, but it suits us well. Come, let us go inside and find you a chamber. You must be quite exhausted—I know I would be glad of a little solitude and a bath!"

When they went inside, Rose did not feel any less awe. If Maria did not think this was grand, Rose was afraid of what else there would be in the world of the ton to belittle her when she already felt like a poor relation.

The entrance hall was not large, but still looked palatial, having three stories of white marble staircases ascending the height of the building. Paintings lined the walls, while the ceiling was domed and bore a scene of cherubs and angels in the clouds amongst the heavens. Before they could discard their bonnets and pelisses, Philip appeared with a notable frown on his face. Rose had never seen his features in any expression other than a charming smile.

"Maria, we have a situation," Philip said as he placed a hand on her back.

"Whatever do you mean?

"Have you not noticed the lack of servants?"

"I have hardly stepped into the house. Where are the servants?"

"At my parents' house. According to the note left by Jacobs, a chimney has fallen through and damaged the roof and upper floors. The house is uninhabitable until repaired. I am afraid it is not safe to remain here. Would you prefer to lodge with my parents or yours? I am afraid it may be somewhat crowded at Everleigh House."

"Then of course we shall go to Mottram Place."

"Let me first send a note to your brother. I am afraid it would be better if you were to wait outside until I can be assured it is safe."

"Is it possible for Bisset to retrieve my gowns?" Maria asked as she stepped towards the door.

"I will see what may be done. I also have need of my wardrobe. If you will be so good to take a walk in the park, then, my dear, until I hear from Mottram?"

Maria sighed heavily, but patted her round belly and walked out of the house again. There was a square-shaped park across from the house and several other terraced houses overlooked it. Maria explained to her mother what had happened. Receiving the news stoically, she followed them into the park, there to arrange herself on a cast-iron bench.

"I think I would prefer to stretch my legs," Maria said, and Rose joined her on the pebbled path through the garden. It was dotted with plane trees, and was in full color with a variety of blooms that made Rose miss her own meager garden at home in Edwinstowe. She tried not to think about removing to the earl's house, and being in close proximity with him again. To herself, she admitted to some disappointment, too, for she could never be quite at ease in his presence. However, she was grateful they had a place to go, even though she felt more and more like an encumbrance.

By the time they had completed a circuit of the path through the garden, Philip had already received word from the earl, and within minutes they were mounting into the carriage once more.

"I think I am more loath to climb into a coach again then I am to move houses!" Maria exclaimed.

Rose was not overly happy about the necessity either, but at least it was a short distance. She could not feel easy about being in such close proximity to the earl again.

She was surprised when they stopped within a few moments and a footman opened the door of the vehicle. "We are here?" Rose asked.

"Yes," responded Maria. "Being only two streets, I daresay we could have walked instead, but travel is so wearying." Rose said nothing, but it seemed a silly notion to drive such short distances.

When she alighted, if she had thought the Everleigh residence grand, then there were no words for the mansion that stood before her.

It was as large as the earl's country estate. It was a beautiful work of architecture in Portland stone, having tall windows the length of the first two stories and shorter windows for the uppermost.

"Welcome to Mottram Place," Maria said beside her. "Will you come inside?"

Rose had been gawking. She nodded and followed her friend.

A butler held the door for them. "Welcome, my lady; Miss Sutton."

Rose was baffled that he knew her name, but smiled at him and looked around. There was a black and white checkered floor, a wide marble staircase and a number of life-sized statues set in alcoves, and this was only the entrance hall!

"Mrs. King will show you to your chambers when you are ready, my lady."

"Thank you, Bromley. Would you please have a bath prepared? Where is Lord Mottram?"

"I am here, Sister." The earl stood in a doorway behind and beside the stairs. Maria went towards him and Rose followed. The countess was already climbing the stairs. *This must be his study*, Rose surmised, following her hosts into the room. It felt much cozier than the rest of the house, and not unlike her own papa's. The walls were paneled in dark oak, a large desk sat to one side, in front of the windows, and a leather sofa and two armchairs surrounded the fireplace.

"I am sorry for the intrusion. Thank you for taking us in." Maria stood on tiptoe and kissed her brother's cheek.

"I am not sure why you felt the need to ask. This is your home, too."

"It was Philip." She waved her hand in the air for explanation.

"Where is your husband?" Mottram asked.

"He will be here shortly. He is dealing with the house and making arrangements for some of our belongings to be brought over."

Rose stood just within the door, feeling like an intruder. She could only pray that she did not feel thus for the entirety of their stay.

"Would you care to sit down, Miss Sutton?" the earl invited her. "I do hope you will make yourself at home while you are here," he added kindly.

"Thank you, my lord." She bobbed a curtsy. "I should like to retire to my bedchamber, if you will forgive me?"

"Of course. I will call Mrs. King to attend you."

"That will not be necessary. I will ask the butler the way. Please, take time to speak with Maria." She smiled at them both and hastily withdrew. The butler told her where to find her rooms and Rose assured him she did not need the housekeeper. Having servants hovering was, quite frankly, disturbing.

As she climbed the stairs, she pondered her new circumstances. Rose had known life would be different in London, but she had not realized quite how much. Despite having known Maria all her life, Rose had been very ignorant about Society. How had she ever thought to come to Town and fit in?

Footsteps approached and Rose longed to escape, but it was not a servant, rather the man she most hoped to avoid at Mottram Place! Was she to share a roof with him after all?

"Ah, Rose."

"Lieutenant Lloyd," she replied stiffly.

"Mr. Lloyd now. I have sold my commission. I can see you are angry at me," Bertie said, looking amused.

"I think I have every right to be." Her voice was shaking. How she wished she could have spoken icily!

"I beg your pardon if you misunderstood my intentions, but since I am only an heir, I must seek an advantageous marriage."

"You will certainly not achieve such an ambition with me," she said tartly, and immediately turned to walk away.

"I wish you luck with your own ambitions," he taunted her. "After all, we are in the same situation, are we not? But should you find yourself without success by the end of the Season, I would be pleased to make you another kind of offer."

Rose did not turn around. Her face was burning with shame. "Does the earl know you are here?"

"Oh, yes," he sneered. "Your fierce protector. You are aiming a little high there, my sweet, are you not?"

When had Bertie become so cruel? This was not the man she had fallen in love with. At least she'd had the fortune to see him for what he truly was instead of sighing over him for the rest of her life. His rejection still hurt, nonetheless.

She looked back over her shoulder. "I wish you well, Bertie." Rose was proud of her forbearance. She had been within ames ace of telling him to burn in the fires of hell.

CHAPTER TWELVE

G ABE WAS ESCORTING his sister to the stairs, for a few minutes after her arrival, when he overheard voices. Sound carried extraordinarily well in the vast house and he heard every word. Evidently Maria had as well, for her fingers dug into his arm. "What is he doing here?" she hissed.

"Accosting Miss Sutton," he growled. "He promised me he would keep his distance."

"The temptation of living here for free must have been too great for him to resist. I will go and comfort her, but I believe it is a good thing she has discovered his true nature. You stay and deal with him." Maria released his arm and climbed the stairs, passing Bertie as he descended.

"Bertie, I was not expecting to see you in London," Maria said curtly as they met each other halfway on the stairs.

"He was just leaving," Gabe growled, clutching the bottom of the handrail and feeling like committing murder.

"Afternoon, Cuz." Bertie smirked at him. "I hope you do not mind. I stayed here while waiting for you."

Gabe swiftly decided he would make it clear to his servants that in the future Bertie would not be admitted without his permission. And never without Gabe himself being present—unless he was dead.

"In my study, now."

"Yes, sir." Bertie saluted to mock him.

Gabe waited for Bertie to pass in front of him, then followed his heir inside and closed the study door behind them. He leaned against the door and crossed his arms. "Explain yourself. I thought we had come to an agreement."

Bertie sat casually, crossing one leg over the other. "I am simply taking advantage of your hospitality while I wait for the funds you promised. I had thought to try my hand at finding a wife as well."

"'Taking advantage' is about right. You were to keep your distance from Miss Sutton."

"How was I to know you would bring her here?"

"She is in London under the patronage of my sister and mother. It was certainly within the realms of possibility that she might visit this house. I do not recall you asking permission to reside here."

Bertie shrugged. "As your heir, I had thought it a reasonable assumption. This old pile was sitting empty."

"To have it thus is my prerogative, I believe. But I will make it very clear, since you always did need your orders to be very specific, you will remove yourself from here immediately. You will not go within a mile of Miss Sutton again without her permission, and never alone. And if I ever hear that you have propositioned her again, we will meet on a field with pistols, and your body will never afterwards be found."

Bertie began to laugh. "By Jove, you want her for yourself! I'll admit she is a tasty armful. Too bad she has no money or connections, or I might just take her for myself."

Gabe did not think. He drew back and slammed his fist straight into Bertie's nose, feeling a satisfying crack before blood begin to spew forth. Gabe tore off his heir's neckcloth and shoved it into the fool's nose to stop the blood from flowing all over his carpets. Bertie screamed in pain, but nevertheless held the cloth to his nose.

"You devil! You broke my nose!"

"You are fortunate that is all I did. I believe I showed admirable restraint." Gabe took him by the shoulders, turned him about and walked him directly from the room, through the entrance hall to the door. Bromley, bless him, was already holding the door ajar, and Gabe shoved Bertie through it. "Your belongings will be sent to your parents' house." Gabe nodded to Bromley. The butler closed and locked the door behind his sorry excuse for a cousin.

"I expect you heard that interview?" Gabe asked. "We were hardly circumspect."

"Every word, my lord."

"Then please express to the rest of the servants, in the strongest terms, that he is not welcome in this house—ever."

"Yes, my lord."

Gabe began to walk forward, then stopped. "Are there any more residents I have not been informed of?"

"No, my lord."

Gabe spun on his heel and marched back to his study, where, having poured himself a brandy, he paced up and down the carpet.

Something told him that Bertie was not about to simply disappear, but intended to cause trouble. The question was, would it be trouble for him or for Miss Sutton, or for them both?

Gabe should have suspected his cousin would do something like this. He had no doubt it had been intentional. Why the devil had Gabe not discovered Bertie was in the house before Rose had?

He wanted to go to her and make certain she was unharmed—and reassure her. Yet he had no right to do so. He could claim only a small acquaintance with her thus far, though he would like to think they were becoming friends. Besides, Maria would speak with her.

Gabe collapsed into a chair and tossed back the rest of his drink. He closed his eyes, allowing the warmth of the spirits to soothe his frustrations. He needed to formulate a plan, and quickly, not only to control his despicable error, but to convince Miss Sutton that he would be a worthy husband.

"Mottram?" He heard Philip's voice from the doorway.

"Come in, Everleigh." He waved his hand at the decanter. "Help yourself."

"Thank you, I could use a drink. But what is your excuse?" He looked over his shoulder as he poured himself a generous portion of the golden liquid.

"You have just missed my illustrious cousin."

Philip raised his brows. "I thought you had dealt with him?"

"Apparently not. It seems he plans to be a menace wherever we are. He had the audacity to proposition Miss Sutton under my roof: on the staircase, if you please."

"He did *what*?" Philip almost choked on his drink.

"You heard me correctly. I told him if he approached her again, his body would not be found."

"I will gladly help you dispose of it."

Gabe raised his glass in acknowledgment and appreciation. "What I need help with most, is how to proceed with the other… situation. Somehow it seems… unseemly to attempt when she is under my own roof."

"I understand what you mean." Philip pursed his lips in thought. "Perhaps you might start by inviting her to a night at the theater? Unless you feel it is too soon."

"I am very much afraid that if I do not steal a march on the Marriage Mart, I will miss my chance."

"Very well. I will see what is playing tonight and discuss the matter with Maria." Philip continued to look at him strangely. "What are you thinking?"

"I think that perhaps you should simply tell Miss Sutton of your intentions."

"And if she is not amenable to my suit, then she will be trapped, living in my house and forced into my company every day," Gabe argued.

"I cannot think she would be anything but flattered, Mottram. And once you go into Society, you will have any number of eligible women throwing their caps at you simply by virtue of being an eligible bachelor."

Gabe shook his head. "Perhaps they will, for a Society marriage, but Miss Sutton deserves chance to see the lay of the land for herself. I do not want her to accept me for fear no one else will offer for her. Besides, I am still not certain how I will be received in Town. It was part of the reason I had hoped to stay in the country and court her there."

"That is very noble of you," Philip said, "but I do not think anyone holds your father's actions against you. At least, I have seen no such malice against Maria and it has been some time now."

"I hope you are correct. I suppose I want more for myself and for her. Perhaps I may show my hand once your house is repaired, Miss Sutton is not reliant on my roof, and there is an alternative for her."

"Very well. My pride would wish to know I was being chosen for the right reasons as well. It was part of what made Maria so attractive to me. She had seen me at my worst and was still willing to have me."

"Thank you. I dare not hope for what you and Maria have, but a partner in life, and perhaps mutual respect, would be welcome."

Philip sighed loudly. "Might I suggest arranging to be in her company as much as possible? If you have already decided you would suit, provide ample opportunity for her to come to the same conclusion."

"I have none of your charm, Everleigh."

"I disagree. You simply choose not to exert it, unless it suits you."

Gabe doubted that very much.

"Shall I invite Jack and Kate to join us at the theater?" Philip asked.

"The more the merrier, eh?" Gabe said the phrase as a question because for him it could hardly be a greater falsehood.

Philip laughed. "How painful was that for you to say?"

"Very. But I can tolerate them, and it will make it less obvious that I am singling out Miss Sutton."

WHEN MARIA TOLD her they were to attend the theater that evening, Rose felt giddy. Perhaps the description was a bit fanciful for a clergyman's daughter, but she loved the whimsical nature of playacting. Her family often spent holidays writing their own comedies and performing them, and to have the opportunity of seeing a real play, performed by professional actors, was thrilling. There was little else to do for entertainment in a small village, besides the monthly assemblies and occasional fete.

Bisset helped her to dress in the same green silk, embroidered with delicate vines and trimmed with fine lace, she had worn at Arden Park. It was cut lower than would be considered acceptable for a rector's daughter in a small parish, but she hoped to distract from that with her mother's pearls. The strand was unique, with a larger pearl, resembling a tear-drop and hugged by two small diamonds, in the center. The matching earrings were made up of a diamond above a pearl drop. Bisset performed another miracle with Rose's hair, leaving a few of her curls untamed to soften her face.

As she made her way down the stairs to the hall, where Lord Philip and Lord Mottram were waiting for them, she wondered if she would often be coupled with the earl. He was also in search of a spouse, and she did not wish to be a burden, but was doubtful he would ever to admit such to be the case. Now she was a guest under his roof, and she feared that to him she must soon feel like an obligation. How could she reassure him on that score? Of course, if she said anything to Maria, she would dismiss Rose's concerns as being silly.

As she descended the stairs, Lord Mottram looked up with what she thought was an appreciative gleam in his eye. It warmed her insides and made her smile in return.

Reluctantly, she had to admit he made quite an appealing physical specimen in formal dress. His starched neckcloth was white, his silk waistcoat a tasteful silver. His broad shoulders were hugged by a precisely cut tailcoat, and his strong legs were encased in black breeches.

"Shall we go?" Philip asked, offering his arm as Maria joined them.

"What is playing tonight?" Maria enquired, once they were settled in the carriage. Rose was thankful to be seated next to Maria, but it was still disconcerting to be in such a small space with Lord Mottram—their knees touching with every turn.

"Massinger's *A New Way to Pay Old Debts* with Kean as Sir Giles Over-reach," Philip answered.

"That does not sound like a comedy." Maria frowned.

"I am afraid not, but Kean is always worth seeing."

"Even I have heard of him," Rose added, her excitement building.

"As have I," Mottram agreed. "But have not yet seen him tread the boards."

"Then you are both in for a treat," Maria said.

There was a large crowd already assembled when they arrived at the theater. Rose was scarcely able to take in the opulence, for the gowns and jewels swirled past in an array of colors as the party was ushered through swarms of people to the earl's box.

The ladies sat in the front seats, with the gentleman behind. Rose was grateful to be able to see, but she was acutely aware of the earl, directly behind her.

Now seated, she was able to look around and observe. It was crowded, and Rose thought all of Edwinstowe's inhabitants might fit inside. Perhaps even those in the next village would do so too. She looked around and noted the affluence everywhere, from the fine architecture of the theater itself, with luxuriant burgundy curtains covering the stage, to the ornate candelabras hanging from the ceiling. But it was nothing compared to the people. What she had noticed in the lobby was overshadowed by a closer view. Many of the fine ladies almost dripped in diamond, sapphire, emerald, and ruby parures, from tiaras on their heads to earrings and necklaces, and fingers covered in jewels. It was likely their gowns alone cost more than her papa's income for an entire year. The gentlemen were more subtly attired, but there was still little doubt as to their position in the world.

However, when she looked downwards, there was another sort of scene—one which more closely resembled a fair in Nottingham.

"Who are they?" Rose asked Maria.

"I see you have found the pit. Shall us just say, decorum is a little more relaxed there than in the boxes. Oranges are not the only thing the women sell, if you understand my meaning."

Rose thought she did, and once Maria had pointed it out, it was rather obvious. "Do you mean to say those sorts of people actually consort with the upper classes?" she asked in disbelief.

"The theater is one of the most likely places to find those sorts of persons."

Rose felt as provincial as she probably looked. It was not as though it was unheard of in her village, but she herself had never before witnessed such a scene.

"Do you know those people?" Maria asked, inclining her head away from the stage.

"Which people?"

"Two boxes away. The Duke and Duchess of Haverstock."

"I am not acquainted with any dukes or duchesses," Rose replied. Unobtrusively, she tried to look at the box in question. "The lady has a glass to her eye, and it seems to be pointed at me! Perhaps she is trying to catch a glimpse of your brother."

"Perhaps... but it is more likely to be you who has piqued her curiosity. Any new, unknown lady is always of great interest to the ton."

"Papa says it is rude to stare," Rose responded, trying not to squirm.

"In any other instance, it would be considered so, but the theater is where people come to see and be seen. If you look around, every matron has a lorgnette to her face, and even some of the men."

It was all so strange. She would probably never get used to the oddities of fashionable life, Rose mused, but then consoled herself with the thought she would not be in London for long.

The play finally started, and the story did little to ease her comfort. It quickly highlighted the snobbery of the nobility, over even the landed gentry, when Sir Giles wanted his daughter to marry Lord Lovell but was rejected from class distinction.

Rose found herself gripping her fan with one hand and the edge of her chair with the other. Is that what everyone would think of her? She knew that not everyone in the nobility was so high in the instep, but it was not too far-fetched a notion. Her own mother had been shunned, and she had been a viscount's daughter. By the arrival of the interval, Rose found herself engrossed in the story despite its theme.

"I must visit the ladies' retiring room," Maria said, with a sheepish smile, and Lord Philip escorted her out, joined by Kate and Jack, who left with a wink.

"How are you enjoying the play thus far, Miss Sutton?" Lord Mottram asked.

"Mr. Kean is a brilliant performer," Rose prevaricated. She did not care much for the plot.

"Indeed, but if it were not for the comic relief of Jack Marall and Justice Greedy, it would be far less entertaining."

"Indeed. I must say I think I would have favored a comedy myself."

"Shall I fetch you some refreshment?"

Rose shook her head. "Thank you, I do not care for anything, but please do not feel obliged to stay with me if you should wish to partake."

"I confess, I would prefer to stay within the confines of the box, if you do not find my company objectionable."

What could she possibly say to that? She could hardly tell him she did not mind his company as much as she had. Thankfully, she was saved from answering.

"I say, Miss Sutton, are you acquainted with the Duchess of Haverstock?"

Rose looked up. "Is she staring again?"

"Again?" He frowned.

"Your sister asked the same question before the play. I confess I have never seen them in my life." Surreptitiously, Rose looked at the silver-haired matron and older gentleman, and wished she had her own pair of lorgnettes with which to examine them in her turn.

"I cannot fathom what their interest may be. They have no marriageable sons or daughters, that I can recall."

Rose smiled. It was kind of him to think a duke might think her marriageable. She supposed the earl must be unaware of her origins. The thought made her wonder who her grandparents were and if they were at the theater that night, or if they were even still alive. Even though she was angry for how they had treated her parents, she was still curious about them.

Then she realized she had no notion of her grandfather's title. She only knew her father's surname.

There was a knock on the entrance to the box, and they both turned, to find several gentlemen blatantly looking her over, even to Rose's inexperienced eye. It quickly became apparent that they were not sober. Rose had never seen anyone this intoxicated before, but their glassy-eyed looks, ruddy cheeks, and smiles indicated it must be so. She stood, wide-eyed, uncertain of how to go on.

"Exchuse me, but we would like to beg an introducshion to your lady friend," spoke a gentleman with reddish hair and dressed in bright blue. Two other men, appearing equally dandyish and drunk, looked on from behind the first.

"Since I do not believe we have been introduced, I will respectfully decline," Mottram said, the words cold and clipped.

"Bertie shaid you were a cold fish, by Jove," the man slurred.

"So my cousin put you up to this, did he?"

"Not exhactly." The man's brows furrowed as if trying to think of the reason. His friends laughed. The red-headed man put up his finger when he remembered. "He shaid he wasn't allowed to shpeak with her."

"In that, he is correct. May I suggest you also remove yourself from her presence? Perhaps, when not in your cups, you may seek a proper introduction to both of us."

Mottram turned his back on the man, barring entrance, and they slunk away, grumbling about lack of hospitality.

"Thank you," Rose whispered. She had been afraid they would cause trouble, and to know Bertie had instigated their intrusion sank her spirits even further.

"I am sorry for that. My cousin's mischief knows no bounds."

She shook her head. "It is not your fault."

"I must also apologize for the fact he accosted you in my house. I had made it clear to him that he was not to impose his presence upon you."

"Please do not hold yourself responsible for his actions. I believe he is what my brothers would call a rum touch!"

"One who is dependent on me for his livelihood. I will ensure he does not trouble you again."

Rose was grateful for the support, but she doubted even the earl could control Bertie.

CHAPTER THIRTEEN

T HE NEXT MORNING, Gabe, Philip, and Jack all went to the War Office to see if there were lists of those discharged that might be in need of assistance. Owens joined them at Mottram Place and they rode together across the Park then up the Mall to Whitehall. As they stood before the five-storeyed edifice of Portland Stone, windows and columns, Gabe smelled the odor of the Thames on the breeze and hesitated.

"I confess, I do not know where to begin. There must be thousands of men in need of a position."

"But how many will want to remove to Nottinghamshire?" Jack asked.

"An excellent question—and one I am prepared to ask as many as needed," Gabe replied.

"None of us has been long back in England, so I think this is an excellent place to begin," Philip pointed out practically as they climbed the steps and went inside. They did not meet with much success.

A bespectacled clerk sat behind a large, dark wooden desk, his ink-stained fingers hovering above an open ledger as he paused to answer their enquiry. He could not fathom such a request. "I beg your pardon, sir. You want me to provide you with lists of those men invalided out since Waterloo?"

"That is precisely what I am asking," Gabe answered.

"Unfortunately, sir, that would take days, if not weeks to compile. We are still trying to assimilate lists of all of the men lost." He waved his hands over the stacks of ledgers on his desk.

Gabe looked at Philip and Jack, who seemed to be as perplexed as he. It had been a year since the battle.

"I am looking to hire some men willing to leave the capital in order to work. Do you have any suggestions?"

"To be frank, sir, you could walk the streets of London and find as many as you need. It is an unfortunate state of affairs, but that is the case."

Gabe frowned. "Our men are on the streets?"

The clerk seemed to sink backwards into his chair and shy away.

"It is not his fault," Philip said, taking Gabe's arm.

Gabe took a deep breath. Philip was right, but he was angry. He could only imagine what he would find when he began to look. They left the building and stopped just outside the door. "Where to begin?"

"Perhaps the Guards' Club? Maybe some of the commanders will know of men from their battalions now in need of work," Philip suggested.

"If that fails, we will scour the streets," Jack offered.

Gabe thought it might be worth doing that anyway. He had a feeling there might be more than he had anticipated, but he would think of some way of aiding those he did not need. After all the country had asked of the men, it beggared all belief that they could be left on the streets.

They found their horses and mounted, riding across St. James' Park, and then Green Park until they arrived at the Guards Club on St. James'.

At once it was familiar and comforting. It felt more like an officers' mess than White's, though it was still much the same on the outside and in: an elegant building of light stone without and dark paneled walls, oriental carpets, leather chairs and card tables within. The scent of coffee and tobacco smoke filled the air, while familiar uniforms of those still serving were dotted throughout the room. Camaraderie and laughter echoed and something in Gabe relaxed.

"Ahoy, Everleigh! Owens! Lloyd! Have pity on us half-pay officers and buy us a drink, will you?" someone shouted from the group already gathered.

"Major Lloyd is an earl, now. Perhaps appeal to him," Jack teased.

"Yes, that is an excellent idea," Philip agreed as he took off his hat, and sat in a chair.

Gabe signaled to one of the footmen and asked him to oblige everyone with a glass of spirits. He joined the others, seating himself in one of the leather chairs.

"What brings you three back to the land of poor soldiers waiting for orders? Are you regretting selling out so soon?" a fellow guardsmen, Lt. Col Ward, asked. He was a handsome fellow with full whiskers, and had risen in the ranks through his own merit on the battlefield.

"I admit to being a little bored at times, but I am not willing to leave my wife and child behind, nor drag them out to follow the drum," Jack said.

"And I will soon be a father," Philip said, a besotted smile on his face.

"Congratulations," Ward said, and raised his glass in salute.

They all drank to that.

"I have been back in England only a month," Gabe replied. "I am still plodding my way through estate management. It is why I am here."

"Oh? Pray tell," Ward said.

"I am looking for some men. A couple of dozen or so, to remove to my village as laborers or craftsmen."

Ward raised his brows, but allowed Gabe to continue.

"Over thirty men were lost. We need good men and I have been told many are left to fend for themselves—even on the streets."

"Unfortunately, what you have heard is true. It will not take you long to see the disgraceful numbers of injured begging along nearly every thoroughfare. But how can I help?"

"We thought to ask if anyone here knew of men who might be interested in my proposition."

"I imagine most of us do. I can already think of a couple of sergeants from my regiment. I will look into it for you."

"I would be much obliged," Gabe said.

"Also, take a stroll to Covent Garden. Many ex-soldiers share tenements around there. They would be glad for some honest work, but with their injuries, no one will hire them. I know that Lord Fairmont started a home in Eastbourne, where soldiers can go to convalesce and also learn a skill when they are well enough. He takes as many as he can, but…"

"There is only so much help one person can provide." Gabe filled in what the Colonel had not said. "Perhaps I will go and look at this infirmary. Maybe that is something I could do at one of my estates. Not all of them are in use."

"I beg your pardon, gentlemen. Captain Gray from the 95th." A young officer introduced himself. He had blond hair and a matching mustache. "I could not help but overhear, and I think I have someone for you, but he has a wife and children. Do you have a place for a family? He is one of the hardest workers I have ever known, but his leg was blown off at Quatre Bras. I've been trying to help where I can, but since being on half-pay, there's little enough to pay my own bills. The wife takes in sewing when she can, and he works in the kitchen of a tavern."

"If you would speak to them for me, and give him my direction should he be interested, I am certain there is work he could do." Gabe had no idea, but he would find something better paid than washing dishes.

The relief on the captain's face was palpable. They stayed another half-hour, reminiscing with the soldiers, before taking their leave and returning to Mottram Place. At once Gabe thought of his monstrosity of a house and how many bedrooms sat empty. It was nothing short of criminal, that all the King's men were not looked after for their sacrifices. He was only one man, but he would do what he could.

"I expect you will soon have a long list of candidates," Philip said after Jack had taken his leave.

"I had not considered there would be families to house," Gabe admitted. "Hopefully, Miss Sutton will know where they might be placed. I expected more unmarried soldiers."

"I think you will have your fill by the week's end. We can also visit Covent Garden in the next day or two, once we have heard from the captain."

"Did I hear you say Rose's name?" Maria asked, peeking into his study at that moment. Miss Sutton stood just behind her and they looked as though they were about to go on an errand. The men rose to their feet.

"Indeed, you did, my dear," Philip answered, going to her and kissing her cheek.

"We have just been seeking veterans to fill some of the positions left empty in Edwinstowe, and we found one possible candidate, but he has a family. Mottram was saying he would need to consult Miss Sutton to see if she knew of a place for them."

Gabriel looked up and saw Rose watching him intently. Her face wore a look of... approval? Perhaps even admiration?

"I had no idea you were considering such a stratagem, my lord. What an excellent idea."

Gabe ignored the warmth that spread over him at her approval. "I have not yet told you of my idea. I had thought first to determine if any injured soldiers cared to remove to the country." He had not wanted to raise hopes if there was no one interested in such work as he could offer.

"I can think of a cottage or two where a family could settle."

"Perhaps I may trouble you to sit down and inform me where there might be places to fill. I drew up a list of my own from our visitations the other day, but you know the people much better than I."

"I would be delighted my lord," she said softly.

"Are you going out?" Philip asked.

"Yes. Rose has need of accessories—gloves, fans, bonnets, that sort of thing. We have received a few invitations, but I imagine more will begin to arrive in a day or two," Maria said.

"Invitations?" Gabriel asked, knowing it was inevitable but still dreading the prospect.

"I have placed on your desk the ones I thought we should accept, Brother. We can discuss them when we return."

Gabe nodded, already feeling the bile rise in his stomach. He wished he might have more time with Rose before competing for her favor.

As THEY LEFT the house and ascended into the carriage, Rose felt a warmth in her heart she could only describe as joy. And to think she had been angry with the earl, that day they had paid visits in the village, for not speaking with the people! All the time, he had been keeping notes of ways to help. She had misjudged him. How many people did the same thing? How many called him cold and aloof when he was simply reserved? Not everyone felt at ease when speaking to others. Her heart softened toward the man, even though she still could not quite feel comfortable in his presence. She would try harder.

"What a lovely thing it is that your brother is doing," she said to Maria once they were settled and on their way.

"Gabe is very tender-hearted and has an acute sense of responsibility. Even when he was working covertly on the Continent, he would find a way to come to me in secret to see how I did. What happened with my father was very difficult for him, but he never forgot about me."

"Of course, he would not," Rose agreed.

"I should have been the one to comfort him, but he would never allow it. He believed everything which happened was his fault, so he stayed away."

"Now he is trying to make everything right."

"Yes." Maria whispered. "I wish only for his happiness. I do not want him to have a cold marriage of convenience. I wish for him to find someone who sees him as he truly is; someone who would be content in the country. A partner in life."

Rose could understand why Maria felt that way. The earl did not make those aspirations easy.

Soon they were set down before the shops on Bond Street. Rose again felt very small and insignificant when faced with an entire street full of milliners, modistes, tailors, jewelers, shoemakers, and the like. Even in Nottingham there were not half as many.

"Magnificent, is it not?" Maria said, noticing the awe on Rose's face. "If there is nothing to your liking here, then there are some warehouses in Cheapside."

"That already sounds more to my liking." Rose only partially teased her friend. She feared her papa's gift to her would not go very far.

"We will start with gloves and stockings. You should have enough gowns, unless something takes your particular fancy. Bisset is a dab hand with alterations."

"You are too generous," Rose said. "I do not know how I may ever thank you enough."

"My dearest Rose, your being here is enough."

Rose doubted that very much, but what else could she say? They entered a very pretty shop, full of anything and everything a lady could desire to go with her toilette. There were drawers of stockings of so fine a silk, and exquisite with beautiful designs from flowers to hearts to paisleys and more, Rose could not imagine how someone might put them on without ruining them. She chose a more plain, practical pair and hoped they would last her the whole Season. Next, she chose a pair of white kid gloves, but there were so many choices in more colors that she had not known existed, she was sorely tempted to buy more. How extravagant it would be to have a pair to match each gown she owned! Yet she had little doubt that was the case for many ladies in Society.

Once she had made her choices, she found Maria selecting some ribbons and lace.

"There you are. Did you find everything you needed?" Maria asked.

"I did. Thanks to your kindness, I needed but one or two items."

"Please, say no more on the subject. I have done very little, I assure you. Let me make my purchases, and then we may return home for tea. I am famished." She laughed as though she was delighted by the notion.

When they returned to the house, they had been gone only two hours. Rose did not want to admit it aloud, but she was excited by the chance to discuss the village with the earl. How she had wished for the opportunity to help the villagers more than she had been able, and now it looked as though he genuinely meant to do his duty.

"Maria? Is that you?" Lady Mottram called from the drawing room as soon as they had shed their bonnets and pelisses.

"Yes, Mama. Coming," Maria answered.

They climbed the stairs to the drawing room, where Lady Mottram was sitting with a teapot and cakes on a tray in front of her.

"Is that still warm?" Maria asked as she took a seat on the gold-coloured sofa. "Oh, look at the cakes!"

"The tea is fresh. I have just had visitors."

"So soon? We arrived only yesterday."

"But you attended the theater last night. Many saw you there."

"Yes, of course. Who was your visitor?" Maria asked as she poured tea for Rose and handed it to her. Rose selected some spice cake and apple tarts while listening to the exchange.

"The Duchess of Haverstock, and Viscountess Coleston."

Rose froze with her cake in front of her mouth. "My aunt?" she whispered.

"Yes, indeed. She was sorry to have missed you. They both had many questions about you."

"I have not seen my aunt since Mama died. It has been quite some time. It was kind of her to call. Papa did not care overmuch for his brother's wife as they did not agree with him taking in my mother. Their estate was far away from his parish, and there were too many children for them to travel such distances. But why would the duchess ask questions about me? We have no prior acquaintance."

"She was looking at Rose last night, Mama. Quite noticeably, I might add," Maria said.

"Is that so?" Lady Mottram looked curious.

Rose remained quiet. It was all so strange.

"What did she want to know?" Maria asked instead.

"The duchess was here first, and she simply inquired who Miss Sutton was. I could not say why the interest, for she has little family of her own. They lost both sons in tragic circumstances before there was another heir to inherit the dukedom. Now a nephew is set to inherit. Then the viscountess arrived—it is no secret the families are not friends. There was some history between them long ago. I forget what it was, but the duchess did not stay long after Lady Coleston arrived. She did, however, leave invitations to a ball in two days' time. She wanted to deliver them personally, since it is such short notice. She was not aware we were to be in Town."

"How kind of her," Maria said, while reaching for another cake.

"Will you have gowns ready by then?" Lady Mottram asked Rose.

"Yes, my lady. Bisset has several ready for me."

"Wonderful! Then I will accept the invitation. I was uncertain whether you would have a suitable wardrobe by then, but it is quite an event at which to make your come out. Practically everyone will be there."

Rose thought the prospect intimidating in the extreme, but could hardly say so. She was becoming more and more sympathetic to Lord Mottram's aversions to Society. "That was gracious of her to include me."

"She made very certain to assure me of that." Lady Mottram eyed Rose more closely than she had ever done before.

Rose desperately wished to escape. Would it be very forward of her to ask to see Lord Mottram, and discuss the future of Edwinstowe, instead of remaining here for this acutely uncomfortable conversation?

"Which gown will you wear?" Maria asked. "Perhaps the cerulean silk with the gauze overdress? It will look splendid with your eyes and hair. Not that you need any extra help, my dear. You would look glorious in sackcloth."

Rose shook her head. "You flatter me."

"Not at all." Maria waved her hand. "But it never hurts to look one's best at one's come out. I am so pleased for you! What a prestigious event at which to begin!"

Rose could only hope she did not disappoint. At the same time, she began to have a sinking feeling about the duchess. Could it be? If so, what purpose did she have in befriending her?

CHAPTER FOURTEEN

G ABE TRIED TO prepare to face the evening ahead, reminding himself that if he could face enemies on a battlefield that he could face the ton. He had been gone a long time, but there would still be familiar faces. He would be with friends and colleagues; with Rose.

He tied his neckcloth and fastened his sleeve buttons. He supposed he should also find a valet while he was looking for help. Many officers brought home their batman, but none of them who had done the secret work had had the luxury of a manservant. It was too risky to involve another person, and it was harder to track one than a pair. He was so used to doing for himself, it would be difficult to have a servant hovering. He would ask Maria if he was up to snuff.

He left his chambers to go downstairs, but his mother hailed him from her open door.

"Gabriel? Is that you?"

He stopped at her door. "Yes, Mother."

"Come inside for a moment. There is something I wish to tell you."

That sounded ominous, but he did as she asked.

"You may leave us now," she said to her maid.

Gabriel waited for his mother to speak.

"It is about Miss Sutton."

His brows raised. "What about her?"

"Do you not find it interesting that the Duchess of Haverstock personally invited us to their ball?"

"I assumed you were acquaintances renewing your friendship. I have been too far removed to recall all your friends."

"Acquaintances is a generous term for our previous relationship. It is why I am suspicious."

"Do you think she has an interest in Miss Sutton?" Gabe could not fathom why.

"Were you aware she called upon me yesterday, followed by the Viscountess Coleston, who is Miss Sutton's aunt?"

"Indeed?" Gabe knew very little about Miss Sutton's family. He supposed it made sense that the reverend was the younger son of a Viscount.

"The two of them together refreshed my memory. You would not recall, but there was a scandal, years and years ago. Lord Edward Byrne eloped with the viscount's sister."

"Byrne, I presume, is the family name of Haverstock?"

"Correct, and I suspect Miss Sutton is the product of the union."

"Is she aware of this?" Gabe did not think it was common knowledge.

"I have not asked, but I did wonder if we should prepare her. The duke was adamantly against the marriage and cast his son off. He was trying to have the marriage annulled, but Lord Edward died before that happened. And any child of the union would have been born after his death."

"Do you think the duke will cause trouble for her?" Gabe felt uncommonly protective of Rose.

"I could not say. I fear it might be so. I do not know what the duchess is about. Perhaps she has told him her suspicions, or perhaps she means to see for herself if Rose is Edward's daughter."

"Why would she risk such a scandal at a ball?"

"Perhaps she believes the duke would not agree to meet the

child otherwise or that he might restrain himself in such a public setting? I am not certain." She shook her head. "The duchess did come here to meet her yesterday."

"Then why not try again before the ball?"

"I could not say. Perhaps I am spinning moonbeams out of clover, but it seems too coincidental. I do not think the duchess vindictive; rather, she seemed somehow hopeful to me. Maybe she suspects Miss Sutton is her grandchild and hopes to get to know her."

Gabe narrowed his gaze. "I would not see Miss Sutton hurt."

"Nor I, which is why I sought your advice. I do not wish her to find out in front of the ton."

"I would think Maria could broach the subject more easily than you or I."

"Yes, I suppose so, but Maria is not here. They went to dinner with Lord and Lady Marsden before the ball. And I did want your perspective. Your father was always good at telling me I was imagining something that wasn't there."

Maria and Philip would not be arriving with them? Gabe was not sure how he felt about that. "I suppose I can speak with her, but there will not be much time. What if she does not wish to go?"

"It is a possibility, and I am sorry for it, but it has been weighing heavily on my mind, since the duchess' visit."

"I will see if I may speak with her now." Gabe left his mother and went to knock on Miss Sutton's door. He did not have the time to send for a servant. This was going to be a devilishly awkward conversation, but he had endured many before with some of his soldiers.

"Yes?" Bisset opened the door. "Oh, my lord. May I help you?" She dropped into a curtsy.

"Would you let Miss Sutton know I would like to speak with her as soon as she is finished with her toilette."

"I am ready now, my lord." Rose answered from behind the maid, who stepped out of the way. When Gabe saw her, he could not remember, for a moment, why he needed to speak with her so urgently.

She was dressed in white silk as befitted a debutante, looking like a goddess come to life. A small bodice and capped sleeves gave way to a flowing skirt adorned with spangles that would shimmer in the candlelight when she danced.

Then he remembered himself. He bowed. "You look beautiful, Miss Sutton."

"Thank you," she said with a soft smile." I owe it all to your sister and Bisset. They have wrought a miracle."

"You are a pleasure to dress. You cannot make a pig look pretty no matter how you dress it, mademoiselle," Bisset remarked behind her.

Rose shook her head as though she did not believe the praise. Again, it was why he was so drawn to her. Any other lady would have preened.

"You wish to speak with me, my lord? I have made a list of places where I think the veterans could be useful."

"That is not what I wish to speak to you about. If you are ready, perhaps we may withdraw to the drawing room while we await my mother?" He knew he had sounded abrupt just then, but he could not take it back now.

He offered her his arm out of habit, though it was perhaps too formal for the circumstance. He was surprised how right it felt when she accepted his support. She fit perfectly next to him and smelled like fresh lilacs on a summer day.

After they had entered the drawing room, he led her to the settee and then went to pour her a drink. "Sherry?"

"Yes, thank you."

He handed her the glass and then took a deep breath. "My mother has asked me to speak with you since Maria is not here."

She looked at him, clearly perplexed.

"You are aware the Duchess of Haverstock paid you marked attention at the theater, and then called here yesterday, asking about you."

"Yes," she replied, a question in her voice.

"Forgive me if this is presumptuous and preposterous, but my mother thinks you might be Her Grace's granddaughter."

He watched her face, and she did not look surprised.

"She did not wish you to be taken unawares at the ball."

Rose toyed with her fan before speaking. "I appreciate her concern. She may be correct, but I am not certain either."

"So you are aware of the possible relationship?" Gabe was relieved he was not giving her devastating news, as he had feared. She had already been disappointed in Bertie.

"Papa told me who my father was, and gave me their wedding certificate, only the night you came to dinner at the rectory. Before that, I had not been certain who my father was, or if my parents were wed."

Her eyes had been red that night, he recalled. She had been crying about something. Gabe saw her chin wobble, and he moved to sit beside her. He hesitated to touch her, but he wanted to comfort her.

"I truly appreciate her ladyship's concern. Is she afraid they will mistreat me? Why would they invite me to their house only to shun me? Or is that the way of the ton?"

"Mother believes the duchess' intentions to be pure, but the duke is another matter. She may not have told him."

"So this could be simply a fishing expedition in which I may be cast back into the water?" Her grey eyes looked up, searching his.

"Perhaps, but I could not say."

"Of course not. Forgive me. I appreciate you bringing it to my attention. Hopefully my Season will not be over before it has begun."

"What are you afraid of?" he asked gently.

"It seems you know my secrets, but there is one you may be unaware of. Papa intends to marry the harpy that was speaking about me. I have just received word. They will marry soon. They have already called the banns."

"And you cannot return there."

She shook her head, fighting tears. He did take her hand then.

"Come, you mustn't cry. Everything will be well." If only he had words of comfort to offer! He felt crippled with inadequacy. What would he say to Maria?

"I appreciate your kindness. I am certain this is the last conversation you wished to have." She laughed on a sob.

Should he say something to her now about his intentions? He still wanted her to have a chance to choose. Footsteps echoed on the stairs, signaling his mother's arrival. He had missed his chance with his indecision. He rose to his feet and helped her up.

"No matter what happens this evening, you may always look to me for help." It was far less than he wished to say.

"Remember, my dances will be empty," she teased.

"Any of them are yours. You have but to say the word."

ROSE WAS TOUCHED by Lord Mottram's words. She was sympathetic to the fact he'd been compelled to deliver the news to her, fearing that he would have to tell her that her parentage might be mistaken. Not very long ago, it would have been the case. She was still coming to terms with finding out about a father, only to learn he was dead. At least her parents had loved each other, and had not willingly abandoned her as the duke and duchess had done her father. How her mother must have suffered, losing her love and then struggling through childbirth, knowing she was dying, asking her brother and his wife to raise her orphaned child.

It was very tempting to lean into the earl's strength when she was so very uncertain about herself and her future. But there was one thing she could not abide, and that was pity. He only felt a sense of responsibility for her, being under his roof and a part of his village, and nothing more.

"MY SON HAS told you of my suspicions, then, Rose? Do you still wish to attend the ball?" Lady Mottram asked when they met her in the hall.

It would be so easy to say no, but Rose did not have the luxury. She could only pray that it would not be a trap to humiliate her. "Yes, we should go, come what may." She forced a smile she did not feel.

Rose remained quiet as they rode to the ball. When they arrived, there was a line of carriages, and they were obliged to wait. To say she was nervous did not begin to describe the emotion churning within her. Not only was she at her first ball, but she might be meeting her grandparents for the first time.

When they alighted in a courtyard, Maria and Philip were there, waiting for them.

"You look beautiful," Maria said, kissing her cheek.

"Thank you. As do you." She barely noticed her friend was glowing in a rose-colored gown.

"Is something the matter?" Maria looked between them.

"Now is not the time," Gabriel said. "I will explain later."

He took Rose's arm on one side and his mother's on the other, and they followed Philip and Maria up the steps into the grand mansion. It was at least as large as Mottram Place, an imposing fortress of golden stone, and it glowed brightly from every window as dusk began to fall.

As the earl spoke their names to the majordomo, she tensed, and she felt a reassuring squeeze on her arm. Who would've thought the earl who hated crowds would be the one to comfort her? She could have laughed if she were not so busy trying not to be sick.

When they were announced, it felt unreal. Her name alongside that of an earl and a countess. Heads swiveled at the name, but she knew it was not for her. Maria had told her that Lord and Lady Mottram had not been in Society for several years.

She was ushered along to the receiving line, and she held her breath when the Duke of Haverstock stood before her, and immediately she saw the resemblance to the miniature in her mother's chest of belongings. Was this what her father would have looked like were he still alive? There was but a moment to study him, while he greeted the earl and countess, and when Lord Mottram introduced her, he scarcely glanced her over and inclined his head, as though she were insignificant. He did not even look at her face. It was certainly not what she would have expected.

The duchess was another matter. She clasped Rose's hand and smiled at her as if she were something very precious. This must be her grandmother, then. Rose could feel Lord and Lady Mottram watching her as they spoke to the duke and duchess. The older matron looked as though she wanted to cry, and Rose felt her own throat tighten. "You are very welcome, Miss Sutton. I hope you will make time to speak with me later."

"Yes, Your Grace." Rose curtsied deeply, and moved along. It was like a daydream—meeting her grandparents, attending a ton ball, being dressed in finery, and surrounded by hundreds of people, each person more glamorous than the last.

It was too much to take in all at once. Would that she could escape now to a garden and consider things.

As they made their way into the grand ballroom, introductions were made, and Rose knew she would never remember half of the names or faces. Occasionally, she would feel Lord Mottram tense beneath her arm, and it was her turn to offer a reassuring pressure on his arm. What an unlikely pair they made! They reached a safe spot before Lord and Lady Marsden, Lord Philip's parents. He introduced them, and as Rose curtsied, Mottram released her arm. He had not yet asked her to dance, but perhaps he had not thought to do so, or was waiting for her to say she would like to, but she dared not.

Others conversed around her, but she stood on the periphery, observing. The contrast between Edwinstowe and the highest echelon of society could not be more poignant. It was more different than night and day, if that were possible, and she had yet to see a genuine smile. There was a practiced politesse and stiffness of manner that was foreign to her nature. Yet, given her nerves, it was likely that she blended perfectly with the assembled.

Thankfully, her conversation was not required as Maria and Philip chatted with his parents and Lady Mottram. She did not hear a word they said until Lady Marsden remarked, "I wonder why the dancing has not yet begun? The duke and duchess are no longer receiving."

Rose knew nothing about the London ways. The music would have already been playing and the dancing in full swing at an assembly.

Then she noticed the quiet and turned. For one second, she wondered if this was how Moses felt when the Red Sea parted, but the entire ballroom watched as the duke strolled towards their party, as though he were the King himself. He did not look pleased as he stopped before them. Oh, no.

"Miss Sutton, I believe?"

She sank into a curtsy. "Yes, Your Grace."

"May I have the pleasure?" The way he said it, she doubted very much that it was anything of the sort. He held out his arm, so it was not really a question, but a command. She did not understand why it was happening, but it would be detrimental to refuse.

"It would be my honor, Your Grace." She placed her hand on his arm as he led her to the center of the floor. She held her head high with as much of a smile as her tense muscles could muster, noting the inquiring stares of the entire beau monde.

He stood before her as others formed sets around them, looking her up and down with a frosty glare that must have frozen many a person in place.

It was hard not to harden her heart and hate... but that would make her no better than he. She said not a word before being spoken to.

"My wife informs me you are the daughter of someone very

dear to her."

Was he fishing? Rose had no intention of obliging him.

"How kind of her to remember me."

He scoffed, if it was called such when a duke made a noise of disbelief. It was clear he thought her an encroaching provincial.

Thankfully, the music began, and she was too worried about making a misstep to bother trying to make small talk. She was very grateful for the practice Maria had provided for her at Arden Park, or she might have made an utter fool of herself.

So this was the man who had raised her father, who had turned his back on him. At least, Rose supposed, he was being civil and doing her this great honor. Ha! She doubted he knew who she was or he would have refused. He might have even created a scene and asked her to leave.

When the dance ended, she was relieved it was over. It was probably a blessing that she had needed to concentrate. The duke made a slight bow as she curtsied at the end of the set. He escorted her back to Lady Mottram, who smiled and patted her arm. "That was very nicely done, my dear. Now I am afraid you will be besieged."

"I doubt he knew who I was," she said where only Lady Mottram could hear her.

"Unlikely," the countess agreed. "However, it was very well done of the duchess. He rarely dances. Your success will now be assured."

Rose doubted that very much. She still had no dowry, which mattered as much or more than any illustrious pedigree.

However, she did have a partner for every dance, with gentlemen who would never take her seriously once they knew more about her. Not once did she have to beg Lord Mottram to save her. He must have been relieved.

CHAPTER FIFTEEN

G ABE HOVERED ON the periphery of the ballroom, only
speaking to people when necessary. It was easier to linger in
shadows, observing that way. If the Edwinstowe assembly had
been under more controlled conditions, such as this, there was
every likelihood he would not have made a complete fool of
himself.

Maria tried to convince him to dance with another, when
Rose already had a partner, but he asked no one else. He told
himself he wanted to be available for Rose, should she need him.
She did not, of course. He had known men would be drawn to
her, and as soon as the duke had given her his stamp of approval,
it had been a mere invitation to dance with the new beauty in
town. Gabe feared his chances were dwindling.

He was pleased with one thing, though. No one had snubbed
either him or his mother. He knew she was nervous for her first
time back in Society. There had been a few looks of surprise, but
if the Duke and Duchess of Haverstock welcomed them, then no
one dared oppose them.

He paused and watched as Rose took a turn with Lord
Tilney. She was more poised, and composed, than she had been
when she had danced with him at the village assembly. 'Twas a
pity, and yet… although he secretly treasured her like that, he did
not relish others seeing her thus.

"She is very beautiful," a voice said beside him, surprising him. He was never caught unawares. Ever. He would have been dead long ago.

"Your Grace." He bowed.

"She is a guest in your house. What are your intentions?"

A direct hit. Gabe consider prevaricating, but the duchess's gaze was very keen. He turned his head back to watch the dancers. "I am hoping she will consent to marry me."

"Have you asked her?" A world of surprise lilted her question.

"I have not," he admitted. "I had thought to court her in Edwinstowe, but then she agreed to accompany my sister for the Season. They are old friends. I thought at least to grant her as much before asking her; she may find a suitable match."

"If not, then you will step in and save the day." Her tone was sardonic.

"Something of that nature," he grumbled. He scarcely knew this woman, yet she had pried his confidences from him. "Why are you asking me this?"

"I have an interest in Miss Sutton."

"She mentioned that His Grace told her you were a dear friend of her mother."

She gave an impatient wave of her hand. "Does she know the truth?"

Gabe was shocked she would also share confidences, and that she knew he knew.

"I believe Reverend Sutton only recently told her of her parentage."

"Yet she did not seek an acquaintance." She mulled that over.

"Can you blame her?" Gabe asked.

"I suppose it depends on what she was told. She could have claimed her birthright and demanded many things of us."

"That would be out of the realm of her character. But I believe you should ask her yourself. I know little apart from what my mother told me. After your visit and apparent interest, she remembered the old scandal of Miss Sutton's parents eloping, and then being cast off. Beyond that, I do not know what she was told."

Beside him, the duchess paused and swallowed hard. Gabe dared not turn and disturb her composure while she gathered her dignity. She was clearly affected by the past, and sought to remedy it.

"Why did you seek me out instead of my sister?" Gabe could but wonder. It was only by the accident of Maria's absence that he knew the whole.

"Because I see how you look at her."

Oh, good God, was he so obvious?

"I know about you and what you have done for the country. I asked Wellington himself."

"Then you know I am hardly a catch. You will also be aware of the scandal involving my father, a few years ago."

"One that seems to be forgotten." She waved her hand towards his mother, who was surrounded by some of her old friends.

"I must thank you for your part in that."

She inclined her head. "You are an earl and a bachelor. That in itself qualifies you as a catch, as you put it."

"Miss Sutton is the one I want, but I want her to choose me." Why was he revealing this to a woman he scarcely knew? Perhaps because they both felt vulnerable where Rose was concerned.

"I have left my portion and an estate to her in my will. As soon as I saw her at the theater, I knew who she was."

Gabe tried not to show outward reaction, but that would surely make her an heiress of sorts. If the relationship was acknowledged, many would want her for the ties with the dukedom alone. Gabe would never have a chance if the fact were made public. Unless the duke refused to acknowledge her, that was, but he had danced with her at his own ball. He would look a fool were he to renounce her now. The duchess had been very, very clever. Gabe would be his own fool for underestimating her. Yet he could not understand what he could do for her.

"What of your husband?" Gabe asked, knowing she under-stood why he was worried.

"He is not stupid, but I do not know if he has yet realized. Likely, after dancing with her, he has put two and two together. I cannot say what he will do now. I never would have believed he would have thrown Edward out. I, too, believed he would forgive them once the deed was done. Then it was too late. I cannot lose her, too." She said the last so quietly that he almost did not hear her.

Gabe remained silent. It was not up to him, though.

"Will you help me, my lord?" she pleaded.

He suspected it was not something she'd often done. "My word holds little weight with her, Your Grace."

"I think you are wrong." She paused again. "I am prepared to help you."

Gabe did turn, then, to look at her again. "How?"

"I will refrain from making it known that she is an heiress—and yes, I can do so even if Haverstock threatens trouble—if you will help me further my acquaintance with her."

Gabe furrowed his brow. "I cannot think my help necessary. She would not refuse to see you."

"How can you be certain?"

"Miss Sutton is very fair. At the very least, she would speak with you."

"Would you perhaps be willing to discuss the matter with her and send word? I had thought to speak with her here, but I am afraid I wish for a more private audience. You may think me a coward."

Gabe realized how vulnerable she was. He felt a kinship with her in that at least. "I believe that would be akin to the pot calling the kettle black. I stand here in the shadows next to you."

"You do yourself a disservice, my lord. There is value in those who linger in the shadows."

He noticed she did not say hide.

"Observation is an asset that many underestimate," she continued.

"I still think my sister would be a better advocate," he argued.

"I disagree. Your sister is preoccupied with her new husband."

That much was true, but Rose was an acquaintance and tolerated him because she had to. He was working on changing that, but it was not a quick process. "She could have anyone."

"Yet you wanted her when she was only thought to be the ward of a country vicar."

"I considered that an advantage," he retorted.

"But the other gentlemen would only see her as a duke's granddaughter with a large dowry."

"And a spirited beauty," he added.

Hoist with his own petard, he realized, as she smiled knowingly at him.

"I will do what I can. Are there any restrictions on where you would like to meet?"

"I would prefer somewhere neutral without other curious eyes or listening ears. I have already brought her to the ton's attention with my meddling. Perhaps it was poorly done of me, but a grandmother wants…" She did not finish the sentence. "I should have met with her first, but I thought to launch her successfully."

"Do not doubt yourself, Your Grace. As long as you keep her dowry a secret, then it will keep the fortune hunters at bay. I do agree that you should meet with her. I will see what I can arrange."

"Thank you, Lord Mottram." She slipped away, leaving Gabe to contemplate just what he had agreed to. He should be grateful that she approved of him, but he didn't want anyone's help. He wanted Rose to choose him for his own sake.

ROSE'S FEET HURT. She had danced every dance, and by the time the evening was over, only the earl awaited her.

"Where are the others, my lord?" she asked, looking about the room.

"I am afraid Maria and my mother were fatigued, and left a little while ago with Lord Philip. They sent the carriage and Bisset back for us."

"I would have left when they did, had I known." She shook her head.

"They were happy to see your success, and did not wish to disturb you. The carriage awaits." He helped her with her silk wrap, and then led her to the door, where a very tired-looking duke and duchess were waiting.

Rose curtsied. "Thank you for a lovely evening, Your Graces."

"I am delighted you could come, Miss Sutton. I do regret that we were unable to become better acquainted. Perhaps you would join me here for tea one day," the duchess said, with a meaningful look, while the earl made his goodbyes to the duke.

"I should be honored, Your Grace."

Bisset was waiting in the carriage to chaperone them on the drive home. Rose appreciated the condescension they showed her by waiting to bid her farewell.

"How was your first ball, mademoiselle?" Bisset asked.

"It was very grand," Rose replied.

The earl made a noise of disbelief. "She danced every dance, including the opening reel with the duke himself."

"I knew you would be a hit, mademoiselle!" Bisset beamed.

"It must have been my coiffure," Rose teased. She was very weary by the time they reached Mottram Place and entered the house.

"I will await you upstairs, miss," Bisset said to Rose.

"Good night, Miss Sutton," the earl said as she clasped the handrail to climb the stairs, then paused.

"What did the duchess have to say to you, if I may be so

bold?" she asked.

He looked surprised that she had noticed. Unfortunately, she had been unable to keep her thoughts from him all evening, wondering why he never claimed a set.

"She was asking about you."

"Was she?"

"She asked me to help arrange a private meeting with you."

"I had thought she would speak with me during the ball," Rose admitted.

"She intended to, but decided it might not be the best place."

"Very well. I would like to meet her. I assume the duke still does not know?"

"She believed he would quickly come to realize."

Rose nodded. At least there had been no disastrous scenes. It had been enough for her nerves that the duke had danced with her.

"You did very well tonight," the earl said softly.

"You did not dance with me," she blurted out before she thought better of it.

"You had no need of me."

"But you did not dance at all?" she asked.

"In case you had need of me. Good night." He made a bow from the waist, turned and left her there, wondering.

She climbed the stairs, slowly trying to sort through the events of the evening. It would take some time. Why, then, was her primary concern the earl? He had not danced because of her?

She was too tired to appreciate what it might have meant. She would think on it tomorrow.

THE NEXT MORNING, Rose awoke and lay in her bed, staring at the canopy while still toiling over the night before. She should have slept more soundly, but there was too much on her mind. She knew she should be considering the gentlemen she had danced with, though she could not think any of them would seriously consider her as a match. Only one of them had not held a title of some sort, and Maria had told her the gentleman was as rich as Croesus and extremely well-connected. Neither of those qualities appealed to Rose. Many of her partners had been handsome, but she had not felt at ease with any of them. Was that a fault in her or them? London Society was so foreign to her very being that she did not know if she would ever feel comfortable. It was only her first ball, though, and perhaps those not hosted by the Duke and Duchess of Haverstock might not be so ostentatious.

Considering the duke and duchess, what was she to do? She was drawn to her grandmother, if she were being honest. Was that disloyal to her parents, even though she had taken an instant dislike to the duke? Rose could easily imagine the blame lay at his door.

Trying to fall asleep again was in vain, so she threw back the covers and dressed for the day. Maria told her everyone slept past noon during the Season, after staying out all night, and Rose could see why. However, waking early was also ingrained in her country ways.

It seemed she was not the only one. Lord Mottram stood up at her entrance to the breakfast room. He was drinking coffee and reading the papers.

It was shocking to think, but she was growing comfortable with the earl. Was it simply because of familiarity, and that she had discovered there was kind heart beneath the exterior gruffness? Or because of what he had done for her last night?

She should not think too much of his kindness. He would have no more interest in her than any of the other high-born lords of the ton. The reason he was being kind to her was because of her friendship with Maria. It was strange to think she had spent as much, if not more, time with him.

"Good morning. I expected you to sleep a little later than usual after dancing all evening," he said with a stiff smile.

"I wish I could," she said, dipping a curtsy before taking a seat.

"I, too, cannot sleep late. I blame too many years with the

army. Shall I ring for tea and toast? Perhaps you would care for something more this morning?"

"Tea and toast, please." Why did it please her so that he remembered? It was not as though it was an exceptional order.

Lord Philip walked in and greeted them. "Good morning. I did not expect to see either of you for some hours yet. May I say congratulations on your success last night?" he said to Rose.

She felt herself blush. She wanted to protest, but then she would seem ungrateful. "Thank you."

"Do the Duke and Duchess of Haverstock intend to acknowledge you?" he asked bluntly.

"I could not say. I gather Maria has told you the whole?"

He nodded.

"I did wish to speak further with you on the subject. I wondered if perhaps you had changed your mind after sleeping on it," Lord Mottram said.

"No. I would rather do so sooner than later. I would rather know."

"Very well. I will arrange it."

"Arrange what?" Philip asked, after ordering something from the kitchens.

"The duchess wishes to meet Rose privately."

"Ah."

"Where did you have in mind?" Rose asked.

"There is a cottage in Richmond that used to belong to my grandmother. No one has lived there for a few years, but there are caretakers."

"That seems a bit extreme," Philip said. "You could meet at my parents' house if the duchess does not wish to return here."

"I still think it would be too public. The servants would know about it. I know your parents are discreet, but servants are another matter."

Even Rose knew that to be true.

Maria sailed into the room, looking as fresh as a daisy. She came immediately to Rose and threw her arms around her. "I knew you would be a success!"

Rosa's heart sank. She suspected it would be like this all day. She had never wanted so much attention, and certainly not to have all eyes of the ton upon her. Beggars should not be choosers, according to the old proverb, she reminded herself. But truly, she was uncomfortable with the attentions of such lofty personages. It only meant she had further to fall when they realized she had nothing to recommend her.

"Have you seen the drawing room yet?" Maria asked. "Of course, I knew it would be full."

Whatever was she talking about? The confusion must have shown on her face; she could feel the earl's eyes on her.

Maria laughed. "Come and see!" She took Rose's hand and led her to the drawing room, where she was met with a veritable garden of floral arrangements.

"How beautiful!" Rose exclaimed.

"And they are all for you! 'Tis hardly surprising that most of them are all roses. I suppose they think themselves clever."

"For me?"

"It is customary to send flowers to those you danced with the night before, or to ladies who you admire. By the looks of this, I would say you were very admired. These are no token arrangements." Rose had never seen such beautiful—or large—arrangements of flowers.

In fact, it made Rose unhappy to think of how many villagers could have been fed on what one of these alone must have cost.

"You had better become accustomed to it," Maria remarked, accurately deciphering Rose's feelings. "It will be like this every day. And with the patronage of the Duke and Duchess of Haverstock, there will be many callers, from curiosity alone."

Rose uttered an unladylike groan. "I seem ungrateful, I know, but I have never wanted this kind of attention."

Maria looked at her sympathetically. "I understand, but you are very beautiful, Rose. I know you are wholly unaware of your charms, but gentlemen love nothing more than flirtation with a beautiful woman. Most of it will not be serious. Many of them consider it a way of enlivening the Season."

"Then how am I to know who is genuine?"

"Why, by consulting me, of course. I will guide you through everything you need to know!"

Now, why did that not make Rose feel better?

CHAPTER SIXTEEN

G ABE DISTRACTED HIMSELF with the business of finding veterans to work in Edwinstowe. So far, he'd had interest from the family Captain Gray had recommended, and one other sergeant who had served under his friend, Felix Knight. It was a start, but he still hoped to fill more of the gap left by the loss of men from amongst his tenants.

Besides, staying busy kept him from dwelling on Rose. He knew not what he could do other than facilitate her reunion with her grandmother. Despite what the duchess thought, Gabe had no illusions about Rose's eligibility once everything became known. And it always did.

He penned a letter to the duchess, then sent some of his servants out to ensure the cottage in Richmond was suitably prepared and warn Mr. and Mrs. Davies of their visitors.

The duchess replied immediately, so Gabe went to find Miss Sutton to see when she was available.

She sat in the drawing room amongst a sea of callers like a queen with her subjects at her feet. The immediate surge of jealousy Gabe felt surprised him. He had been expecting it, yet it still rankled that he was beholden to such base emotions. She was not yet his and she might never be.

"I beg your pardon. I should like a quick word with Miss Sutton, if I may."

Of course the gentlemen protested, as was expected. What Gabe hated most amongst the set was their practiced responses and lack of genuine feeling. Rose looked relieved when she reached his side. They stepped out into the entrance hall.

"I am sorry to disturb your court, but I must reply to Her Grace about a convenient time for your meeting."

"You are sorry to disturb me? I am indebted to you," she replied dryly.

Was this not what she wanted? Gabe furrowed his brow. "Shall I ask them to leave?"

"Of course not." She shook her head.

Gabe would never understand women. She had told him she had a problem and he could easily resolve it.

She smiled at him in the most enchanting fashion. "You dear man. You are so used to fighting battles that you would slay all my dragons for me."

"If you wish." He nearly choked on the words. The look she gave him left him feeling more confused. It was not full of disdain and dislike as he had come to expect. He could not recall an occasion when he had ever been addressed as a dear man.

"As to your question, I do not believe we have any engagements tomorrow, during the day. I am anxious to have it over with, truth be told."

"Very well. I will answer her, and hopefully make an arrangement for tomorrow." He began to turn to return to his study.

"Drat."

He turned back sharply. "What is the matter?"

"I was hoping for an excuse to avoid riding in the Park with one of those gentlemen," she whispered.

"None of them are to your liking?"

She shook her head. "I suppose I should accept, but none of them have any genuine interest in me."

"How could you think not? Anyone would be interested in you."

Her eyes widened, and her breath caught on a gasp. Had he said something wrong again?

"I am simply the latest *on dit*."

That made him smile, but he understood what she meant. "Would you care to drive through the Park with me? If, that is, you need an excuse to deny these other gentlemen."

"You would do that for me? What about your own prospects?"

"I do not think they would be harmed by tooling you about Hyde Park during the fashionable hour."

"I cannot ask you to sacrifice your own matrimonial search for my benefit. It was not my intention you should abstain from dancing on my account."

"It was my pleasure, as it would be to take you driving this afternoon. Truly, though, I could say the same of you. If you are always to be seen in my company, people will believe we are courting. Would that be so terrible?"

"Of course not, but you can look as high as you wish for a wife."

"Let me worry over that." He knew that mattered to some, but not to him. After what he spent the last decade doing, he knew there were more important things.

"Perhaps being seen with the new Incomparable will help my cause."

That seemed to amuse her and she smiled brightly, as she had the first time he'd seen her. "Now who is being ridiculous?" She stood on tiptoe and kissed his cheek. "Half an hour?"

"I will be ready."

She went back into the drawing room and he touched his cheek in disbelief, as though an angel had descended from heaven. He was a besotted fool. He had little doubt she kissed her brothers in just the same manner, and it meant no more. Except it meant, perhaps, she thought a little better of him than she had, and that he had been given an opportunity to spend more time with her and further his cause. One day, maybe, she would understand it for what it was. He dared not hope that her aversion to these suitors would continue, but he would take the advantage as long as he had it.

Now, he deliberated, he must quickly see if he could borrow Philip's curricle. He might as well make the most of their parade through the Park, and if they were in an enclosed carriage, they would require a chaperone. It was awkward enough to speak to Rose alone, and the last thing he needed was his mother or sister listening to him bumble.

Gabe was relieved to see all the dandies and Corinthians leaving his house. It was something he would have to tolerate, but he did not have to like it. Philip's curricle was a shiny black lacquered affair with matching blood cattle. It stood waiting at the front for them, the matched pair held by a groom. It had been some time since Gabe had driven such a vehicle, but he knew how to handle the ribbons.

Miss Sutton had put on a fetching bonnet trimmed with yellow ribbons to match her gown. He missed the floppy straw hat she had worn in the country. She would think him even more ridiculous than she did already were he to say so.

"What a smart vehicle," she said as she stopped outside. "Bang up to the mark, as my brothers would say."

"It belongs to Lord Philip. He was ever fashionable, and a good judge of horse flesh."

"No more so than you, I dare say," she remarked, as he handed her up onto the seat. "I saw your Pedro, remember? Is it true you mean to begin breeding horses at your estate?"

"I do. Pedro should be appreciated for generations to come."

"He was your war horse," she said, as though just realizing it. "Then I like him all the more for keeping you safe."

Gabe did not know how to respond to such a humbling statement. Thankfully, he had to concentrate on negotiating the traffic to the Park. "This will be your first visit to Hyde Park?"

"Yes. I am grateful for a little piece of country in Town."

"Unfortunately, you will need to go out early in the day for that. At this hour, it will be very crowded."

Rose would soon see what he meant. The carriageways were blocked with vehicles, the paths lined with pedestrians and riders on horseback. Ladies wore beautiful gowns with bonnets and parasols, and the gentlemen were also handsomely dressed.

"Welcome to the fashionable hour in the Park, where people come to see and be seen."

"Like a horse at auction," she reflected.

"Very much like that, I am afraid," he agreed.

"You must hate this. I did not understand what it was I was asking of you."

"I did, and rest assured I would not have agreed had I not been willing. We can always leave the path and go into other areas of the Park. It is very vast."

"I am not certain we could go anywhere quickly," she remarked as she looked around. Crawling would be an over-idealistic description of how fast they were moving.

"I do believe those soldiers are waving to you." Gabe looked over to where she indicated, and tensed.

"Is something the matter?"

"I believe it's you they are hoping to be introduced to," he said, spying a few familiar faces. "Should I avoid them?"

"Not on my account, sir."

It took a while for them to maneuver the curricle towards the group of soldiers on horseback.

"Major Lloyd! I was not expecting to see you amongst the crowd here," Colonel James said with a friendly smile.

"Even I come out of the shadows on occasion," he quipped.

"Would you be so good as to introduce us to your lovely guest?" Captain Wembley asked.

"Colonel James, Lieutenant Sheffield, and Captain Wembley, may I present to you, Miss Rose Sutton of Edwinstowe?"

All three of them tipped their hats to Rose.

"Stealing a march on everyone else, are you Lloyd?" the Captain asked, looking a little too smart in his uniform for Gabe's liking.

"No, I am simply her humble servant."

"We are neighbors in the country," she explained. "How do you do, gentlemen?"

"If this is what your part of the country boasts, maybe I will take up one of the posts I heard you are offering," Wembley remarked.

"It might be better than half-pay," the Lieutenant agreed.

"I am afraid it would require dirtying your hands," Gabe retorted. It was common practice to tease the Royal Horse Guards about sullying their uniforms.

The colonel pulled up closer to Gabe. "I'll say, is it true about your cousin?"

"What about him?"

"He lost over five thousand at the tables last night. Then he started a brawl right in the middle of the Guard's Club."

Gabe wanted to sink into the curricle. "The impudent fool. He lost every bit of what I settled on him."

Colonel James whistled. "Enough to set him up for life."

"I thought so," Gabe said through gritted teeth. "I hope he has not already spent it and can honor the debt."

"I hate to be the bearer of bad news." The colonel maneuvered his horse, which was becoming restless.

"Thank you for telling me. I would rather know." Gabe shook his head in disbelief. "I wonder how long it will be until he comes crawling to me for more."

"Not long enough, I daresay. I know some Navy Admirals who could use some men. You only have to say the word."

"I will keep that in mind. I have a feeling this is not the end of it." They left the Park soon after. Gabe did not know what Rose had overheard, but he feared it to be a great deal too much.

ROSE WOKE EARLIER than normal and could not remain still. At least she had met her grandmother already which eased her anxieties somewhat, but there was still much unknown, such as if her grandfather would accept her, or if he would apologize for forcing her father to leave, resulting in his being killed.

Rose took a walk in Green Park with Bisset, needing to do something to expend her energy and pass the time. It was much emptier than Hyde Park, and mostly she passed children with their nurses. However, it only passed about an hour of her wait. At least they were to leave before noon. She was ready and waiting in the drawing room, a half-hour before the appointed time, when Maria came in with her brother following behind.

"Are you certain you do not wish me to come?" Maria asked with concern, taking Rose's hands in hers.

"I am sure. I have already met her once, so that helps."

"Oh, very well. I do not see why my brother is allowed to go and I am not."

Lord Mottram just stood there, looking pensive. "Her Grace asked me to help."

"At least it is a nice day for the drive," Maria said as she looked out of the window.

Soon they were in the carriage and on their way. It was very quiet within. Rose enjoyed seeing more of the city and then the countryside. When they drew close to Richmond, she saw some very large estates along the river, and rolling hills dotted with sheep. They turned on to a country lane, overgrown with hedges and flowering vines emitting a sweet fragrance. After a mile or so, they pulled up before a quaint cottage much like her home in Edwinstowe. It was a modest brick structure covered with ivy and pink clematis.

"This was my grandmother's house. She chose to live here after my grandfather died."

"I can see why. It is perfect."

They pulled up before the front of the house and alighted. They were greeted by the caretakers, Mr. and Mrs. Davies. The inside was very well-appointed, with beautiful carpets and Queen Anne furniture, and landscapes covering the walls.

"My grandmother spent her days painting," Lord Mottram said, when he saw her admiring them.

They were mostly of scenes that Rose enjoyed—rolling hills, trees, flowers, and a river in the background.

"Most of them were painted here. Those scenes are from the back garden. The property extends all the way to the Thames. I can show you later, if you wish."

"That would be lovely, thank you."

"Would you like to see the house?"

Before they began their tour, however, a carriage pulled up in front of the house.

"It looks as though it will have to wait until later."

Lord Mottram stayed with her until the duchess was shown into the room.

"Her Grace, the Duchess of Haverstock," Mr. Davies announced.

"Welcome, Your Grace," the earl said with a bow. Rose curtsied.

"Thank you for arranging this for us," she said to Lord Mottram.

He inclined his head. "I will leave the two of you alone. You have much to talk about. Mrs. Davies will be in with a tea tray shortly."

"Thank you, my lord." Rose said, then turned back to her grandmother.

"Well, my dear, where should we begin? I was not sure if you would wish to see me," the duchess said frankly.

"I am uncertain. Everything is happening so fast. Papa only told me about my father less than a fortnight ago.

"Lord Mottram indicated as much to me. I was very surprised to hear it."

"Indeed, I was astonished by the news. I had... thought myself to be a natural child."

"Reverend Sutton allowed you to believe this?"

"It never occurred to Papa that I didn't know. He is a dear, but he was very distracted when Mama—his wife—died."

"They brought you up as their own?"

Rose nodded. "My mother died when I was young. I knew about her, but never my father. My mother asked them to bring me up as their own daughter. Of course, there were whispers when I was a child, but I was well loved. Papa and Mama had five more babies after me."

"I am very glad to hear it, but I wish I had known about you." She took a seat near the window.

"I wish the same, but there is no point to dwelling on things we cannot change."

"Spoken like a vicar's daughter. Come, let me have a good look at you." She patted the space next to her on a green and cream striped settee. Rose sat down, and considered her new grandmother as well.

"I am afraid you see but an old woman before you, but I looked very much like you in my youth."

Rose could see that. She was still very handsome, but her hair had silvered and her eyes told the story of loss and pain.

Mrs. Davies brought in the tea tray and set it on a small table before them.

"Will you pour, my dear? My hands are rheumatic, and I find it difficult. I take it with a little milk."

Rose poured tea into a porcelain cup and handed it to her.

"You must have questions."

"Oh, I do, but I do not know if there is any point in asking them. As I said before, it will not change anything."

"You must wonder about your grandfather, and how he will receive you," she said shrewdly.

"Yes," Rose agreed, "but I cannot say if I wish him to acknowledge me."

"You blame him for what happened?"

"Is that blame wrongly placed?" Rose did not think so.

"No. Robert believed your father would regret his impetuous marriage."

"My mother was hardly ineligible as the daughter of a viscount."

"An unwealthy viscount, who was also one of His Grace's bitterest political enemies."

"That does at least explain his antipathy a little more."

"And he already had selected a bride for Edward."

"Does he regret what happened?"

"We have never spoken about it. Even after the ball, when he must have realized who you were, he said nothing. It is not every day that I demand he opens a ball with a young lady. I would like you to meet him. However, I wanted first to make sure you were amenable to the idea."

Rose studied her cup. "I daresay," she said carefully, "if he is willing to speak to me, then I will agree. It does not mean I forgive him."

"I understand. I do not believe he has forgiven himself. I mean to acknowledge you if you will permit it, Rose. I have lived twenty-four years without my son and, for almost as many years, have been deprived of my grandchild."

"If I may… will you allow me to meet with His Grace first?"

"If you wish."

Rose sipped her tea, thousands of questions whirling through her head, yet she was not comfortable asking all of them. Frankly, knowing her grandmother was a duchess was still beyond the realm of her understanding. Papa had always encouraged them to believe that God created everyone equal. He treated everyone the same, from the poorest to the richest. If her grandfather was an equally radical politician, then she was not certain she wished to know her grandfather if he opposed fair treatment for all of God's creatures. Thus far there was little she could like about him.

"There is also something else you should know. I have left you an estate and a portion in my will. It might improve your marriage prospects, but it appears you were doing very well

without either our name or a dowry. That is also your information to share or not, although when I acknowledge you, it will
certainly be expected that His Grace and I dower you according-
ly."

Rose shook her head. It was too much. "I do not know what
to say." She was very afraid that all the gentlemen who had paid
court to her would do so in earnest if that were discovered.

"It is yours by birthright, Rose. I have no one else to leave my
estate to. It would have gone to your father, so it should be
yours."

"Tell me about him," she said, then settled back to two more
hours of stories about her father.

CHAPTER SEVENTEEN

G ABE WAS HAPPY that things went well between Rose and her grandmother. Whether or not they went well with the duke was another matter. Gabe had not ridden inside the carriage with Rose and her maid in either direction, wanting to maintain the proprieties, and also to give the former time alone to think. At least it was what he would have wanted had their situations been reversed.

Before the duchess had departed, he had overheard that she would send Rose word once she had spoken with the duke.

As for himself, he had no more ideas of how to further his courtship. Maria had accepted so many invitations for every day of the week that there was little time unaccounted for into the near future. He also could not sit at Rose's feet in the drawing room every afternoon, like her other suitors, waiting for crumbs of her time. Even if he were capable of such a thing, he would never know what to say.

When they stepped down from the carriage, Rose escaped to her chambers and Gabe sought his study, where Philip was going through some ledgers.

"Save me, Mottram," Philip pleaded.

"From which inconvenience in particular?" Gabe could think of plenty.

"Take your pick. The house repairs, the Season, being an

expectant father." He held up an elegant hand.

"There is little I can do to help with any of those."

"But you can. I need a diversion. Let us find Owens and do something. Perhaps we can find some recruits along the way. I was given the name of a tavern from one of the other sergeants between Covent Garden and Seven Dials."

"I am sure Maria will love to hear that we are off to Covent Garden," Gabe said dryly.

"I believe you have just made a jest," Philip said appreciatively. "Let us go and find Owens."

Soon they were on their way and Jack was only too happy to join them. They set out for Seven Dials as the rest of the fashionable world was heading toward Hyde Park.

"You have been a busy fellow," Jack remarked to Gabe, as they rode in a hackney towards the theaters and market of Covent Garden, which was connected to Seven Dials.

"I have, rather," Gabe agreed without saying more.

"How proceeds your courtship, then?" Jack asked.

Gabe clenched his jaw. He no more liked talking about his personal life then he did going into a crowd. "There is no courtship currently," he said.

"That is not how it appears," Jack retorted.

"Am I so obvious?" Gabe was truly appalled if that was the case. He had not at all meant to appear to be singling Rose out.

"I suppose not. I might have had a hint." He looked at Philip.

"Do not shift the blame to me," his brother-in-law said. "My wife, on the other hand..." He left the rest on spoken.

"I simply do not wish to embarrass Miss Sutton."

"Maria says you are spending more time with her than she is, so I would think that counts for something."

"I do think perhaps she is softening toward me a little. It does not mean she would consider me for a husband."

As they moved from Mayfair towards Covent Garden and beyond, behind the Opera House and St. Paul's Cathedral, away from the mansions on the Strand, the buildings shrank and were much more crowded and dirty. Some carriages were now re-employed as vendors' carts and hacks instead. Pedestrians wore practical greys and browns and hurried about their business.

Later at night, the atmosphere would change, but it would be easier to find what they were looking for at this time of day. They dismounted from the hackney and paid the driver when it was impossible to drive further into the square. Their task would be much easier on foot.

"I can't say as I've been here during the day before," Philip mused.

"Nor I," Jack agreed.

Early in the morning, it was more of a market for goods. Flower sellers, fruit stands, pies, pasties, and gingerbread were available for purchase. The center of the square was lined with small shops that overflowed into the outdoors, where the working class could buy shoes, hats, and fabrics. A group of dirty children chased after an even dirtier mutt, which had stolen the rag ball they'd been playing with.

"What was the name of the place?" Gabe asked Philip.

"The Crown."

"Of course," Jack muttered, "along with half the pubs in England." They passed on through the market, closer to the theater where they had been recently. Just beyond were the dirty tenements, gin houses, opium dens, brothels and gaming houses, where wild oats were sown, and many a wounded soldier came to attempt to drown out the pain and forget.

"Are you sure you want to look here?"

"No, I do not seek addicts, but perhaps not all are beyond saving," Gabe said thoughtfully.

The tavern they came to was nothing more than a hovel. Gabe could smell the sweat and stale alcohol before even going through the door. Just outside, a body was huddled under a threadbare blanket, sleeping off blue ruin or worse.

"Perhaps we can speak to that one later," Jack said, looking at the still lump.

They went on inside, and Gabe was hard-pressed not to cover his nose. It took a moment for his eyes to adjust to the darkness and smoky haze. Even at this time of day, the taproom was full of custom. Several men sat on stools along the bar, while others sat at plain wooden tables scattered about the room.

"Where to begin?" Jack asked as he looked around.

"That one over there." Gabe pointed to the figure he surmised most likely to be a soldier. He had a distant look in his eye, yet there was also desperation and defeat. Resignation. His clothes were worn, and his beard was full and grizzly, as though it took too much effort to groom himself.

"I will take this one," Gabe said, as Philip and Jack turned to see who they could approach.

Gabe slid onto the bench across from his quarry, but the soldier did not even look up. He stared, lost into his empty mug.

"Can I buy you something, soldier?" Gabe asked.

The man grunted, as if speaking were beyond him.

Gabe waved to the bar-keeper for him to bring two mugs of ale.

"What regiment were you in?"

"The 95th."

"Sergeant…?" Gabe asked.

"Bateman," the man said with obvious reluctance.

"Major Lloyd," Gabe said, and offered the man his hand. He looked skeptical, but took it and returned the shake.

"And what are you doing with yourself now?"

"What do you think?" He growled and held up his arm that was missing the lower half.

"Does that mean you cannot do anything?" Gabe prodded to see if the man had fully given up or if he still had a spark of life.

"It means no one will have me."

A barmaid put two mugs of ale in front of them and Gabe slipped her a coin.

"Have you any family here?"

"No. Family's in the north, but cannot stand to look at me.

Me ma wailed the whole time I was there."

"What kind of work can you do?"

"I was a rifleman. Can't do that anymore."

"And before that?"

He shrugged his shoulder. "Me pa was a tenant farmer. That's the only other thing I know."

"Sergeant, it just so happens I am looking for some workmen, but there is a catch."

There was a slight spark of interest in Sergeant Bateman's eye, but Gabe still saw the skepticism.

"There is always a catch."

"My estate is in Nottinghamshire. It would mean removing there, but with work, wages, and shelter."

The man stared into his ale.

"You need not answer now. Think on it. Here is my steward's address. If you are interested, go to see him there." Gabe placed enough coins on the table for him to hire a hack, have a few good meals and perhaps buy a new coat and shoes if he chose to rather than spend it all on drink.

Gabe stood. "If you know of any other soldiers who wish to work hard and would be willing to move, send them my way. I will be glad of anyone, regardless of their injuries."

He left the sergeant staring into his ale, but Gabe was hopeful his words would bear fruit.

Gabe watched as Philip and Jack also spoke with some others around the room. He waited for them outside.

The air wasn't much fresher out there, but he was relieved to be out of the closed space.

He started when the lump under the blanket began to move. Gabe prepared himself to speak to whomever emerged, but the lump merely shifted then went motionless again.

"This is proving to be harder than I thought," Gabe admitted as Philip and Jack emerged from the tavern, and they walked back through the market to find a hack.

"Give it time. They have learned to be skeptical about everything since the government has left them to rot," Philip remarked.

Gabe did not want to give it time. He wanted to help these men, but he could not force them.

RAIN BEAT AGAINST the window early that morning while the rest of the household slept, so Rose kept to her chambers' sitting room, rereading a letter from Tommy and trying to form a response.

Dearest Rose,

I hope you are enjoying London, but I must share bad tidings. Papa wed Mrs. Winton this past week. He did not wish to interrupt your Season, but I think it was Mrs. Winton's doing. She is every bit as managing and meddling as you feared. Already she has hired a governess to tame the children's "wild, improper behaviors" as she calls them. They are not allowed to dine with the family or spend their evenings in the drawing room anymore. The once happy home feels like a mausoleum. I pray Michaelmas comes quickly, though I feel guilty for leaving George, Julia and Letty behind to the woman's devices. She has already threatened to send George to Eton or Harrow in the autumn. I suppose the only positive she brings to the union is pots and pots of money. I should not burden you with this, but I must speak of it to someone. How I dearly wish you had found someone to marry here so that you might provide some comfort to the girls. Mrs. Winton is no replacement for you or Mama. Papa seems as determined as ever to see good in her.

I do hope to see you soon, though I also hope for your sake you find a satisfactory match. You would not be happy here anymore.

Your loving brother,
Tommy

Rose could not stop the tears from falling. What a wretched, wretched business! She should have made an effort to dissuade Papa, but in her heart, she knew he would not have listened. He always saw the good in everyone, though Rose had no idea what he saw in the old harpy.

If there had only been someone eligible for her to have wed in the parish, she would have sacrificed the Season for the children. Immediately, she thought of Lord Mottram, but as quickly dismissed it. She was hardly an eligible wife for him, though perhaps that was not true anymore. It was hard to think of herself as the granddaughter of a duke. However, she had not been brought up to run a grand house.

Moreover, the earl did not appear to be trying very hard to find his own match. She thought back to the few events they had attended, and the only women he had spent much time with were herself and Maria.

She pursed her lips. Why was that?

"Dismiss the silly notion at once," she told herself.

"You do not even like him," she scolded, but then knew it was no longer true. She could remember several instances where she had misjudged him, though he was still very cold in his manners. Could she be happy with one such as he? Most of her other suitors seemed so silly she could not take them seriously. At least Lord Mottram did not shower her with meaningless compliments.

A knock on her door startled her, and she realized her quill had been dripping a large puddle on her paper. Quickly, she placed it in the standish and blotted the ink. She stood and wiped at her eyes while she called for the person to enter.

The door opened, and Lord Mottram stood in the doorway.

"Good morning, Miss Sutton," he said formally, looking rather handsome in his buff breeches and riding boots with a dark blue jacket.

Rose tried not to blush lest her thoughts give her away. He could not know she'd been considering him as a match.

She curtsied.

"I have had word from your grandmother. Would you care to join me in my study to discuss it?"

"Yes, of course. I will be down at once."

He left, leaving her unsettled. Why had he not sent a servant? Flustered, she attempted to wipe the ink from her fingers, then looked in the glass and tucked a few stray pieces back into her knot. Now she would feel self-conscious around the gentleman, confound her wayward thoughts, even though Tommy had put the idea into her head.

She had little notion if Lord Mottram would even consider her, though he had been all solicitousness towards her in London – and even back in Edwinstowe, if she thought about it.

As she made her way downstairs, she could but wonder if marriage to him would only mercenary for her siblings? Could she be happy with him? For some reason she did not think she could marry him in cold blood. It was one thing to think of marriages of convenience in theory, but another when there was a person to espouse.

"Yes, my lord?" she asked from the open doorway. He was standing by the window, looking outward.

"Please, come in." He held his hand towards a seat.

Suddenly Rose felt very shy in the earl's presence. Before, she had not been comfortable with him, but this was entirely different. She sat expectantly.

"Your grandmother says His Grace is prepared to acknowledge you."

Rose felt her chin tremble. It was very unexpected, this rush of emotion.

"Is it not good news?" Lord Mottram looked perplexed.

"I suppose it is. Forgive me. Did she say how I am to meet him as his granddaughter?"

"She said that will be your choice. She has suggested a night at the theater or a drive in the Park. Either situation would signal to the ton that Their Graces accept you. By the next day you will be known everywhere as their lost grandchild, I expect. You are already without their name, of course."

"Would I be expected to take their name?" She had considered it, of course, but somehow it seemed unreal.

He tilted his head to the side and clearly pondered this. "I would suspect so."

"It seems somehow dishonorable to Papa."

"Perhaps your grandmother will know what is best, though Maria, or my mother, would be happy to give their opinion, I am sure."

"What is your estimation?" Somehow she wanted to know his judgement.

"I would think you could retain your name. Perhaps you might add theirs? Many people take both."

"As in Sutton–Byrne? If they insist, that might be the best solution."

"Besides, if you marry soon, it will matter little."

"How true. Thank you, my lord." She felt her cheeks heat at the mention of marriage.

"I wish you would not call me that. At the very least, Mottram would be preferable, though that still feels like my father."

"I understand. Being called Byrne will feel as though they are speaking of someone else." She smiled in sympathy.

"You seem sad. Is anything else amiss?"

So many things, she wished to blurt out, but she did not. "I have had news from home and I am a little out of sorts."

"Has something serious occurred?" He looked concerned.

"No one is ill. It is just that Papa has married Mrs. Winton. Tommy says she is not kind to the children—wanting them to behave like statues, it seems. I wish there was something I could do, but I cannot live under the same roof with her. When all is said and done, marriage will probably take me far away from them."

"That is a difficult situation."

Rose felt somehow disappointed. It was not as though she

expected the earl to make her some kind of declaration or offer, but somehow there had to be a way she could help her family. She sighed and stood up. "Forgive me for unburdening my problems on to you. I will seek Maria's advice."

"I will help however I may." He moved forward from where he stood as if to reach for her, but then stopped.

"That is very handsome of you, but you have been more than kind. I fear you have neglected your own search for a wife in helping me with my situation. We had agreed to help each other, after all."

"I do not see you as a hindrance."

If Rose had hoped he would say more, then she was to be left wanting. Marriage to him would be tiring, she reflected, always trying to draw conversation from him. It was a foolish notion anyway. She would have to hope whomever she married would allow her siblings to visit often. Realizing he was still watching her and her thoughts had drifted, she forced herself to reply. "Thank you, sir. I believe I would prefer a drive in the Park to the theater, for my first meeting with His Grace as my grandfather, but surely I should reply to my grandmother, and relieve you of the duty."

There was a flash of hurt in his eyes, which took her aback.

"It is no trouble, I assure you, Miss Sutton, but, if you wish to pen the note yourself, I will see it delivered promptly."

Rose hated that she'd hurt him, but what could she do? Theirs was a strange sort of friendship at best, but he had done a great deal for her. Boldly, she stepped forward and put her hand on his arm.

"I must beg your forgiveness. I have not been very gracious, but I do appreciate all you have done for me."

"I assure you, Miss Sutton, it has been my pleasure." There was a warmth in his eyes that Rose had not seen before from him. It made her smile, and it gave her hope. Maybe Tommy's idea had more merit than she'd known.

CHAPTER EIGHTEEN

G ABE FOUND HIMSELF wool-gathering, even daydreaming of Rose. Yesterday she had seemed to warm to him and give him hope. Yet he dared not declare himself – especially not before she was acknowledged by the ton as the duke's granddaughter and heir to part of their fortune. If he were to snatch her up now, he feared the gossips would be cruel; and besides, he still wanted her to have choices… not to mention the fact that it would be wrong with her living under his roof. He was grateful for the time he had spent with her and he hoped she would consider him once he was able to court her properly.

He heard the clock chime ten, and knew his man of business would arrive shortly for their meeting. He rang for some fresh coffee as Williams entered the room.

"Good morning, my lord," he said politely with a friendly smile. He was not long down from university, but very sharp and keen to work hard. Gabe trusted him despite his boyish face.

"Good morning, Williams."

The man was extremely efficient and usually provided simple choices for Gabe to decide between, but today he seemed unsettled. He watched as his secretary seemed to be choosing his words carefully.

"What is it?" he asked.

"I fear I have some good news and also some bad news, sir."

Williams looked at him frankly.

"Then let me first have the good."

"Very well. I had three veterans apply to me yesterday for positions, and they are all amenable to the terms. I have arranged for their transport and will provide them with letters of introduction to Reverend Sutton and your steward at Arden Park."

"Excellent. Now give me the bad. I conjecture it has to do with my cousin?"

"Unfortunately, yes, my lord. I looked into the matter of his gambling debts as you requested. He owes amounts far larger than the sum you settled on him. He has paid enough to hold them off a while longer, but even if he returned to full service, he would not be able to meet them without a large deposit of funds."

"And the only way to have that occur is by gambling more," Gabe muttered.

"Or by marrying an heiress," Williams pointed out. "I have also discovered that he sold his commission for the funds."

Gabe suddenly felt sick. Would Bertie honor their agreement to keep his distance from Miss Sutton once word spread about her fortune? If it was true, and Bertie had already spent all the funds Gabe had given him, then he would be desperate. Would that Gabe could be certain Rose would not take Bertie back, but he had no right to dictate to her otherwise.

He did not think Rose would want to marry his cousin now, but if her heart was still engaged, she might be tempted if Bertie decided to be charming. However, Gabe would not put it past his cousin to attempt some form of trickery to force her compliance.

"What would you have me do, my lord? The gambling debts, I understand, are not your responsibility, but some of the tradesmen have applied to me."

"Pay the tradesmen. It is not their fault, and they cannot hope to see payment for their hard work. However, please make it understood that they are not to extend him further credit."

"Of course, my lord."

"Is there anything else?"

"Only a few documents requiring your signature." He placed several neatly organized letters before him, and gave brief explanations for each. Once Williams was gone, Gabe pondered what options there might be to deal with his scapegrace cousin. He felt helpless to stop the storm about to break. Bertie had transgressed any number of times on the Peninsula, and Gabe had felt just as helpless then.

The only solution would be to send Bertie far away. But how could he accomplish such a thing without having him impressed? It would be easy enough to do, and he was so very tempted. However, it would break his aunt and uncle's heart, though Bertie was like to do that himself soon if his ways did not change. It was likely he was already too embroiled to prevent a catastrophe.

"You look as though you're contemplating having to put down a horse," Maria said as she came into the room.

"That would be even worse," he said, standing and receiving her kiss on the cheek.

"Would you like to tell me about it?"

"I suppose it might to do to have your opinion," he conceded as he waved her towards a chair and took the seat opposite her.

"Has it to do with Rose?"

"No, though I could probably use your advice in that quarter as well," he answered quietly, wishing the door was closed.

"Then what has you so upset?"

"Bertie. Word of his debt has reached even my ears, so I know he's in dun territory. I settled five thousand pounds on him to keep him away and he has already run through it."

"That jackaknapes!" Maria exclaimed indignantly.

"A kinder word than I would apply," he agreed wryly. "I have been racking my brain for a way to deal with him that would not distress our aunt and uncle, but I fear it is too late and he will be desperate enough to take drastic measures. I made it clear he would get not a penny more from me."

"Perhaps you should tell them. They might be able to reason with him."

"Certainly, I have been unable to appeal to any sense of honor in Bertie. I suppose I should try speaking with Uncle Severn. I had hoped to spare him such an interview."

Maria reached out and took his hand. "I know, Brother, but you cannot undertake Bertie alone. It sounds as though you have tried everything."

"I was considering finding him a post in the East India Company," he admitted.

"If our uncle thinks that is best, mayhap he can convince him to go."

Gabe nodded. It was not a conversation he looked forward to.

"Now, what is this about Rose?" she asked anxiously.

Gabe glanced at the open door, then rose to go and close it. In all likelihood, he would hear her coming downstairs, but he would not take such a chance. Once he was seated again, he took a deep breath. "I think she no longer has a disgust of me."

"Well, that is something indeed." Maria's eyes twinkled with amusement.

"Is it not?" His lips twisted wryly. "However, in all seriousness, she has accepted my assistance in the matter of her grandparents, allowing me to spend more time with her than perhaps I otherwise would have done. She is to drive in the Park with the duke this afternoon, if the weather improves." The rain beat heavily against the windows as he spoke. "Yet I cannot, as a gentleman, court her openly or properly while she is a guest under my roof."

Maria sighed. "No, indeed! I will ask Philip how much longer the repairs will take. I would not like for you to miss your chance with Rose on our account."

"She has also confided in me the news that her father has married Mrs. Winton. She was quite distraught about the children."

"Good gracious!" Maria exclaimed. "That will work to your

advantage, I would think, dear brother."

"How so?"

"She will wish to be near them, of course." She tossed her hand as if it should be obvious.

"Of course, I would rather she should marry me for my own... charm, as it were."

"Have you decided to display it, then?"

"A direct hit." He held up his hand to cover his heart. "I am trying as best I know how. Yet I cannot send her flowers or write foppish poetry to her, especially while she is living here. It would be devilishly uncomfortable for both of us if she did not welcome my advances."

"I would say so. However, if you were to speak freely with her, as you do with me, I do not think she would be able to resist seeing what a prize you are. You do rather keep your light hidden under a bushel."

"It is hard to go against my nature, especially after a decade of needing to be secretive in order to survive."

"I understand, but you must make an effort to do so, especially now. She will feel a sense of desperation, knowing Mrs. Winton will be what awaits her should she return home unmarried. God forbid the woman should arrange something for her!"

"I would certainly offer her a marriage of convenience if she had to return unwed. I had hoped she would choose me. I do believe she sees me as something of a friend now, which is a vast improvement. However, given her new status as a duke's granddaughter, she will be much sought after."

"I agree, but knowing Rose as I do, I cannot think a grand Society match would suit her at all."

"I hope you are right, Sister. I still cannot imagine anyone else as my spouse."

"Have you tried? It seems to me you are always lying in wait for Rose at parties, yet you do not dance with her."

"She said a similar thing to me, but did not realize the reason."

"Perhaps a word or two of suggestion might not come amiss," Maria said thoughtfully.

"I do not wish you to do my work for me." Gabe was appalled at the thought of his sister meddling.

"I intend no such thing, but Rose might not consider herself worthy of marrying the Lord of Arden Park."

"That is what appeals to me most about her, I think."

"Really?" Maria said knowingly. "It could have nothing to do with her beauty."

"That certainly doesn't hurt." Gabe allowed a small smile to escape.

"Allow me to place a few subtle hints in her ear, and then I will see what my husband can do to hasten the process of moving us back into our house."

Gabe only hoped he did not regret this.

ROSE'S HANDS WERE clammy beneath her gloves as she awaited the arrival of the duke. He stood very much on his dignity, which she found off-putting, and even though he had decided to acknowledge her, it did not mean he would suddenly become affable.

As she waited in the drawing room of the earl's town house, having been ready half an hour early, she thought back to when she had felt similarly about the earl, and he had continued to surprise her. Perhaps her grandfather would do the same. She could but pray.

"His Grace, the Duke of Haverstock," Bromley announced.

"That will be all," the duke said to the butler and closed the door behind him.

Well. Rose stood and dropped into a curtsy. "Your Grace."

He was dressed in buff breeches and a bottle green coat, with a cream-colored waistcoat and held a cane.

"Granddaughter." He condescended to make her a bow, which surprised her. She knew not what to say, and did not think he would appreciate her babbling, but it did not preclude her being a good hostess.

"May I offer you tea, your Grace?"

"I cannot abide the stuff. I suppose we might as well take a turn around the Park. We can talk just as well while we do so."

"As you wish." Would she ever become used to the gruff, arrogant manner he bore like an escutcheon?

There was a burgundy and cream-colored landau waiting for them in front of Mottram Place, the matching bay horses being held by a groom in livery matching the equipage.

Her grandfather handed her into the vehicle, then took his place beside her. "To Hyde Park, Jenkins," he said to the coachman.

As the vehicle made its way through the traffic to the Park, Rose debated what to say. "If I might enquire, what are your feelings, sir?"

He barked a laugh. "What do I think of you? Or the fact that you exist?"

"Both, I should say. I was certainly surprised to find out about you, a few weeks past."

"Her Grace mentioned you were unaware of your origins until recently. I will say, the moment I saw you I knew you were Edward's child. You look exactly like him, but prettier, I suppose. He was a very handsome lad."

"Why did you decide to accept me, when you rejected my mother and her marriage?"

He grunted. "You deal in plain speaking, miss."

"I am afraid I know no other way."

He was quiet for a while, and Rose thought he would refuse to answer, but at last he did. "I was wrong in the matter of your father and mother. When you are a parent, you will understand better, but you must believe I wanted what was best for him."

"Even after they had married?"

"Many would not agree with you that an elopement is a true marriage," he argued. "But we did not know about you."

"Would it have made a difference? My mother would still have been ruined. Losing her husband to the army so soon after their marriage must have been devastating in itself, without having a child to bear alone." She could not hide the bitterness in her voice.

"I am sorry for it. I had no notion he would run off to India. I had no opportunity to say goodbye or make amends and I must live with it. But Her Grace seems to think your uncle and his wife did well by you."

"Indeed, they brought me up as one of their own."

"And you are here to find a husband? Why did you wait so long?"

"An ape leader, am I? As long as we are speaking plainly, sir, my mama died, and I had to bring up the other children. I also had a suitor who went away to war—and did not return." It was not a complete falsehood, she reasoned to herself. The Bertie she knew and loved no longer existed.

"I think we can find you a proper match now. I believe your grandmother has told you of your inheritance?" He looked sideways at her.

"Vaguely."

"I put Edward's portion into the funds every year... just in case. It is now worth well over 50,000 pounds."

Rose swallowed hard. She could not even fathom that kind of fortune.

"All of it is yours, and your grandmother will leave you an estate in Buckinghamshire that was part of her settlements."

"I do not know what to say," she replied. That was a vast understatement.

"I will say this, girl: you may marry as high as you wish. Is there any gentleman you have a preference for? They may appeal to me for your hand."

Rose opened her mouth to deny it, but then her cheeks heated as she thought of the earl. But he was not hers. Did she want him to be? "There is no one yet, Your Grace. I am still quite new to Town."

"In my day, none of this matchmaking was necessary."

Rose refrained from commenting on his views.

"If you need help arranging a match, your grandmother and I will give you a list of suitable candidates."

"I think it will be for the best if I try to find someone on my own."

She could tell he wanted to protest from the way he stiffened beside her, but he did not argue. "May I at least advise you if I think someone to be unsuitable?"

"You may advise me," she conceded, "but only that, if you please. I have Lady Maria and Lord Philip to warn me who the fortune hunters are."

"Humph."

Was she supposed to thank him? She was still rather angry with his treatment of her parents, even though he did admit he was sorry for it. Papa would advise forgiveness, but it was very hard to forget that, because of him, her father had been lost to her.

Rose looked askance at her grandfather and realized with his bushy eyebrows and full whiskers that she felt sorry for him. A duke must lead a lonely existence with no one ever questioning them, and likewise having few boundaries for their power. He was an old man and had little happiness, it seemed. At least she had been given that. She had never lacked for anything and her days had been full of laughter. She tried to soften her feelings towards him. Perhaps it was his way of trying to make old mistakes right.

They pulled in through the gates of the Park, and his gaze narrowed. "Prepare to be toadied to," he muttered.

Rose doubted she would appreciate that either, but he had always been a duke. He must be used to it.

"I will introduce you as my granddaughter," he stated.

"Very well, but I would like to keep Sutton in my name." Rose knew in her heart that it was the proper thing to do and if she did not stand her ground in these matters, he would try to run roughshod over her as he had her father.

He looked at her long and hard. "You are full of pluck, just like Edward, too. I have no right to argue on that point. Very well, what shall it be? Sutton-Byrne or Byrne-Sutton?"

"I think Sutton-Byrne has a nice ring to it." She was very grateful to Lord Mottram for suggesting it. Losing her name would have felt like losing a crucial part of herself.

They soon came upon the crush of Society, since it was the fashionable hour. Rose was glad she had experienced it before so she was better prepared to deal with the attention.

"There is Lady Jersey. An introduction to her will have the news all over Town before supper," His Grace commentated.

The duke tipped his hat to her, but did not stop. Apparently, he did not mean the news to be all over Town by supper.

Another lady in a bright jonquil gown with garish orange and pink flowers and matching bonnet was waving at the duke.

"Vulgar mushroom," he grumbled. Rose tried not to laugh. She could see Mrs. Winton doing such a thing.

"There are Lord and Lady Moncrief. He is a fine fellow and a staunch Tory. Jenkins, pull over!" he commanded as the vehicle slowed to greet his friends.

"Good day, Your Grace," Lord Moncrief said.

"My lady," the duke greeted the gentleman's wife. "May I introduce you to my granddaughter, Miss Rose Sutton-Byrne? She is Edward's gal."

"Pleased to meet you, young lady," the kind-eyed, portly man said. "Edward's daughter, eh?"

"We have just found her," he explained.

"What a miracle!" Lady Moncrief exclaimed.

"Indeed, and she's in Town looking for a husband, much to my chagrin."

Rose tried to keep a sweet smile on her face instead of grimacing at His Grace's sudden exuberance.

"She does have the look of him. She will have no trouble procuring a match, I declare," her ladyship remarked with authority.

"Especially not once they hear of her inheritance," the duke mentioned, as though it were a secret. He was clever, she had to give him that, though somehow she wished he could take back the words. Rose did not relish the change in circumstance. She did want to know her grandparents, but not to be an heiress with all that it entailed.

They drove on, and there was more of the same, though His Grace was selective who he chose to speak with. Already, Rose was flagging from the constant smiling and trying to keep everyone's names straight.

"I cannot take much more," her grandfather said once they finally had a small break in the procession. "Do you wish to continue?"

"Absolutely not," she said emphatically.

He surprised her by laughing. "You don't have a fancy for this any more than I do, then?"

"I am afraid not."

"Let us sneak to Gunter's for an ice. Just don't tell your grandmother."

Still trying to reconcile this nobleman beside her, Rose was eager to comply, if only to leave the crush of Society.

"Humph. I almost forgot. Your grandmother wishes you to move to Byrne House for the rest of the Season."

CHAPTER NINETEEN

G ABE WAS RELIEVED to have the interview with his uncle over with. It had turned out he was not surprised to hear of Bertie's troubles.

"I had hoped the army would cure him of his wild ways," Uncle Severn had admitted. "He never could quite keep himself from thinking he should have what you did."

Gabe had no response to that. He had seen it before, often with younger sons jealous of their elder brothers. "I have found him a post with the East India Company, if you think he'd be willing to go. He would serve as an apprentice of sorts to one of the senior officers, as befitting his rank. His opportunities would be endless, if he was willing to work hard."

"Your aunt will be devastated," his uncle said. "However, it is better than him ending up in a debtor's prison. I know you have been generous to him. Even finding him this post is more than he deserves."

Gabe agreed wholeheartedly, but could hardly say so. "I will leave it to you to tell him, if you will. It will be better coming from you." Gabe handed him a letter with the East India seal. "These are the details of to whom and where he should report. The ship sails in three days' time."

Uncle Severn accepted the letter and nodded. Gabe could not have felt worse if he'd had to tell them Bertie had died in the war.

At least it would have been with honor in that case, he told himself.

All of it was exhausting. It had taken him some time to convince an official at the East India Company to take Bertie on. Apparently his reputation preceded him. Now, if his scapegrace cousin would but accept the post.

Gabe left feeling drained by everything. He wished he could make things move along more quickly so he could begin his new life as a country gentleman, though he did not relish the prospect of doing so without Rose.

He returned home to find a carriage being loaded with trunks. Had Philip and Maria finished their house repairs so soon? Gabe knew it would help him, but the thought of not seeing Rose every day left him feeling unsettled and decidedly peevish.

He handed his horse to his groom, and then walked inside to see what was happening. His sister was standing in the entrance hall, saying goodbye to Rose. What the devil?

"Gabriel, you are just in time to say farewell to Rose."

"Are you returning to Edwinstowe?" he asked, wondering how soon he could follow without looking completely desperate.

"No. My grandparents have asked me to finish the Season under their protection. They feel it might be their only chance to spend time with me."

"I have told her she does not have to go if she is uncomfortable with the notion," Maria said. "Please tell her she is welcome here."

"Of course, you are more than welcome, Miss Sutton. You must not leave on account of putting us out."

"You have been all that is good to me," Rose assured them. "However, I think I must go."

Gabe tried to keep the disappointment from his face, but somehow this was much worse than her going to Maria's house. There, he would not feel as out of place when visiting. They walked her out to the duke's carriage that had been sent for her. He felt his throat thicken and felt ridiculous for such emotions.

She was not his to lose, yet he feared she would be lost to him all the same. In a rare display of gallantry, he handed her up, but did not release her hand immediately. He bent over it. "Will you save the next dance for me?"

"It would be my honor to dance with you. I do hope we will still be friends." She smiled down at him before ducking into the carriage.

"I will always be of service to you," he said, as he closed the door gently behind her, and tapped on it to signal the driver to go.

He felt Maria's hand on his arm. "At least you may court her now," she said reassuringly, though he still felt despondent. "And her behavior just now was very... encouraging."

"Do you think so?" Like a love-sick fool, he was still watching as the carriage rolled away from his house.

"I do, but dear brother, we need to make a plan."

"Plans are my area of expertise," he said with more optimism than he felt.

Philip was in the study, poring over sketches when Gabe and Maria entered. "I will ring for tea," she announced as Gabe walked over to see what Philip was looking at.

"Come and see this. I thought to make a few improvements while the workers are there anyway. There was some water damage and it is a good time to update the plumbing."

Gabe looked at the designs and sketches but scarcely saw anything. "My plumbing could stand to be improved," he remarked absently.

Philip chuckled then looked up at Gabe. "Why the doldrums, Mottram?"

"Rose has left to stay with her grandparents for the remainder of the Season," Maria explained.

"Ah. A tragedy indeed."

Gabe scowled.

"Let him be, my love. Now he can court her properly, but we need a plan."

"We?" Philip asked.

There was a knock on the door, and Bromley entered. "A message for you, my lord." He handed a note to Gabe on a silver platter.

"It is an invitation," he said as he opened it. "An evening of dinner and dancing, given by the Duke and Duchess of Haverstock at their villa on the Thames, to introduce their granddaughter, Miss Rose Sutton-Byrne."

"They certainly have not wasted any time," Philip mused.

"I should say not," Maria agreed. "When is it to be?"

"Two days hence."

Maria tapped her finger on her chin in thought. "That is the night of the Worth ball, but we were not attending anyway, of course."

Worth was the brother of General Newsom, the traitor Gabe and Maria's father had protected. Gabe had no inclination to associate with Newsom's brother, either. It would be deuced awkward. "I am surprised we received an invitation."

"To Worth's or Haverstock's?" Maria asked.

"Worth."

She waved her hand. "It is a mere formality. Of course, we never attend, but they cannot afford to snub us, or likewise."

"Will it be a crush, this dinner and dancing?" he asked.

"I suspect it will be a few select members of the ton... meaning a hundred or so of their dearest friends."

Gabe groaned.

"You should send her a floral arrangement tomorrow morning, with a note asking her to secure that dance."

"Do you think so?"

"But do not send her roses. I happen to know she likes them, but they are not her favorite." Maria wore a devilish smile.

He looked up, waiting for her answer. "Are you going to make me guess?"

"I happen not. Violet was her mother's name and also happens to be her favorite flower."

"That is her scent." He spoke without considering what he was revealing.

"I believe you are correct," Maria agreed.

"What else is there for me to do?" He leaned back against his desk, crossing his arms over his chest.

"Spend as much time with her as you can."

"I have already been doing so."

"And look how much progress you have made, but you need to be different from her other suitors. They will offer her poetry, drives in the park, invite her to the theater, try to secure the supper dance…"

"This is completely unnatural for me. I am not one for grand gestures."

"Be that as it may, if she is the one you want, then you must make her wish the same."

"If only it were so easy."

"You should also think of some others to dance with, so it does not appear you are singling her out."

"Even though I am?"

"Perhaps it would make her uncomfortable to know that at this juncture, and if she sees you with others, perhaps it might also serve to make her realize how eligible you are." Maria winked at him.

"Play games, you mean?"

Maria waved her hand dismissively. "Courtship is all a game of sorts—akin to chess. You must anticipate the other's moves before they do."

Gabe disagreed. He was an excellent chess player, but felt fathoms out of his depth in this game.

"How do you feel when you see her with another gentleman?" Philip asked, looking up.

Jealousy. Inadequacy. Rage.

"Precisely," Maria said in that knowing, sisterly way.

"Very well. I shall make an effort to pay attention to others."
He was going to loathe every minute of this, he knew, though he

should consider others if Rose rejected him.

"I will make the introductions."

THE TWO DAYS Rose had spent with her grandparents were like a whirlwind she had been sucked into and from which she could not find the ground again. Her grandmother decided to throw a welcoming party in her honor, despite the fact that she had hosted a ball in the last fortnight.

When Rose protested, the duchess would hear none of it. "Nonsense. I should have spoken to you before the ball, and it was my cowardice that prevented my doing so. We shall do it properly now. I think, perhaps, dinner and dancing on the river would be just the thing. I will invite young people for you to become acquainted with," she remarked, having a one-sided conversation.

Rose dared not argue. It would be a waste of breath. Her grandmother was a force of nature not to be contained. If Rose had been concerned about the duchess overworking herself, she quickly realized Her Grace had a team of persons well versed in throwing such parties at short notice. It seemed she had an orchestra, a florist, a secretary to write the invitations, and decorators to create anything she wished.

Rose felt incredibly guilty about the luxury and the expense. The last thing she needed was anyone fussing over her. It was as though the duke and duchess thought this was a way to make amends, when she would prefer merely to spend time with them.

The duchess had brought in her modiste to create Rose a new gown for the party in two days. Even Rose knew that was an impossibility unless multiple seamstresses worked night and day.

When she became overwhelmed with plans for her party, she would sometimes escape to find her grandfather amenable to a game of chess and arguing about politics.

It was hard not to feel as though she was losing her sense of self. At least with Maria, she had been friends since childhood, and shared a familiar village. All this pomp and splendor made her long for home and the simplicity of village life. Lord Mottram was wealthy, but it was somehow different. She found herself wishing for his calm presence, and wondered if he would remember his promise to dance with her. She would have laughed if someone had told her when they left Edwinstowe that she would soon be longing to dance with him!

The morning of the party, she received several bouquets of flowers – most of them roses. She read through the cards—not really remembering many of the people. However, there was one simple bouquet of violets which stood out amongst the sea of pink, yellow, and white roses. Immediately, she was drawn to it—especially when she wished she had her mother there to guide her. What would she think of her being presented by the very people who had destroyed her life? Rose still couldn't credit those events to the people she met. Perhaps Papa was right, that with age came a realization of the things you had done wrong, and wished to put right.

She opened the card and smiled.

My dear Miss Sutton-Byrne, would you do me the honor of standing up with me for the supper dance? Your obedient servant, Mottram.

As ever, he was short and to the point. It was hard to imagine the stoic earl calling her "my dear" in person.

She took one of the bundles out of the arrangement for later. Perhaps her new maid could arrange them in her hair to go with the lavender silk confection her grandmother had ordered. It was the most exquisite gown she'd ever seen. She felt like a princess. Instead of the usual plain scoop necks and puffed sleeves, it had two crossed pieces which formed a 'V' and then tied over her shoulders. The glacé silk of the skirt flowed as she walked, revealing matching slippers, and the duke had produced a parure of amethysts to match the gown.

It was the first day of summer, and the weather was fine. A makeshift ballroom had been set up under a tent beside the river, with tables and tables of food, as well as tables for dining covered in white table cloths. Arrangements of roses of all colors stood in the center of each table. Hundreds of candles sparkled, along with lanterns to brighten the path alongside the water.

The sun was in the evening sky and twinkling across the river, which was vastly clearer, and smelled fresher, than in London. Most of the guests would arrive by boat and while there was not a formal receiving line, a sord of ducks was there to greet them with their noisy chattering and quacking. Rose remained with her grandparents to welcome as many as they could. She smiled and accepted invitations to dance, but her eyes were continually searching for Lord Mottram—because, of course, it would mean Maria was there. Of course it would. She desperately longed for a familiar face.

The orchestra began playing in the background, and Rose prayed that nothing had happened to her friends. She knew they would be there unless something drastic had occurred. But she had promised the set to Lord Suther, Their Graces' nephew, so she was forced to join the dancing.

There were to be no minuets or quadrilles. That was the one thing she had asked of Her Grace. Rose feared she would look a fool, but she had decided she wanted to be herself, since she was to have their name. If she had to make a grand match, then at least any suitors would know what they were getting. Once she had seen that jigs and reels were included at other balls, she had felt more comfortable asking for them.

Likewise, her grandmother had insisted on only inviting young people, as she called them. Anyone with a suitable pedigree was to be there, both male and female. She could hardly exclude either sex. Rose would need friends amongst both to succeed after marriage.

Lord Suther bowed over her hand, and was all that was civil.

He was not exactly young, but he was a relation, and it was proper that he led her out, since her grandfather refused to dance something so uncivilized as a reel or a jig at his age.

Soon Rose was caught up in the dance, determined to enjoy herself, and not worry if Lord Mottram had arrived.

She saw Maria first, speaking with her grandmother, and Lord Suther led her back to her chaperone when the dance ended, so the earl had to be present somewhere. It was only because she had saved the supper dance for him that she was concerned, she assured herself.

Her next partner was Lord Tilney, someone who had danced with her at every dance thus far and had been present for every at-home Lady Mottram had held.

"You look beautiful, Miss Sutton-Byrne," he said with a warm smile—a little too warm, in her opinion.

"The name is quite a mouthful to say, is it not?"

"I think it is wonderful that you have found your grandparents again and they have welcomed you into the fold."

"It is." She could also imagine how wonderful he thought her inheritance and ducal connections were. She should not be so cynical. He had paid her attention before.

A familiar face was awaiting her when Lord Tilney returned her to the duchess.

"Quinn Foster!" She was delighted to see her old friend.

He bowed to her. "Is your next set spoken for?"

She shook her head and took his hand. "Only the supper dance is bespoken."

As they took their place in line, she was about to burst with the desire to hear news from home.

"Is it true, then?" he asked, before she could inquire about the latest news.

"That the duke and duchess are my grandparents? Did you not read the invitation?"

"I meant the fact that you are an heiress."

"Unfortunately, it is." She deliberately did not meet his eye.

"It means you may marry as high as you like." He sounded despondent.

"You know I have never had ambition." She took a turn with next partner. Was Quinn jealous? He had never had any true interest in her before. Maybe he thought he had, but she had never taken him seriously. She chose to ignore his boyish churlishness. Besides, she needed to make a match now; she could not wait for him to reach his majority.

She looked up and saw Lord Mottram dancing in the next row, smiling down at the beautiful Lady Alice.

Rarely had she seen him smile, and it produced a very unwelcome emotion within. Jealousy, indeed. She forced her feet to move forward and back to Quinn.

"Has anyone been courting you?" he asked, with a petulance similar to her own feelings.

"We would never suit, Quinn, and you know it. You have years before you will be ready to settle and start a family."

"That is not true, and I have never made it a secret how I feel about you," he argued.

She looked at him with the affection she would her siblings, and the wind seemed to fall out of his sails. "You flatter me, Quinn, but you know you are as a brother to me."

He did not meet her gaze for the rest of the dance, and then returned her to the duchess with a stiff bow.

"He looks forlorn, like a lost puppy," the duchess mused.

"I have known him since he was a boy, but he has always been as a brother to me."

"I hope you let him down gently. He certainly won't be the last."

Rose hoped it would not be as bad as that, as she watched Lord Mottram lead Lady Alice back to her chaperone, who was smiling knowingly.

CHAPTER TWENTY

F INALLY, THE SUPPER dance arrived. Gabriel had suffered through several dances with silly young ladies, feeling completely out of his depth, while attempting to smile and be charming. At last it was time for the real reason he was there. He only hoped Rose had saved the dance for him. His party had been too late for him to speak with her beforehand and reassure himself, but she had already been dancing with one partner, and then another and another. She was exuberant and smiling—not quite laughing—and it was torture to watch her in the arms of other men.

He was incredibly nervous as he walked towards her and the duchess, but he was determined not to show it. He bowed before them. "Your Grace, Miss Sutton-Byrne."

"I expect you are here to dance with my granddaughter?" she asked, measuring him with a glance and, dare he say, a twinkle in her eye?

"It would be my honor. If you still have the dance available?" Gabe hoped the desperation he felt was not apparent as he looked at Rose. She wore the violets he had sent entwined artfully around her elaborate coiffure. He had not seen them from afar, but it filled him with pleasure. She was even more beautiful than ever, with the rosy glow and smile he had seen on her face that first day in the village after his return.

"Of course," she responded with a smile. "I have saved it for you."

He bowed in gratitude and held out his arm for her. When she wrapped her fingers around his arm, it was like a caress as opposed to the stiff formality of the other ladies he had danced with.

The strings of a waltz begin to sound, and as they took their position, he felt himself smile naturally with anticipation.

"I chose this song and dance particularly," she said sheepishly. "I did not trust myself to waltz with anyone else."

Gabe could not believe the pleasure he felt at that admission. Was she saying she would welcome his courtship?

"I am honored," he said as the dance began. He wanted to tell her how much he missed seeing her—especially their quiet times together at breakfast. He'd not been able to drink his coffee in the breakfast parlor since she had left. "Are you enjoying your visit with your grandparents?" he asked instead.

"It has been rather overwhelming. Perhaps, once this party is over, it will not be so busy, but I am far more comfortable with a quiet, country life. I am happy to know my grandparents, and I know my time with them is short."

"I am happy for you, then."

"And what of you, sir? How has your time here been? I realize it is only been a few days since I left Mottram Place." Her large blue eyes looked up at him and he almost forgot his steps. She was so close, he could lean down and…

He swallowed hard and forced himself back to the ballroom and the hundred guests around them. "Everleigh, Owens, and I have continued the search for workmen. We have four so far who I have agreed to employ in Edwinstowe."

Her smile was so bright, he wished he had a portrait of it. "That is wonderful news!"

"Your father has agreed to help them become established in the village."

"You have been working with my father?"

"We have been corresponding. I did not think it right to send them there without someone to guide them."

She nodded. Then he led her in a series of turns. Every step, every touch, every turn became imprinted as a memory he would relive over and over later. He dared not say anything yet, but hope ignited as it never had before.

When the dance ended, he led her to one of the tables laid for supper. He filled her a plate of delicacies, from lobster patties to buttered prawns and veal pie.

"I hope this meets your satisfaction, but I did think I had seen you eat some of these dishes before."

"You are very observant, my lord, though I could feed half the village with this amount of food!" she teased.

"I cannot deny being observant. It is my service to the Crown, I am afraid."

"I am pleased to see your skills translate to civilian life."

As others moved closer to join them, he thought he had better speak before he lost his chance. "I wondered if I might ask you to do something this week."

"Something? What would that be, pray tell?"

He realized she was teasing him. "Whatever you should care to share with me. The Tower? A museum? Or the theater, mayhap?"

"I should like any of those things, sir. Which do you suggest?"

"May we join you?" Maria and Philip approached before it was decided.

"Yes, of course," Rose answered.

Maria sat at their table while Philip went fill a plate for her. "You are the belle of the ball!" She kissed Rose's cheek, then drew back. "But you do not like this attention at all, do you?"

"You know I do not," Rose answered, looking down at her plate. "However, it is a small price to pay for knowing my grandparents. It will be over soon."

"Unfortunately, word is spreading about your dowry. I do not think it will be pleasant for you presently."

Gabe sat and listened to the exchange, not quite tasting his food.

"I was afraid of that. How, then, do you know if someone values you or your money? I do not know these people or their reputations well enough to discern their true natures. The only thing to guide me thus far is if they were paying court to me before my grandparents' announcement."

"That is something," Maria agreed.

"Yet I cannot be comfortable with any of them. Even Quinn Foster claimed to have strong feelings for me."

"Did that little pup importune you?" Maria asked indignantly.

"He is harmless, I assure you. I can handle him. For some unknown reason, he fancies himself in love with me, but he is of an age with my brother James, and I cannot think of him as more."

Gabe felt more relief at her words than she knew. He was afraid she might be tempted to accept the boy simply because he was familiar and would allow her to return home.

"Have any of them asked to court you?" Maria continued.

"Not yet, but my grandfather has agreed to consult me before agreeing to any such thing. It was one of my conditions for coming to live with them."

Good for her, Gabe thought, but did not say so.

"I did not want a repeat of what happened to my parents," she added quietly. "He did say he was sorry for what occurred, but that he had only wanted what was best for my father. As a woman, everyone else always knows what is best for one," she added sardonically.

"I was most fortunate in my father and brother," Maria conceded. "They were very patient and allowed me to choose."

Gabe watched Rose's face.

"I suppose my grandparents would not force me to a hasty decision, but I cannot be comfortable here forever. This…" she waved her hand around, "is not me. I had hoped for a quiet country gentleman."

Even Gabe knew that would be difficult for her to find, given her new circumstances. The duke and duchess would exert pressure on her to marry a peer of fortune and standing. Since her grandmother had agreed to help him, he thought his suit would be welcome. If only he could be sure of Rose's feelings on the matter. She would feel obligated to say yes to him.

"You must make certain who you choose will offer you happiness. I could not abide to see my dearest friend in a marriage of convenience. We will do our best to guide you, of course." Maria squeezed Rose's hand.

"I appreciate it more than you know."

Gabe excused himself to fetch a selection of puddings for Rose and himself, when he caught a flash of red from the corner of his eye. He turned to see his cousin, Bertie, in full dress regimentals, standing next to Rose.

His vision began to blur red with anger, and he stopped what he was doing and marched back over to see what was the matter. Rose looked distressed and his cousin would have to answer for it. He would not have been invited, of that Gabe was certain.

"Is my cousin troubling you, Miss Sutton?"

He could see from the distress on her face that he was. Even Maria was looking at him with fear.

He looked to Bertie, who smelled strongly of spirits. "What is your business here? Should you not be packing for India?"

"What I want is to claim my bride," he said smugly.

Gabe looked back at Rose, who looked horrified at those words. A crowd was already beginning to gather around them.

"Is this true?" he asked Rose quietly.

A small shake of her head was answer enough for Gabe.

"I am afraid you are mistaken, Cousin. You renounced your claim on her and your promises when you returned from war. If you will recall, you denied to me that there was ever any such agreement." Gabe kept his voice lowered so the crowd could not overhear.

"Is there a problem here?" the duke boomed as he approached, while the duchess was trying to lure the crowd back to dancing.

"No problem, Your Grace." Bertie attempted a bow and almost fell over.

"Is this true, Rose?" he asked his granddaughter. "I do not recall meeting this… individual before."

"Perhaps this discussion would be better conducted elsewhere," Gabe suggested.

"I only asked my betrothed for a dance," Bertie said loudly, having the intended effect as Gabe heard a few gasps from around them.

"We are not betrothed, Lieutenant Lloyd," Rose said in a low voice.

"You might wish to rethink that, Miss Sutton. For who would want you now that I've ruined you?"

"I do," Gabe said, with a meaningful look at Rose, hoping she believed it. Gabe could control himself no longer. He felled his cousin with one hard punch that may well have broken a few bones in his hand, wishing her did not have to restrain himself further.

"Have him removed at once!" the duke boomed to some of his footmen.

ROSE WATCHED THE scene unfold before her in abject horror, as if it were a play on stage and not actually happening to her. Never in her wildest imagining could she have foreseen this happening. What had she ever done to deserve this but be loyal to Bertie for five years? He had not even tried to speak with her privately. He had come there with every intention of forcing her hand. She felt absolutely sickened.

Maria's gentle hand on her arm helped her to her feet, and then she was being guided up the hill towards the house.

Everything felt as if it were in slow motion, yet she had no control.

Her grandmother was there along with the duke. They were speaking in hushed whispers, while Rose was immobile with shock.

"Do not worry, my brother and my husband will see that he is taken care of for good this time," Maria said.

"He has ruined her with his words, I am afraid," the duchess said, her voice shaking.

Her grandfather placed a brandy in Rose's hands and lifted it gently to her lips. The fiery liquid burned down her throat, but it did help her regain her wits somewhat. "None of it is true," she said, pleading with them to believe her.

"We know, my dear," Maria said, sitting beside her and wrapping an arm around her. "My cousin has lost a fortune and is desperate. Gabriel had arranged a post for him with the East India Company and I gather he did not wish to take it."

"It will not matter, will it? No one will have me now, despite my fortune."

"He will expect your grandfather to force him to marry you," the duchess answered.

"Please do not make me!" Rose cried.

"You will not do anything you do not wish to," the duke growled. "I will expose him for the charlatan that he is and that he spread falsehoods to force your hand. He deserves to be called out for this!"

"You will do no such thing!" Her Grace scolded.

Rose could only nod as tears filled her throat and streamed down her cheeks.

"I think I would like to retire." She stood and hugged her grandmother then kissed her grandfather's cheek. "Thank you for doing all this for me. I am terribly sorry it has ended in such disappointment."

"You are not a disappointment, young lady. It is unfortunately a consequence of being an heiress. I simply cannot believe he would make such a scene here, at our house!"

"He will not get off Scot-free, I assure you." Rose could now see the duke who had forbidden her parents' marriage. No wonder they had resorted to elopement.

"You are certain you wish to be alone?" Maria asked.

Rose forced a smile. "Yes. Will you please stay here tonight, since Philip and your brother are dealing with your cousin?"

"Of course. We will put her in the room next to yours, my dear," the duchess assured her.

"I will return and see the guests off. Hopefully most of them have gone by now," the duke muttered as he left the room.

Maria escorted Rose upstairs and performed the duties of maid for her. She helped her out of her gown, then unpinned her hair and began to brush it soothingly.

"Everything will be well. You wait and see."

"I hope so, but he has sowed the seeds of doubt in everyone's mind. I am an unknown, and there will always be whispers, despite my new name and despite my grandparents' status. I do not know if I am strong enough to return home unwed, Maria."

Maria seemed to concentrate on brushing her hair, though Rose could see she was thinking about something.

"Did you hear what my brother said before he drew his cork?"

I do.

Rose had heard. It was part of the reason she wanted to be alone. She wanted to think about what it could mean. "I am sure he spoke in anger and out of responsibility for his cousin's actions. I would never hold him to something said in the heat of anger."

"Anger at my cousin, not you. Rose, do you think you could be happy with Gabriel? I know, at one time, you did not seem too comfortable with him. Am I wrong? I know many people misunderstand him."

"No, you are not wrong, but I also know he is a kind and honorable man. I have seen it time and again since my first impressions were formed. I would even like to think we have become friends."

Maria smiled. "I am glad to hear it."

"He has never indicated that he harbored that kind of interest in me. He came to Town to find his own match."

"Are you certain of that? His interest in you, that is."

Roses own feelings toward the earl had certainly changed, but she tried to consider his behavior towards her. "It has been all that was proper, but until tonight I would not have thought he had any interest in me as a wife."

"Then he hid it well, my friend. He was waiting to court you until you were no longer under his roof. I should not be stealing his moment from him, but I think you need to be reassured. He has no interest in any other lady. He had formed an attachment to you before you decided to come to London for the Season. Tonight's unfortunate events have forced his admission."

"Once he knows I am ruined, he could well change his mind."

"My brother is not so inconstant!" Maria defended his lordship. "He, more than most, is aware of what a falsely tarnished reputation can mean."

"Of course he does. I did not mean any insult. I am just very afraid. I do not wish to be forced into marriage with Bertie."

"You will not!" Maria protested. "My brother would not allow it."

Those words should have felt heavy-handed, but they filled Rose's thoughts with wonder about the earl and what marriage to him would be like.

Maria left Rose to try to rest, which was laughable. She tossed and turned with uneasiness. Despite Maria's words of reassurance, she could not think Lord Mottram truly wished to marry her now, but she also knew, after what he had said, that he would offer for her. How was she to know for certain if he wanted her? Things had been going so well before Bertie had arrived. If only he had let well alone! Did Bertie really think she would want him after his antics—and falsely ruining her good name?

When the light of dawn crept in her window, she threw back

the covers, giving up hope of sleep. She dressed and slipped outside, hoping fresh air would calm her nerves. The dew was still on the grass, but she was drawn towards the misty river anyway.

"Miss Sutton," a deep voice said from behind her, causing her to jump. She turned to see the earl standing there, looking windblown and tired, as though he had been riding all night. He looked very dear, and she dared not hope.

"Forgive me, I was worlds away."

"Lord Philip and I have just returned. I wanted to reassure you that my cousin will bother you no more. He is in the hold of a ship bound for India. I can only regret, yet again, that I did not prevent this."

"You must not think that you are in any way responsible for a grown man's actions!" she protested. "He knew exactly what he was about when he came here last night."

"But I knew what he was long ago. I protected him instead of soiling our good name, thus allowing him to hurt others. He thought to take advantage of your goodness, and then last night he did his best to sully *your* good name. If it would not distress my aunt and uncle, I would have called him out."

"I am very glad you did not."

Rose desperately wished Bertie had not come between them. She was beginning to hope that Lord Mottram did indeed hold her in esteem—that they could possibly have had a real marriage. Even though she was innocent of Bertie's claims, there would be a scandal—the very thing he wished to avoid.

"Miss Sutton, you must have heard my words last night. I did mean them. I had intended to offer for you once I thought you could return my regard. I had hoped for you to have a choice in your husband—and I had hoped that you would choose me."

She felt her chin tremble.

"Now my cousin has left you little choice, and I would offer you the protection of my name. I only hope, that in time, you will be able to be content, and perhaps even happy. Miss Sutton, will you do me the honor of becoming my wife?"

Rose wanted to cry. It was what she had just realized she wanted, but not like this. Yet what choice did she have?

"You are too good, my lord, but I cannot hold you to such words when you were defending your family's name."

"I assure you, that is not why I do so."

Roses heart filled with some unspeakable feeling that threatened to overflow. How could she have been so blind? "Can you assure me you are not offering for me only because of your cousin's misdeeds?"

"I will admit, to you, the only reason I offer now is because of them, but rest assured, I would have offered in due course. I have admired you since I first saw you, that afternoon when your brother was hurt. I knew, even then, that you were the one for me."

"Why did you never say anything?" She looked up at his handsome face in disbelief.

"Would you have welcomed my suit in the beginning? I know how people perceive me. Am I mistaken in thinking you indifferent to me at first?"

"No," she admitted. "I thought you cold and arrogant. Forgive me for misjudging you."

"You are not the first. There is nothing to forgive. The fault lies in me. But I am trying. I had hoped slowly to convince you of my qualities, and if not for the time under my roof, I might not have had any opportunity." His eyes were twinkling with humor. How had she not seen it before?

"You are succeeding, sir." She stepped closer and took his hand. "If you can be certain you truly wish to marry me, then I would be honored to be your wife."

His hand reached up and caressed her cheek, then he leaned down until their foreheads were touching. "You have made me a very happy man, and I will spend every day of our lives trying to be worthy of you, Rose."

She didn't know if she instigated the kiss or he, but their lips met and he kissed her so softly, so sweetly, that it was nothing like the slobbery mauling Bertie had called a kiss. Her heart squeezed with the tenderness of it. They fit together so perfectly, his warmth and scent of shaving soap surrounding her, his strength making her feel protected and loved. Her arms twined around his neck, drawing him closer to her, and his arm slid around her waist. He was more elegant with his kiss than he was with words, reassuring her that indeed he was not indifferent. His kisses cherished her and held promise for future happiness. How had she ever thought him cold?

CHAPTER TWENTY-ONE

Gabe's spirits were lighter than they had been in years. Bertie was, by now, over the ocean and Rose had agreed to become his countess. It all felt too good to be true. He had expected she would need a great deal more convincing, but instead had acceded quickly. She even seemed—dare he say—pleased? He mused on her reaction. He certainly had not anticipated the kiss or the heat that had flared between them. Already she was warmer towards him than he'd ever hoped, when he had feared she would barely allow a buss on the lips! Hopefully she would not want a long betrothal. After that kiss, he no longer had patience.

Like an eager green boy, he had immediately gone to receive the duke's blessing and had agreed upon settlements. However, after a brief rest, he still intended to ride back to Edwinstowe for Reverend Sutton's permission.

After tearing himself away from Rose, he was now riding back to Mottram Place to pack and inform his secretary of his absence for a few days. When he slowed to cross Hyde Park he was hailed by Colonel James.

"Sir," Gabe said, slowing Pedro down as the colonel, looking grave, pulled away from his other soldiers to speak with him.

"What has happened?"

"It is your cousin again, I am afraid. Last night, he tried to kidnap Lord Rutherford's daughter. Rutherford called him out, of course. They say he'll be thrown in a debtor's prison if he survives the duel."

"But that is impossible! He is on a ship bound for India. I saw him placed there myself, with strict instructions to the captain to keep him there until they were far away from England!" Gabe cursed under his breath.

"He must have escaped, Major. I am quite sure it was Lieutenant Lloyd I heard tell of. Rutherford is furious. He has made it clear that he caught Lloyd before anything happened to his daughter, and he will ruin anyone that dare hints his daughter is anything less than pure."

"I do not think he will have any difficulty with that. My cousin has a long enough record of nefarious deeds that will surely support such villainy being his fault entirely." Gabe wanted to sink into the earth. He cared little for his cousin, but the thought of what it would do to his aunt, uncle, and cousin Louisa was unthinkable. How had the rat managed to escape the ship? And why could he not be content with the chance Gabe had offered him? Doubtless because he had been the one who had arranged it. "When?"

"Tomorrow at dawn, on the Heath. Rutherford only came to me because he thought he was still on half-pay under my command."

"Thank you for telling me. I had not yet heard, but unfortunately, I am not surprised. Perhaps if I had been harder on him earlier in his career, I could have prevented this."

"Word at the clubs is he was desperate. He could not pay off his debts."

Gabe still could not believe his wretched cousin had found a way off the ship!

The colonel clapped him on the back. "I used to take my men's failures personally, but there's no answering for why some turn rotten. That cousin of yours has had every opportunity to make a good name for himself, yet chose the easier, cowardly path every time. No, Major, you cannot blame yourself. His choices were his."

Gabe doubted that he bore no responsibility, but the ship's captain would certainly have something to answer for. "Perhaps, but it will be my mess to clean up." He bade the colonel farewell and left the park, mulling over what to do.

Instead of leaving for Edwinstowe as he wished, he must now stay for the duel.

THE NEXT MORNING, he left well before dawn to ride out to Hampstead Heath. Duels were no longer legal, but they still occurred amongst gentlemen in cases of honor. Bertie could hardly be called a gentleman after his behavior these past weeks, yet Rutherford afforded him that courtesy, which was surprising.

Gabe should have been the one to call Bertie out, but he really had had no right to do so in Miss Sutton's honor before now. Nonetheless, he was not at all surprised that he was witnessing his cousin in such a state.

The Heath still held the mist and the eerie quiet of pre-dawn. As Gabe approached on Pedro, he saw a few people had already gathered.

He remained in the distance, not wanting to draw attention to his presence. He was hardly there in support of his cousin, who would get what he deserved. If Bertie was killed, he would be the one to bear the news to his aunt and uncle. He supposed he would be the one to tell Rose as well. Was her heart still broken for the beau she had waited five years for? He did not think so, except perhaps for the man she had thought Bertie was. Gabe rued the thought of having to mourn at all for his unwanted relation, who had always held him in contempt. How would that delay their wedding? They could hardly have a grand affair mere weeks after a duel, and yet every feeling repulsed at the thought of waiting to make Rose his countess. But mourning was not for the dead as much as it was for the living, and he would honor his aunt, uncle, and cousin, should it prove necessary.

The question was, would Bertie behave honorably and delope, or would he prove foolish yet again and try to shoot Rutherford? Bertie's deluded sense of entitlement would be offended that he was not acceptable as a spouse for the marquess' daughter. Gabe held little hope this would end well. If his wayward cousin did live, what would he do with him then? Let him rot in debtor's prison?

He watched as the two parties gathered at a distance from each other, then while the two seconds met to check weapons. His cousin was dressed in unrelieved black, as was Rutherford. The seconds handed the principals their guns, after which they walked their twelve paces in opposite directions before turning to face one another.

Bertie anticipated the signal. Instead of deloping, he took aim at Rutherford, the stupid lout. He had never been a good shot, but he winged the marquess in the arm. Now Bertie was a sitting target, and Rutherford was a crack shot. Before his cousin could turn and run, Rutherford's bullet hit him directly in the knee.

There was no doubt in Gabe's mind that the marquess could have hit him clean through the heart, but it would have been too easy a death for Bertie. A shattered knee was well known to be one of the most painful injuries, and an unsurprising choice for someone wishing to teach a lesson to a blackguard of the first order. Briefly, he wondered if he could have shown such restraint had he been aiming at his cousin for his sins against Rose—and every other woman from Badajoz to England. Now, Bertie would be lucky to walk again, if he survived the surgery and infection likely to follow. It would probably have been better had he died that day.

The surgeon was running to examine him, while others went to console Rutherford.

Gabe decided not to interfere. Bertie would not be bothering anyone for some time, at least. In bitter silence, he turned Pedro back toward the London Road, wondering what he was to say to Bertie's parents.

‌≫≫≫✕≪≪≪

"YOU ARE CERTAIN this is what you want?" The duke had called Rose into the library to speak with him after Lord Mottram had left to return to Town.

"Yes, Your Grace."

"Perhaps it is time you called me grandfather," he said gruffly. Rose hid a smile as he continued. "Because if he is not who you truly wish for husband, we can weather the storm. I appreciate that Mottram did the honorable thing and offered for you, but he is known for being somewhat of a cold fish."

"He is not so once you know him, grandfather," she said softly.

He grunted, though she could see the term of endearment pleased him. "I will admit he was generous when we spoke of settlements. He insisted that all of your inheritance be put aside for you and any future children, which, of course, endears him to me, if nothing else."

Her grandmother came into the room. "Why is everyone about so early?"

Rose looked at her grandfather, who gave her a nod of encouragement to tell the news herself. "Lord Mottram has just offered for me and I have accepted."

A crease of distress formed between Her Grace's brows. "You are certain this is what you wish?"

"Oh, yes," Rose said, feeling very content with the decision, especially once she said it aloud.

"Well, then, your happiness is all that matters to me. Have you settled on a date?" She looked from one to the other.

"No, Mottram and I thought to leave that to you ladies. He spoke briefly to me of settlements and promised to have his solicitors send them over later. He wanted mainly to seek my blessing."

Her grandmother nodded with approval. "He certainly is an

excellent match by any standards." She sat next to Rose and sighed. "I hate to lose you so soon after we have found you."

Rose took her grandmother's hand. "You have not lost me. I dare say you will see more of me than if I had never ventured to London."

"I imagine that is true."

Rose decided to return to Town with Maria so she could tell her the news along the way, though she was disappointed that Gabriel would not return for a few days. How she wished she'd been able to go with him and tell her papa and siblings the news herself! It would not have hurt to see the look on Mrs. Winton's face when she heard the news, either.

But she must be content in knowing that soon she would be his wife. It was still difficult to believe how wrong she'd been about him and how much she now craved his company.

Papa would have used that knowledge to point out a lesson from the Bible, she mused.

"Will you come in for tea?" Maria asked as they arrived at Mottram Place. "It will be some time before the duke and duchess return and you will soon be mistress here, anyway," Maria pointed out with a smile.

"What a sobering thought," Rose admitted, then was shocked to find Gabriel still there. He looked pleased to see her. Rose was certain her own pleasure showed on her face, and she was very conscious of Maria seeing the look that passed between the two of them.

"I believe the babe needs to rest. I will see myself to my chambers." She patted her growing belly with a coy smile and took herself off upstairs after closing the door behind her.

"Remind me to thank my sister later." He took Rose's hand in his and drew it up for a kiss.

Rose felt it from her head to her toes. Never, in her wildest dreams, would she have thought Gabriel could be so charming. He continued to hold her hand in his.

"Why are you still in London? Not that I am displeased to see you. Quite the contrary, I assure you."

"I wish it were good news, but something has happened. Would you care to sit down?"

Rose nodded as he led her to the sofa and sat close beside her. Surprisingly, she felt comforted by his nearness instead of nervous. "What is it?"

"My cousin somehow escaped from the ship. He did not sail to India. I would not have believed it had I not seen him with my own eyes."

"How? And what does it mean?"

"I have not yet discovered how, but it means he has already caused a great deal of trouble." He went on to describe how his cousin had tried to kidnap Lord Rutherford's daughter, and had been shot in a duel.

"I am sorry he is such a trial to you," she said earnestly, but could not regret Bertie receiving his comeuppance. Still, she would not wish him dead. "Do you think he will live?"

"That I could not say. The bullet would not have killed him where it hit, but infection might. I have not yet heard a report of his condition. It happened only this morning. I planned to pay a call on my aunt and uncle soon."

"Do not let me keep you. I am certain you wish to see how he does."

"On the contrary, I only wish to see how he does for purely selfish reasons." A rare mischievous glint shone in his eyes.

"I have difficulty believing that." She had seen evidence over and over of his inherent goodness.

"Trust me when I say I do not wish anything to delay our wedding."

She looked up at him and saw an entirely new Gabriel before her. His face had softened in tenderness, and his eyes were dark with want—for her. It was hard to believe.

"I do not wish to hurry you if you prefer a long betrothal, but I am eager to make you my wife."

"What a lovely thing to say!"

"Is it? You know I am no connoisseur of words."

"You are doing quite well in my opinion. You simply needed to practice."

"I simply needed motivation… and temptation." His head was moving closer to hers and she thought he might kiss her again.

"Is that what I am?" She looked up with genuine surprise and could see it was true.

"Since my sister has been obliging enough to leave us alone for a few moments, I would not want to waste the opportunity to show you," he whispered before his mouth descended on hers.

Slowly, tenderly, he caressed her lips as if worshiping her, and making promises to her, before he deepened the kiss, and made her forget herself entirely.

When he was finished with his demonstration, she lay her head on his shoulder, feeling content, and looking forward to their wedding. "If Bertie dies, how long will we have to wait?"

"I believe four weeks is the required interval for a cousin, but either way the wedding would need to be small."

"Small suits us anyway, do you not think?"

"You do not prefer a grand London wedding?"

The thought made her shiver. "My new grandparents might, but they will have to be content simply to be present."

"You would prefer the church in the village?"

"If it is not too small for you, yes. I would love for my papa to marry us."

"Then it shall be as you wish, my dear. Then a wedding breakfast at Arden Park? I am sure between my mother, my sister, and your grandmother, they will be happy to arrange it all."

"Indeed. Please say we may deny Mrs. Winton. She likes nothing more than to manage the affairs of others."

"I believe the duchess can quash any pretensions your papa's new wife may have. You will have to see her from time to time, however."

"But with our own home nearby, we will not have to share a

roof!" It was a blessed relief, and she could still see her siblings often.

He laughed and it was the most blessed sound for its rarity.

"I hope to hear much more of that laughter in our future."

"For you, I will try."

After she had been a few more minutes in his arms, he sighed. "I suppose I should go and see how my cousin does. If his condition is stable, then I will leave to speak with your papa tomorrow."

"Will you ask him to have the banns called on Sunday?"

"If that is your wish."

"It is, but I also wish that I could go with you. I have no need to remain in London."

"Your wish is my command, my lady." He rose from the couch and bowed.

"That will take some getting used to, mind you, and the village will think you have married beneath you."

"Then we shall spend the rest of our lives proving them wrong." He kissed her once more, reassuring her more with his actions than words. It was some time before he went to visit his cousin, after all.

EPILOGUE

S O MUCH FOR a small, intimate affair, Gabe thought. He looked out over the congregation, in the small church that was packed well beyond its capacity. In Gabe's opinion, the gathering held well beyond what he would call close friends and family. He waited anxiously, with Lord Philip by his side, the tolling of the church bells signaling to the village the blessed event now occurring.

He looked at the empty front pew, trying not to think of the crowd. He would do anything to have Rose forever, even if it meant standing before this assembly trying not to panic.

It had been a whirlwind of three weeks since the banns were called. Once he and Rose had spoken with her papa, they had been summoned back to London for an engagement ball held by the Duke and Duchess of Knighton. The dowager duchess was the Duchess of Haverstock's aunt, and would have been highly offended if the entire family had not been allowed to celebrate. Gabe knew better than to argue. Besides, Felix Knight was one of his closest friends.

Then, of course, Arden Park had been fully opened for as many guests as could be packed inside. Rooms that had not seen the light of day in decades now held illustrious guests, including Rose's grandparents. Gabe's mother had organized the wedding breakfast, while Rose's grandmother had overseen the trousseau.

Not to be outdone, the church had been decorated with enough flowers to masquerade as a garden, thanks to Mrs. Winton—or should he say Mrs. Sutton now?

Uncle Severn had written to wish he and Maria well, but did not feel able to attend the wedding. Gabe remembered the shame of his own situation not long ago, and wished he could take that from his aunt and uncle who did not deserve to bear their son's shame. Bertie had somehow managed to survive, but he might not be able to walk again. Gabe could only pray he would never be a bother to them, though he would not hold his breath on that account. But he did not want to think about his cousin on his wedding day.

When the music began, and the doors to the nave opened, Gabe could not take his eyes from his bride. She was, again, like a beacon—a ray of sunshine drawing him to her. He relaxed a little, knowing all eyes were on her instead of him, which was as it should be.

She wore a lavender gown of silk, tight at the bodice, flowing into layers at the bottom. A crown of violets circled her golden curls, which he knew was partially for him, partially for her mother.

Which only made her look as though she had descended from the sky. Certainly, she was his angel, undeserving as he was.

The duke escorted her down the aisle, while her papa stood ready to officiate. It had all worked out very neatly, in fact, the reverend eager to let the past be in the past, and forgiveness reign supreme.

Rose was smiling brightly at him, and Gabe could but smile back. He doubted many of his fellow soldiers would have recognized him anymore, since these days he seemed to be wearing a perpetually besotted grin.

He took her hand from the duke, who gave her begrudgingly, it seemed, with one last warning look at Gabe. He did not mind, knowing the duke wanted only the same thing Gabe did—Rose's happiness.

Rose looked at her papa, who smiled kindly and then began.

"Dearly beloved friends, we are gathered together here today in the sight of God…"

By some force of luck Gabe was able to repeat his vows. He remained in awe and wonder of his good fortune in securing such a treasure as Rose. Somehow she was able to see beneath his exterior and did not mind what she found beneath. None of that would have been possible had it not been for a blessed series of events beyond his control, and for whatever had made it happen. Some would say fate, some would say God, but he thought them one and the same.

"Those whom God hath joined together, let no man put asunder."

Gabe could not agree more.

"I pronounce that they be Man and Wife together. In the Name of the Father, of the Son, and of the Holy Ghost. Amen."

No one had objected. They had both pledged their troth. She was well and truly his wife. The communion, the prayers, signing the register, were a blur in his memory. And to think he had almost not come back to England, not wanting to face the shame. Yet so much of what he had feared had never come to pass. Had he not returned, he would never have known this happiness.

They walked back down the aisle, congratulated by their guests, then they ran through a shower of rose petals to the waiting carriage.

"What are you thinking, my love?" Rose asked once they were seated and driving back to Arden Park for the breakfast.

"Many things," he replied. "Mostly how grateful I am that I decided to come back to England… how lucky I am to have found you."

She laid her head upon his shoulder. "I would argue that I am the lucky one, but we were meant to be together."

"Could you have imagined such a thing before you left for London?"

"Do you mean my marrying you? Never! But that was because you hid your true self from me. Now that I know you, I cannot be sorry you hid your charms from others. Otherwise I could not have stood a chance."

"I did not wish for anyone but you."

"And I would not have believed you had I not witnessed it for myself." She shook her head as if in wonder. "But I will not question it, as I am too happy." She tilted her head up to look at him and, indeed, she was too delectable to resist. If she arrived at the Park looking well kissed, then so be it.

She was entirely worth returning home for.

About the Author

Like many writers, Elizabeth Johns was first an avid reader, though she was a reluctant convert. It was Jane Austen's clever wit and unique turn of phrase that hooked Johns when she was "forced" to read Pride and Prejudice for a school assignment. She began writing when she ran out of her favorite author's books and decided to try her hand at crafting a Regency romance novel. Her journey into publishing began with the release of Surrender the Past, book one of the Loring-Abbott Series. Johns makes no pretensions to Austen's wit but hopes readers will perhaps laugh and find some enjoyment in her writing.

Johns attributes much of her inspiration to her mother, a former English teacher. During their last summer together, Johns would sit on the porch swing and read her stories to her mother, who encouraged her to continue writing. Busy with multiple careers, including a professional job in the medical field, author and mother of two children, Johns squeezes in time for reading whenever possible.

Milton Keynes UK
Ingram Content Group UK Ltd.
UKHW020630140823
426838UK00016B/756